MAVERICK HEART

Wild Cow Ranch 1

Natalie Bright
Denise F. McAllister

Maverick Heart
Natalie Bright
Denise F. McAllister

Paperback Edition

CKN Christian Publishing
An Imprint of Wolfpack Publishing
6032 Wheat Penny Avenue
Las Vegas, NV 89122

Paperback ISBN: 978-1-64734-263-0
Ebook ISBN: 978-1-64734-262-3

MAVERICK HEART

Dedication

*For my friend, Jodi Koumalats, who told me
more than once,
"You can do it. You're a writer."*
– Natalie Bright

*Many thanks to my best friend, Elisabeth
Ghyssels Bragg Klemis,
who has always believed in me.*
– Denise F. McAllister

Chapter One

A twinge of claustrophobia hit Carli Jameson as she waited to enter the arena. Squeezed together with thousands of pounds of horsepower in such close proximity, a memory from her younger years with other inexperienced riders popped into her head. A spooked horse, kicking and squealing. Nowhere to escape. Crowded "alleys", as the horse crowd called them, always made her heart race, but now she was with seasoned show horses and they stood waiting patiently to go into the ring. Carli loved all aspects of horse showing—the physical and mental parts of the sport, the bonding with people and her horse, even the smells of horse sweat and manure.

She nudged her horse Beau slightly with her calves, and he walked forward as they stood on the back edge of the group, nearing the narrow space where competitors waited for the next event. Dust fogged the air over the crowded holding area at the Georgia International Horse Park. Carli blocked out the distraction of the other exhibitors and focused on her horse.

"Remember to push him." Her friend and business partner Mark Copeland used a hand towel to wipe the dust from her English boots. "Don't let him get lazy or strung out."

"He's acting a little weird, like he's sleepy or something. I hope he perks up in the ring."

Leaning down she patted Beau's neck. "You'll be all right, sweet boy."

"You know who's in this event. Try to steer clear of her." Mark edged closer and kept his voice low. "Remember the last time she cut you off? She'll do anything to win."

Carli frowned. "She's a barracuda in the show ring. Have you seen Josh? He promised he'd be here."

"Just focus. That boyfriend of yours is probably already in the stands." Mark patted Beau's neck and walked away.

Adjusting her helmet and settling into the saddle, she checked to make sure her boot toes were snug inside the metal stirrups, heels down. Concentrate on your breathing. Calm your nerves. Don't transfer any anxiety to Beau. He always did well in the show ring but could be unpredictable if he lost his focus.

Suddenly a hand touched her knee and a voice asked, "Excuse me. Carlotta Jameson?"

Carli looked down from atop her horse at a pudgy woman wearing a pin-striped suit and a silk blouse that matched her orange hair, except for the pink highlights that framed her face.

"What?" Carli frowned and squinted at the woman.

"Are you Carlotta Jean Jameson? Can we talk?"

"What? No." Carli glanced up and noticed riders edging closer to the arena. "I've got to go. I'm in this class." Her head turned from the woman to the in-gate and back again. Placement in this event was important and she didn't want to mess up her chances. She needed a good spot so that the judges could see her.

Ignoring the woman, Carli cleared her mind and clicked her tongue. Beau moved ahead. She had to get in front of another horse. Then she saw her rival, Savannah, "the barracuda", was already in the ring at a trot and heading for a perfect place on the left. Only a few seconds more and Carli and Beau would be in the ring.

"Let's do this, Beau," she said under her breath, more to herself than to him. A horse show veteran, she knew Beau would be able to sense any nervousness from her. Patting him on the neck again with her black leather glove, she then buckled her chin strap.

"It's urgent, Carlotta. I'll wait for you so we can talk," the woman called after her.

"You have the wrong person." Carli looked over her shoulder to the woman as she nudged Beau to move.

Nobody had called her that name in close to twenty years. She had spent most of her life burying the ties that name represented. Her body tensed and her face flushed with irritation. She sensed Beau go rigid. He shuffled and jerked his head, anxious to get into the ring and get to work. But also acted odd.

Aluminum shoes made a clip clop cadence on the last part of the cement aisle leading into the covered show ring. Carli trotted Beau through the in-gate and to the right to stop him on the rail. Most of the riders were already in position and Carli would have to continue past them to find her place.

Two judges stood in the center of the arena with clipboards in hand. They looked at Beau and Carli as she trotted by too quickly. This could either be good or bad. Maybe Beau would catch the judges' eyes, or maybe they were annoyed she was late. Carli wasn't sure. Her stomach fluttered. She had to settle down. The woman in the alley hadn't done them any favors.

The audience quieted, and for a minute all was still in the show ring. Riders patiently waited and didn't move from their spots on the rail. Finally, one judge nodded to the announcer his readiness. "Judge, that's your class. Riders, trr-ott your horses." The "trot" came out as two syllables, his voice rising at the end.

Up and down Carli posted to Beau's trot. They were in perfect sync and she was finally able to breathe evenly. Rhythmic sounds of the horses filled her ears, hooves evenly padding over softly packed dirt. She wasn't going to think about her encounter, or how that woman knew her legal name. Block it out. Focus. She was not going to think about that blue-eyed Josh either.

Right when she felt good and relaxed, Savannah appeared at Carli's left, too close. It seemed she deliberately slowed her horse's trot to be neck-in-neck, blocking Carli and Beau from being seen by the judges. Carli gripped the reins until her fingers ached, her teeth set in a tight clench.

The beautiful and evil Savannah, up to her old games. Carli might have to come up with a few tricks of her own.

Savannah edged her horse closer to Carli's and blocked the judge's view again as all the horses made their way around the arena like a live carousel.

"Move up," Carli whispered, trying to be discreet since riders shouldn't be talking in the show ring. Instead, she should be looking forward, head up, shoulders back, and heels down to appear like a perfectly framed portrait of horse and rider working in unison.

Still, Carli had to get out of the well Savannah had put her in. And Beau was starting to get annoyed with the other horse near him. His ears pinned back, and he almost stopped. Oh, geez, keep going, Beau!

"Move up. Quit blocking," she whispered again.

Savannah tilted her head slightly towards Carli, nose in the air, the edges of her lips pressed into a smirk.

In the nick of time the announcer's voice came over the loudspeaker. "Canter your horses, please. Can—ter." Savannah took off into a fluid canter.

Carli waited as long as she possibly could to leave as much space between her and Savannah before she cued Beau into the next move. One judge watched riders on the right of the arena and the other judge studied riders on the left, their backs to each other.

Beau took off beautifully on the left lead exactly as he was supposed to do, and even though Carli detected something out of whack with his movements, her confidence soared. The first place win was within her reach. They passed Mark who leaned on the rail next to several other trainers, and she rolled her eyes. She didn't know if he had seen Savannah's maneuver.

"Just keep going and wake him up. More leg," Mark said as she passed by. But Carli knew the incident with Savannah might affect the outcome of how she would place.

After the walk, trot, and canter in one direction, the P.A. clicked with the announcer's voice again: "Exhibitors, reverse at the tr—ottt, please. Reverse at the trot."

Carli took a big breath through her nose and patiently bided her time, even if only for another ten seconds. Just as the judge looked in her direction, she expertly bent Beau around to the left at the trot and, even though he felt suddenly sluggish to her, they got right back on the rail. What's with this horse? Don't quit on me now, Beau. She knew what was coming next, so got ready, but didn't jump the gun.

"Exhibitors, canter your horses, please," the announcer's voice rang out over the arena. He enunciated every syllable. "Can-terrr, please. Go at the can-terrr."

Carli cued Beau by touching his left flank slightly with her spur so that he would lead with his right front leg. At first, he did nothing. No response. C'mon, Beau! Don't mess up now. She touched him stronger with her spur. Her face showed nothing, although her heart thudded. Still, she was hopeful of claiming first place. Oh, good Beau, that's it! Let's go. It was as though they floated around the ring barely touching the ground. She peeked at the judges as they wrote on their clipboards, their faces set in deep concentration. Hope they didn't see Beau's mistake. And before she knew it, it was over.

The announcer's voice declared the end of the class. "Exhibitors, line up in the center, please. Bring your horses to the center."

Carli glanced at Savannah. Not wanting to be anywhere near her adversary, she chose a spot at the opposite end of the line, straightened her spine, and sat tall in the saddle. This was it. Beau had been very good for the most part, although she wondered why he had slowed down at times. Mark gave her a thumbs up from across the arena, but he wasn't smiling.

After all contestants were in the middle of the show ring, the announcer instructed, "Back your horses, please. Back your horses." They all complied. Except for Beau. She tried twice, but he just wouldn't do it. He was sluggish, sleepy. Carli was embarrassed as one judge stood in front of her waiting for Beau to back, but then marked his form and moved on. He tipped his hat, almost sympathetically.

First place. She knew it was lost. She and Beau had worked so hard to be here today. All the hours spent in the saddle practicing, and now this. They needed this win.

Carli willed her face to appear relaxed and calm, but the feeling of wanting to run away as far and as fast as she could made her hands shake and her stomach tremble. She took a few ragged breaths and smiled bigger. What was wrong with Beau?

After a few more minutes of marking their scorecards, the judges turned the paperwork in to the ring steward. More waiting and then the announcer sounded over the intercom calling placements starting from ninth through third. The audience clapped for those as they exited the arena.

"In first place, number two-twenty-three, Zippo's Delight, ridden by Savannah Martin. Number seven-forty-seven, Colonel Beauregard, ridden by Carli Jameson, has been excused. Riders, the third-place winner will now move up to second, and so on down the line."

Carli stifled the scream of shock and disappointment that lodged in her throat. A first place was exactly the boost she and Mark needed to help their training business.

Trying to coax Beau into a trot towards Mark, but settling for a slow walk, she glanced at Savannah who was smirking. Her attention turned to the alley and waiting at the end stood a tall cowboy wearing a bright purple shirt and a big smile on his face. Her heart fluttered. Josh. They had been dating for several months and she felt he might be the one. But as they came closer, she realized his attention was fixed on Savannah, not on her.

He patted Savannah's leg. "You did great." He didn't even glance in Carli's direction.

Savannah leaned down closer to him and gave him a wide smile. "Thanks, babe. I couldn't have done any of this without your help." She puckered her lips and sent him an air smooch.

Josh helping Savannah? Babe?

As Carli passed them, Savannah called over to her, "Looks like you were having some trouble with your horse. Maybe he had an extra nip of something in his water?" She giggled.

Josh smiled but ignored Carli.

Tears welled up in her eyes, but she blinked them away. What in the world was going on? Josh and Savannah, together? She felt like she had been sucker punched. Gritting her teeth, sparks of anger exploded in Carli's brain. Apparently, she and Josh were over. What a jerk! Men! First, not placing in the class, and now this. The world was conspiring against her. But before she could reply to Savannah's cutting remark, she felt a hand on her boot.

"I must talk with you Ms. Jameson. Please."

Carli looked down to see the neon-haired lady again. "We have nothing to discuss. You've got the wrong person."

In the instant she argued with the woman, Carli also glanced over to see Savannah dismount and walk into Josh's big bear hug. They linked arms and disappeared around a corner.

The other riders from her class had long since ridden past, but she was frozen. She couldn't make sense of what she needed to do or what she was seeing. Josh and Savannah?

Frank Gibby, an official with the horse show, walked up to Carli and stood next to the neon-haired woman. "Carli, if you have any questions about the disqualification you can come to my office."

"No, sir. She's not going anywhere. I am Adelphia Fenwick, attorney-at-law, and I must speak with her first. I've been searching for this young lady for several months and I'm not letting her out of my sight."

The official pushed back his silver belly Resistol and glared at the lawyer over the top of his glasses. She stared back and firmly stood her ground.

Mark appeared at Carli's side. "What's going on here? Carli, you need to move Beau out of this alley.

The other event is waiting to come in. Hey, Frank. What's the problem?"

"Carli is disqualified. I think there might be something wrong with her horse. They excused her from the class."

"He wasn't acting right, but there's no need for the DQ." Mark took Beau's bridle and led him out of the ring into the sun. "Carli, you go with Frank. I'll be there as soon as I put Beau in his stall. I think our vet, Amy, is on the grounds. I'll call her to come take a look at him."

Carli followed Frank to the show office, and the neon-haired attorney tagged along right behind her. This can't be happening. Her throat squeezed shut and no words came out of her mouth as she looked towards the door when Mark finally stepped in.

He was visibly upset, his voice raising in protest. "I don't know what just happened. Beau was acting out of sorts and she had a problem getting him to back. But why disqualify her?"

As Mark and Frank continued their embroiled conversation, even touching upon possible drugging, Carli mumbled, "I've got to go back to the stalls and check on Beau. Maybe the vet is there now." She needed some air.

Carli left the office and leaned against the outside of the building willing herself not to burst into tears, yet at the same time her blood still boiled with anger at her ex boyfriend. Young girls in tight English breeches nearly collided with her as they were all abuzz about the latest heartthrob, their ponytails swinging. She remembered those silly, carefree days. Carli's dizzy head couldn't make sense of anything today. The neon-haired lawyer stuck to her side like glue.

"I must insist we talk, Ms. Jameson," and then she laid a hand on Carli's shoulder. "Are you feeling alright? You're as white as a dove."

The lady stood close, face-to-face, and stared her

right in the eyes. Carli was trapped. She swallowed but couldn't answer.

"You are Carlotta Jean Jameson, aren't you? You may call me Del. I have been retained to find you by parties connected with your grandfather's estate in Texas."

"What does that mean? I've never even met either of my grandfathers." Carli backed up a step.

"It means, young lady, that you are the next in line, on your mother's side. Her only surviving heir. Everything goes to you."

The idea of a mountain of debt and some run-down shack that she owed back taxes on ran through her mind. And then the reality of the situation stunned her. Only surviving heir meant one thing.

Her mother was dead.

Chapter Two

Carli chewed her lip and stared at the neon-haired attorney as they stood outside of the horse center's administrative offices. She just could not deal with anything else today.

"Ms. Fenwick. You have the wrong girl." Del opened her mouth to speak but Carli kept talking. "I have to check on my horse. He might've been drugged."

Carli turned and walked as fast as she could, almost at a jog, towards the stalls. Ducking behind the stands, she wormed her way in and out of the crowd gathered at the concession stand and dared not look back. She hoped the lawyer had given up on trying to follow her.

The smells of hot dogs and fries filled her nose. She was probably hungry since she hadn't eaten all day, but the thought of food made her feel sick to her stomach.

Disqualified? This was crazy. It's gotta be a mistake. What was wrong with Beau in that class? Did someone really drug him or was he sick?

Carli slipped into the stall with her horse and slid the door behind her almost closed. Beau greeted her with soft, adoring eyes and a swish of his tail. Wrapping her arm around him, she buried her face in his neck and breathed in his earthy, sweaty smell. I'm sorry, boy. Hot tears trickled down her cheeks and she fought to keep them under control. No matter what happened next, she'd never let them see her cry.

Amy, her veterinarian friend, walked up to the stall. "I think he was drugged, Carli. His lips are numb and he's real sluggish. I checked him out right after your class when Mark brought him back. It could've been a hefty amount of Bute or any number of drugs. I'm not sure which, but I could draw his blood if you want."

"Will he be all right, Amy? And who in the world would do this?"

"He should be fine within twenty-four to forty-eight hours. Keep an eye on him and let me know. I'll get the blood to my lab and give you a call with the results. As far as who would do this, do you have any enemies?"

"I appreciate your help, Amy." Carli's hatred for Savannah bubbled up inside her chest. Her head ached and she wondered if Savannah could have anything to do with this nightmare. Carli wasn't sure she even wanted to continue with the horse show world and all its drama.

Was she that much of a threat that Savannah felt the need to ruin Carli's life? Steal her boyfriend was one thing. She'd survive that, but to get her disqualified? Why would Savannah go after her and, ultimately, try to destroy her entire business? She was certain that Savannah knew something about what was happening today, maybe even had planned harm for Beau and Carli. But, why?

Everything Carli had worked for seemed to be falling apart. What would her clients think of her disqualification? She might lose their business. Horse show people could be finicky and jump ship in a heartbeat—stay with the top trainers, avoid the crooked ones...even if there was no truth to it.

Wiping her drippy nose on the sleeve of her shirt, she removed her jacket and Velcro collar, folding them neatly and placing them inside her bag. Giving Beau one more pat on his nose, she walked into the alley. She removed her helmet and smoothed her hair. Feeling gritty, she found a paper towel in the tack trunk to wipe her face. With a deep breath she dabbed her lips with the gloss from her pocket.

Her heart had calmed somewhat, but if she happened to see Savannah she didn't know if she'd punch her or burst out in tears. Neither option would help her situation. The comment Savannah had whispered as they left the show ring suddenly came to mind. Something about Beau's water. Carli's blood ran cold. What had she done?

"Time to face the music," she whispered to herself and walked back to the administrative office. Del stepped forward and opened the door for her. Carli frowned at the woman's intrusion. Walking into Frank's office, she pretended a confidence she did not have.

As she walked into the office, Mark stopped in mid-sentence and turned towards her. "Is Beau doing all right?"

"He's going to be okay. Amy looked him over. This is a huge mistake. I'm not sure what was wrong with Beau in that class, but I would never drug my horse, Mr. Gibby." Carli tried to control her emotions as she stood in front of his desk, but her voice came out sounding shaky and childlike. Burning with anger again, she couldn't think of anyone who would do this. But of course, it was Savannah. She stood between Carli and that precious first place win. Who else could it be?

Frank Gibby explained they weren't accusing her of anything. "It's just that the horse did not perform, even appeared ill or out of it to the judges so they excused him from the class."

Mark leaned across the desk to stare him in the face. "Frank, let's be reasonable here. Someone must have it in for Carli. You know Carli's good reputation. Something just smells fishy, dontcha think? Did you ask Savannah Martin about this? She has the most to gain. Look, it put her in first place. We've all heard those stories about people walking past a horse's stall and slipping something into the water bucket. I wish we had spent the night by the stalls to protect our horses. Was anyone patrolling the facility? You have a security problem."

"Now look, Mark. You're way out of line naming other exhibitors. We can't go accusing others without any proof. I'm sorry. You know I respect you and Carli. You're good people and I've always liked you both. But I have to abide by the judges' decision. They excused the horse from the class. That's all there is to it."

Carli stood quietly listening, but then said, "You know, Savannah did say something weird to me right after the class. Something about did Beau have an extra 'nip' of something in his water. Why would she say that?"

Carli couldn't believe this was happening. Not after all the work she had put in on Beau, all the hours. This might even cost her some customers. No one would want to ride with a trainer who had been disqualified, especially if there was suspicion of drugging. And without this win, her overall points would be too low to qualify for All Around at the end of the year. Everything in her life was crumbling.

"I need to make some phone calls," Mark turned to stand in front of Carli. "You may as well get ready to head home." He placed his hands on her shoulders. "Don't worry, we'll get through this."

Carli walked back to the stalls in a daze. She worked in a mind-numbing motion to gather her gear. The situation seemed hopeless and she felt powerless to do anything.

Stepping inside the stall with her horse, anger swelled her heart. Why would someone taint her horse's drinking water? She picked up the bucket and slung it against the back wall of the stall with all her strength. Beau raised his head and side-stepped in alarm at her sudden movement. Water turned the wood dark and ran in rivulets to the ground.

She leaned against Beau, her arms resting over his back. The lawyer lady suddenly appeared staring through the bars into the stall, patiently waiting. Carli could feel her eyes watching. Her mother was gone. Carli couldn't bring herself to voice a comment or ask questions about a woman she hadn't seen in thirteen years.

Stories had circulated from people who had known her mother on the horse show circuit, mostly in the Midwest and West. Michelle Jameson was a wild child, grew up on a ranch in Texas, had lots of odd jobs but did not stay in any one place for very long. Carli didn't know her birth father's name. She wondered if her mother even knew which guy was responsible.

Put up for adoption when she was a baby, luckily, a nice, older couple had loved her unconditionally. The elderly Fitzgeralds stepped up to foster Carli, gave her a home and allowed her to pursue her passion for horses, but they were both gone now. They never adopted her or changed her name. Carli always carried the self-inflicted "brand" that her mother didn't want her, that she had given her away. Packed her up like a Goodwill donation so that she could go on with her party life unencumbered by a baby.

As soon as Carli could afford to live on her own, she did. Pretty much raised herself through young adulthood and was proud of the life she'd made. She didn't need to rehash old garbage or relive those painful memories again. She didn't need family.

Couldn't care less about who or where her mother's people were. Joe and Linda Fitzgerald were the only family she'd known or needed.

They were kind people with no other children, and they had given Carli a happy home. More importantly, they allowed her to chase her dream of working with horses. But Carli always felt like an outcast, especially when she noticed her schoolmates had a real mother and father at home.

When Carli was fifteen, Linda Fitzgerald had received a call from out of the blue from Carli's birth mother, Michelle. Seems she wanted to see her daughter after all those years and was passing through town. The Fitzgeralds were hesitant but had let Carli make the decision. Curiosity won out. She wanted to see the woman who had abandoned her.

Her foster parents drove her to an Atlanta café which specialized in gourmet cheeseburgers, her favorite. They stayed in the car while Carli went inside. Knowing they were outside was comforting in some ways.

There was no doubt who her mother was, because it was like looking in a mirror at her older self. The same hazel eyes. Michelle had a bright yellow top on with her jeans tucked inside cowboy boots. Her hair fell over her shoulders making her look much younger than her years.

Carli followed her to a booth, and they ordered. They stared at each other more than they talked. Carli was relieved when Michelle grew nervous and indicated it was time to leave.

"You barely touched your food." Michelle hadn't eaten much from her plate either.

"I'm not hungry."

Michelle paid the check and they walked outside.

"I guess we won't be seeing much of each other again," said the stranger who happened to be her mother.

"Guess not." Carli shrugged her shoulders. She wanted to wrap her arms around her mother's neck. She wanted Michelle to say that she'd never leave her again. That having a daughter was the most important thing in her life. But the woman looked back at her with emotionless eyes that were the same color as Carli's. There was no love there. No regret.

And then Carli remembered they did have one thing in common. Horses. She never even thought to tell her mother about her riding. Carli watched Michelle climb into a dented, blue car. She had stood frozen in the parking lot and had stared at the back of that car until it disappeared out of her life.

The people she seemed to care about the most usually ripped her heart to pieces. Her birth mother. A father who was out there somewhere. And now she could add Josh to that list. More reason to not care and to never trust anyone. People always let you down.

She could take care of herself. Always had. Always will. And she would've won a first place if someone hadn't drugged her horse. Her hard work was thrown out the window. She wanted to scream at the top of her lungs. She might vomit or start sobbing uncontrollably. Why had that lawyer showed up today of all days and opened up those memories?

Her soul had been torn apart that day, but she'd never let anyone know it. She would have to convince Del Fenwick that she wanted no part of any inheritance. Carlotta Jean had died a long time ago in the parking lot of a burger joint in Atlanta.

Chapter Three

Inside Beau's stall, Carli brushed his side a little strenuously. Although his halter was chained to the wall, the horse strained to turn his head and look at her.

"Sorry, fella, just got a lot on my mind. You doing okay?" Carli whispered.

"We can talk anytime you're ready, and I know this is overwhelming. We are working under the deadline of a court date. It's very urgent." Del watched Carli with her horse.

Mark peeked over the gate holding up two coffees and a couple of bags from the concession stand. He ignored the attorney. Carli could smell the greasy fries.

She unhooked Beau so he could relax. He wasn't showing any visible signs of illness although it was pretty evident in the show ring that he wasn't himself. Maybe he had been given some kind of drug. They would keep a close eye on him and have the vet check him again at home.

When she came out of the stall and looked in the bags, she said, "You trying to kill me? I usually eat yogurt or a salad."

"This is called stress eating." Mark tried to

manage a faint smile. Carli sat and Mark carefully unpacked the sack containing one hamburger, one chicken sandwich, fries, two pieces of apple pie wrapped in aluminum foil, and all the napkins and condiments he could find, laying it all out on a cooler.

"I can share." Carli looked up at Del, who shook her head.

"No, thanks. I'll give you two a minute. Maybe you'll have time to visit with me later. I've got to go to my car anyway and get my briefcase." Del disappeared into the crowded alley.

Carli turned to Mark. "So, what's the latest?"

"Well, news spreads fast around a horse show. Or should I say 'gossip'? Everyone knows you didn't even place. They're speculating whether you gave drugs to Beau. And a lot of people are whispering about Savannah and Josh hugging and everything."

"Great," Carli said between sips of coffee. She set the cup down and unwrapped the pie, remembering she hadn't eaten all day.

"One of your students' mother found me right away, said they'll have to rethink Tiffany's riding program, what with her heading to college soon. I think that was her subtle way of saying they don't want to be with a trainer whose reputation has been 'tarnished' by a DQ and possible drugging. Something about being with a 'top' trainer."

"You've got to be kidding." Carli shook her head. "I didn't do anything wrong. Someone is trying to frame me. Besides, riders are DQ'd for a lot of different reasons. It's not the end of the world, for heaven's sake."

"People are funny, Carli, especially wealthy folks in the horse show business. It's all about image." Mark unwrapped the burger and took a giant bite.

"Tiffany and I have worked really hard with her horse Rocky. We've come this far."

"When things go wrong you find out who your real friends are."

Carli looked at him. There was never any romance between them, but she realized what a good friend Mark was.

"Thanks for sticking by my side. I can't tell you how much I appreciate you and our working relationship. One of the best decisions I made was to join you in a business partnership. And I know this mess is going to affect your income as well. I'm sorry, Mark."

Settling into one of the fold-up-in-a-bag chairs, Mark took a sip of coffee. "Hey, partner, it's not your fault. We'll figure something out. Now let's eat this healthy dinner. By the way, what did that crazy looking lady want with you in the alley before your show class?"

Carli picked through her sandwich to just eat part of the grilled chicken. Before she could answer, they heard that annoying woman again.

"That 'crazy lady' has important business with Ms. Jameson." Stopping right in front of Carli, Del said, "Sorry for the bother again, but I really do need to speak with you. It's a legal matter that requires your attention." Her face glistened with moisture. Trickles of sweat ran down the side of her chin. She had removed her suit jacket, folding it over the top of her briefcase.

Mark walked closer to Del. "Now is not the time, ma'am. She's had a rough day."

"You have the wrong girl," Carli said. "We have nothing to discuss."

Del ignored Mark before turning her attention back to Carli. "You are Carlotta Jean Jameson and I'm almost certain you're the one I've been searching for. Why are you reluctant to admit that and talk with me?"

Mark's head snapped around to Carli. "Carlotta? Is that your real first name?"

Carli had never told Mark anything about her past. Looking down, she mumbled. "I don't use that name anymore. Can you give us a few minutes please, Mark?" It put an end to his questions.

She had to admit that she was curious, but Texas? What a foreign sounding place.

"Sure. I have phone calls to make and I'll go talk with Frank." Mark gathered up their food wrappers, stuffed them in the sack, and picked up his coffee with the other hand, then walked back towards the equine center.

Del occupied the vacant seat, set turquoise reading glasses on her nose, and rifled through her briefcase. She flipped through some white papers bound neatly in a purple folder.

"It appears, Ms. Jameson, that an old deed has been uncovered that shows your grandmother, Jean Jameson, was the rightful owner of twenty-two thousand prime acres of land in the Texas Panhandle. Your mother, Michelle Jameson, would have been the new owner since your grandmother passed away but now it seems that your mother has also passed away. I'm sorry if this is upsetting news to you."

Carli hesitated. To admit that Michelle was her mother would mean she would have to face whatever was in store for Carlotta Jean. She swallowed the lump in her throat. "Yes, Michelle is my mother's name. It's just a slight shock. I didn't know she had passed. We haven't spoken in a long time. I don't even know the names of my grandparents. And now you tell me I own a ranch? I still think you may have found the wrong girl."

"I am truly sorry for your loss." Del looked at her over the glasses, sympathy and concern showing in her eyes. "That leaves you as the only surviving heir. Your great-grandpa, Norwood Jameson, left his entire ranch to his only daughter, Jean. I'm guessing you were named after your grandmother. However, there's a dispute." Del flipped through her papers before continuing. "A Mr. Billy Broderick claims he's the rightful owner. There's a hearing scheduled for Monday morning in Amarillo to review the documents and allow a judge to sort this out. I've been retained to find you and make sure that you attend since we're talking about a large amount of money here, even if you decide to sell the land and never live on it."

"I don't have any money, Ms. Fenwick. I can't pay for any land in Texas. Besides, I need to take care of my horse, make sure he's not sick; plus, I have my own business to look after. I can't just take off somewhere...to Texas, of all places." Carli stood and folded up her chair. "You have the wrong girl."

"I would be willing to represent you and make the travel arrangements for the two of us. You don't have to worry about a thing. Go with me to the hearing on Monday, find out what you can, and let the judge rule on this issue. What have you got to lose? We leave on Sunday."

"That's tomorrow!" This was all coming so fast. The attorney was silent for a few minutes while she allowed Carli to take it all in. "Can you answer me one question? What happened to my mother? I haven't heard from her since I was a teenager. I don't even know who my real father is."

"Not sure," Del said. "The information on that is unclear. I can look into it for you if you want, do a separate investigation."

"I'm not sure I can go to Texas so soon! I have Beau and our customers' horses to look after. Not to mention work. I can't just drop everything."

"We need you at the hearing, Ms. Jameson."

Mark spoke as he walked up the alley. "You have to go somewhere? Don't worry, Carli. I'll take care of the horses. Where are you going?"

"I may have inherited some land in Texas." Even though they had been friends for many years, Mark knew nothing about her family or past.

"That's exciting. Is it something you can liquify for cash? You can buy more acreage like you've always wanted. Go on. I can take care of things here."

They both smiled. Mark was always there to support her.

Carli looked at Del. "Okay, I'll have to ask my boss tonight about taking off work, but I'll be ready to leave. What time?"

"I'll reserve our flight for tomorrow around noon and two hotel rooms. We'll get a good night's sleep in Amarillo and be ready Monday morning for the hearing. Shouldn't take too long. I would expect you'd also get to tour the property. I understand it's warm there this time of year so dress accordingly. Bring business clothes for court. I'll text you the details. And I'll send a car to pick you up and take you to the airport. I'll meet you at our gate after you go through security."

Del put the papers away, closed her briefcase, and extended her hand to Carli. "Thank you so much, Ms. Jameson, for speaking with me. I appreciate your time." She was gone like a tornado—one minute, a whirlwind; the next, vanished like it never happened.

Mark's eyebrows raised. "Well, it's been an exciting day. First, there's horse show drama with the DQ and possible drugging, then there's boyfriend trouble, and now legal proceedings and a boat-load of cash!"

Despite his teasing Carli frowned. "Probably a mountain of debt, more like it, or some dilapidated barn full of rattlesnakes. Don't forget family drama that I want no part of. Mother, grandmother—both dead. Not that I ever knew them or that they ever cared. Then there's this place in Texas. Never been there, but I've heard it's flat, dry, hot, with a bunch of pick-up truck-driving cowboys who all carry guns. And what do I know about cattle ranches? And then that lawyer. I'm not looking forward to traveling with her. She's very pushy. You sure you don't want to come along? I might need some business advice."

"Naw, who's gonna take care of Beau and the other horses? You don't want to worry about them while you're gone. Just stay in touch. Let me know how it's going." Mark folded up his chair and slid it into the canvas bag. Carli opened Beau's stall to get him ready to leave.

"You're right. I can't trust anyone else with the horses. I'll go to Texas. Hopefully, it'll be over before I know it. Thanks again, Mark. For everything. You're the one true friend I can always count on."

Next on her list was to contact her boss. Her job as an assistant in a real estate office didn't cover the bills every month, but it was a job and it allowed her flexible hours to pursue a business with Mark. She was sick of wearing work outfits, dealing with people who could never make up their minds about wall colors and floor plans. She was also tired of the stupid jokes from her broker boss, advances from his business associates, and not to mention doing a lot of his work when he was out on long lunches.

If she could spend all day in boots and jeans, she'd be the happiest girl in the world. But dreams can't pay for electricity.

Mark walked closer to her and stopped. She thought he was going to give her a hug, but he hesitated. Instead, he nodded his head, picked up the cooler, and walked away. She could have used that hug.

Chapter Four

Carli and Mark loaded Beau and the gear. There was nothing left to do but go home. The horse show was over for her. She led her horse outside, weaving through the trucks and livestock trailers.

"I'll have to bring the trailer back to transport our clients' horses, but let's get you and Beau home first." Mark swung the back gate open. "You don't mind if I borrow your trailer, do you?"

She had saved her money for years in order to afford a used white truck. Then a good deal came along from a neighbor who agreed to cut the price on a trailer in exchange for riding lessons for his kids. One of her real estate customers had detailed it with blue and purple pinstripes running along both sides of the Chevy pickup truck and trailer.

"Of course, you're welcome to use the trailer."

They finished stashing their gear and Carli grabbed a warm bottle of water from the cooler. What a day. She felt totally zapped and her brain had a disconnect. It was almost too much to think about. What if all the clients left? They wouldn't, would they? She'd have to start over, but the worst part was the loss of credibility and show points. And then there was Josh.

Her eyes blurred with unshed tears. Was he still mad after their little misunderstanding? At this point, she couldn't even remember what they had argued about because it had been three days since they had last talked. Obviously, the boy had been busy. Maybe if it had been with anyone but Savannah, it wouldn't have stung so much. The entire weekend had turned into a horrible embarrassment for her and her career.

"You can drive. I need to catch up on these emails. And by the way, you've never mentioned that your first name is Carlotta and that you have family in Texas."

"I don't want to talk about it." She edged her rig out of the parking lot. Just before pulling onto the highway, she saw Josh and Savannah standing under a tree next to the arena. Savannah toyed with the top button of his shirt as they both gazed into each other's face and laughed. Josh leaned in and planted a gentle kiss on her lips. Savannah didn't close her eyes, instead stared over his shoulder and gave a casual wave to Carli.

Carli swallowed the lump in her throat. She hated them both. Was there anything else that life could dump on her today? Her shoulders sagged and her head throbbed. She took a big swig of warm water. Mark never looked up from the phone in his hand.

After the burn of seeing her boyfriend kissing her worst enemy, her mind wandered back to the neon-haired lawyer. Michelle was dead. Funny how she felt no great sadness over the news of her mother, only regrets. She drove the entire way home in silence.

Her mood calmed and a slow grin formed on her lips despite the day as she turned onto her street. Almost home.

Carli loved her cozy, little bungalow on Saddlebag Lane. Even the street name was endearing. She turned onto her drive, shaded on both sides with tall trees now turning from green to colors of the fall.

It wasn't much, only had two tiny bedrooms, one bath, and the kitchen was about as big as an airplane's lavatory. Not that she was an enthusiastic cook or was home a lot. She didn't really need much, but she loved it just the same as if it were a huge gourmet kitchen.

It was nice to be close to Beau; she could glance out her window anytime to see him munching his hay. She didn't own the place; instead, rented the old country house. Among his many other investments, Mark had agreed to partner with her on the cost of leasing the barn and five acres. That was enough for what they needed for Saddlebag Equine Center, their horse training business. They boarded client-owned show horses that mostly stayed in stalls, so acreage wasn't a priority, and they had a round pen in which to lunge the horses. The clients' board and training fees helped to pay the leasing expenses as well as feed and hay.

Mark led Beau out of the trailer, then unhitched and hitched it back to his truck. "I'll talk to you later. Try not to worry too much and let me know what time your flight leaves."

Try not to worry? What in the world was wrong with that man?

As Carli gathered and sorted dirty laundry to stuff in the washing machine, her mind darted back and forth about the crazy things that had suddenly happened in her life. No more boyfriend—it was obvious Josh had dumped her for Savannah who steered her horse close to Carli and Beau's path in the horse show, nearly causing Beau to break stride. But he didn't.

Then the gossip that maybe Carli had drugged her horse came out of nowhere. It was suspicious, and she couldn't help but wonder if Savannah was the mastermind behind that big, fat lie. Someone was very clever and made it look like Carli was guilty of wrongdoing. Would people ever believe she was innocent?

She didn't want to have to depend on her job at the real estate office forever. Sometimes she hated it there, especially because of her boss who enjoyed playing golf more than running his business which made more work for her. Carli dedicated her free time to building the horse training business with Mark so she could eventually quit the real estate job. That had been her plan anyway. Now that might be all thrown to the wind.

Turning on the washer, she measured soap and softener. Her mind conjured up a vision of the orange-haired attorney, Del, telling her at the horse show that her real mother was dead, and that, crazy as it sounded, Carli was now the sole heir of a Texas ranch. She couldn't help but giggle out loud. Maybe she was imagining it. Couldn't really be true. All these things can't happen to one person in one day, could they?

The washer wobbled and made a loud clunking sound. It probably was on its last leg, but Carli couldn't worry about that now. She was tired and emotionally spent. She dabbed peanut butter and jelly on one piece of bread, wrapped it in a paper towel, and slumped onto an old, rusted lawn chaise in the open carport for a few minutes. The fall air smelled of dusty leaves and pine trees.

She tried to remember anything about her mother's family, but facts and events were foggy. Practically nonexistent. There had been nothing in the Fitzgeralds' papers after they had passed. When Carli was about ten years old, her foster parents, Joe and Linda Fitzgerald, took her on a driving vacation to see the Grand Canyon and other Western sites. They were always so kind and bought her lots of junky souvenirs. Tucked away in a box, she thought she might still have an old postcard of the canyon and a red bandana.

On that trip, Carli remembered driving and driving and driving. She barely could recall the names of states they had passed through. Was it Texas or Oklahoma? Carli hated that part of the vacation. It had been dusty and hot, hardly any trees, and the emptiness of the land had made for a boring drive. The bigness of the sky made her nervous. Cows grazed on both sides of the highway. She watched closely for a horse, but never saw one. How could anyone live there?

They had turned off of the highway and driven on a dirt road. When they pulled up in front of a stone-covered house, a man and woman came out onto the wraparound porch to meet them. The Fitzgeralds hadn't explained much, only that these were some of her birth momma's people and that they wanted to meet her. Carli had known from a very young age that the Fitzgeralds had taken her in as a baby.

The lady said hello and called her "Carlotta Jean", which she hated. She always went by Carli. That was her name.

The man was strikingly handsome and looked just like she might imagine a cowboy would. He wore a wide-brimmed Western hat, a blue scarf tied around his neck, jeans, and wide chaps with four-leaf clovers fashioned in leather work trailing down the side. His belt buckle was a showy piece of inlaid silver and gold with the word "Champion". Carli didn't get close enough to read the date or the rest of the writing clearly.

The lady was just as attractive. Her reddish-blonde hair formed a curly frame for her smiling face, a smile that reached her sparkling hazel eyes. Eyes the same color as Carli's and Michelle's, she had realized many years later. The lady wore a red and white Western shirt with poufy sleeves. Her jeans were tucked into turquoise boots.

They seemed genuinely nice and invited everyone in for sweet iced tea and oatmeal raisin cookies.

Carli could recall the buttery taste of those cookies, but she couldn't remember anything the adults had talked about that day.

Later, on the way home, Joe and Linda had seemed upset, talking in hushed tones. Carli had tried to hear but it was all so confusing for her at that young age, so she stopped listening and just stared out at the desolate landscape. It echoed how she felt inside—alone, not really belonging to the right family, any family. Even today she couldn't recall their names, a highway number, a town's name, or anything about where they had been. The Fitzgeralds had moved her from Florida to Atlanta soon after that trip.

Over the years, she had pushed any thoughts about her birth family away, carried on with her life, and made a home of her own. It might not have been as upscale as some people in Atlanta bragged about, but she didn't care about all that stuff—driving a fancy car, wearing stylish clothes, living in a pricey neighborhood. She was comfortable in her little place and felt safe there.

Enjoying the view of the fall trees from her carport, she leaned back and inhaled deeply. The air was turning cool with a promise of the winter fast approaching. Carli needed to put the washing into the dryer, so went back inside but made herself a cup of hot cocoa first. She always had a weakness for chocolate.

Sipping slowly, she gazed around her simple living room. There wasn't any grand decorating scheme, just used furniture picked up here and there at yard sales, comfortable and well worn. She stared at a colorized drawing of Robert Duvall dressed as the character "Gus" in the movie "Lonesome Dove". Never knowing anything about her birth father, Carli sometimes fantasized that someone like Gus could be her real father, that one day they'd meet, and he'd give her a bear hug and say that he always loved her. The picture barely hung on one wall, a corner skewed, held up by double-back tape.

A riding student had discarded a Cowboys and Indians magazine at the barn so Carli brought it home. The magazine was worn from the countless times she had turned the pages. The ads for the art galleries fascinated her. She loved art, especially Western art, but she certainly couldn't afford the real thing. Happy, though, to surround herself with things that brought her joy she had bought a few picture frames at the Dollar Store to mount the magazine pages. They added color to her white walls and made her smile.

One of her favorites was a picture from a magazine she had picked up at the Booth Western Art Museum in Cartersville, Georgia, nearly two hours from her house outside of Athens. She and Mark traveled to various horse shows all over Georgia and occasionally to Tennessee. It was on one of those trips to Chattanooga that she had been able to run into the museum for barely an hour.

Mark wasn't so keen on staring at pictures, so he stayed outside with the horse trailer eager to get back on the road. On the way to the ladies' room, she remembered being awestruck by the contents of the building. She couldn't help but wander through the treasures.

Carli was in heaven inside the museum. Transported to another world as she viewed the large oil paintings, she also read many of the letters from U.S. presidents, some handwritten. And then, the bronze sculptures stopped her in her tracks. How could the artists make their creations appear so lifelike?

Her favorite bronze stood only two-and-a-half-feet high and was atop a rectangular, gray pedestal. It depicted a Western cowgirl in chaps, boots, and spurs, leaning against a fence. The girl's arms were bent behind her, her left leg propped up on the lower rail, a horse bridle loosely dangling from her fingers. Carli thought the cowgirl had an independent attitude, much like herself—as though the girl might be relishing the fact that she had just worked hard riding her horse, was tired and sweaty, but felt fulfilled and happy that she was capable of doing things herself. She didn't need anyone to do them for her. She was living her life to the fullest, on her own terms.

Carli walked around and around the sculpture that day, taking in every detail. She read the inscription on a plaque: "She never shook the stars from their appointed courses, but she loved good men and rode good horses." The quote was credited to Dr. Margot Liberty, an anthropologist of the Plains. It made Carli think about her love for horses, working the land, and striving to follow one's dreams. It was at that point that she decided to make her own way and stop obsessing over a birth family that had never wanted her.

Carli wished she could have the actual sculpture in her home, but of course could never afford such a priceless work of art. And it probably did belong in a museum where thousands of people could enjoy it, rather than one person keeping it to herself. For now, Carli was happy to have a nice page from the museum's magazine that showcased the artwork in all its 8 x 10 inches of glossy glory. And every time she was able to finagle a quick trip to the Booth Museum, she hurriedly visited "her" statue, her kindred spirit.

It might look tacky to other people, her cheaply decorated small house with only magazine pages to grace the walls. But she liked the Western theme, and it was home to her.

As she folded freshly dried jeans and hung up her English breeches in the closet, she thought again of the Jameson family ranch and the people they might have been. And the thought of Michelle came to mind again, which was strange because she never thought of her birth mother. Well, if she was honest with herself, she frequently wondered about the woman who had abandoned her, and asked the universe, "Why?" But that got her nowhere in life, so she had moved on, rarely thinking about the lady who had given her life.

And now she was gone. What had really happened to her mother?

The lawyer lady said she must be dead or alluded to it. Carli couldn't conjure up any sad feelings. After all, didn't that woman leave her behind? What kind of mother does that? What kind of human being walks away from her own child, her flesh and blood?

Carli pulled away from her thoughts and figured she'd better pack for the flight to Texas. Maybe she'd find out some answers to questions that had haunted her, even if she had stuffed them way down deep where no one could find them, even her. Admittedly, she had stayed hidden from the past, pretending she didn't care. Should she have reached out to her mother again? But then, that one lunch had hurt so deeply she didn't want to relive that pain, the feeling of abandonment. That stupid attorney. Dragging up all these emotions and questions again.

One thing for certain, her life might be about to change. It was hard to say if it would be for the better or worse.

Chapter Five

Around nine Sunday morning, a sleek, dark blue Cadillac Escalade pulled into the gravel driveway of Carli's house outside of Athens, looking out of place on the dirt road. Up early packing, feeding Beau, and thinking of a dozen other things she needed to do besides get on an airplane. Surprisingly, her boss had told her to take all the time she needed which destroyed her plan of telling Del she had to work. That would have been the perfect excuse, and she even wrestled with using it anyway. But lying wasn't something she ever did, so instead she'd dug her suitcase from the bottom of the hall closet.

She wished they didn't have to leave so early but remembered the airline recommendation about getting there an hour or two before the flight, plus allowing for traffic and security lines. Carli could count on one hand the number of times she'd flown somewhere. For as long as she could remember, if there was any travel to do, it involved a horse trailer and one or more horses.

The car driver was very polite—putting her carry-on bag in the trunk. She felt like an intruder, stepping into another world that was never meant for her. Should she sit up front with him or in the back by herself?

Hank made that decision for her, his name being offered as he opened the back door.

"You can call me Hank. This way, Ms. Jameson. I have your airline ticket with me." Carli said hello back and climbed in. She sank into the soft leather seat like melted butter.

"May I offer you a beverage?" The eager-to-please Hank displayed a wide grin that stretched from ear to ear revealing perfect teeth. He even leaned in and opened a mini fridge stocked with various sizes of bottles with brightly colored labels. Carli picked out a fancy water, the name of which she'd never heard of. It hissed as Hank twisted the lid and handed it to her.

She sat so far away from him, they were unable to carry on much of a conversation, only small talk about Atlanta traffic, flight times, and where she was headed.

"Have you ever been to Texas?" Hank asked.

"Not that I can recall." Carli sipped her water, the bubbles tickling her nose.

After some time, Hank pulled curbside and hurried around to open the door for her. "Gate 32," he said as he handed her the bag. "Have a nice flight, Ms. Jameson."

Atlanta traffic had lived up to its notorious reputation on the way there, as did Hartsfield Airport now. It held the title of the world's busiest airport. Throngs of people darted this way and that, all with their own personal agendas of getting to their destinations.

Carli stood in the security line for what seemed like an eternity watching many different ethnicities, ages, genders, and fashion choices of people who also followed the snaky line up to the TSA agent's podium. After showing her identification and boarding pass, she made her way over to the conveyor belt and placed her belongings in one gray bin. Her boots went into a separate bin, only because the attendant shifted her carry-on and placed them there. Carli mumbled, "Sorry." Nervous and at a loss as to the procedure, she worried that she looked guilty about something. Walking through the metal detector, she promptly heard beeping sounds.

The agent said, "Your belt. Remove it and place it in a bin on the conveyor."

Carli spotted Del's neon-orange head before she saw the rest of her waiting on the other side. She looked impatient, but maybe that was her nature. Binder and papers in hand, bifocals on her nose, Del didn't pay attention to those around her.

It took Carli several more tries before she made it through the metal detector. Her belt seemed to be the main issue.

Slowly Carli approached and Del looked up. "Oh, good, we're about to board. We're First Class so we'll be in group one. I have several documents for you to review during the flight. And I hope they give us a good lunch and lots of coffee. I'm famished. Do you have a carry-on?"

Carli wondered if she would be able to tolerate Del's incessant talking and energy. That woman most certainly didn't need any more caffeine. It was going to be a long flight to Texas.

Carli's mind went to Mark and the horses. She knew he would take care of them. Already, she was missing Beau. This was like an out-of-body experience—flying First Class with this strange woman, getting involved in legal proceedings, possibly inheriting a ranch, discovering what happened to her mother, her grandmother—she wasn't sure what to make of it all. The water she had sipped in the limo sat like a fizzy lump of dough in her stomach. The attendant announced their group number.

Carli sank into another leather seat, took a deep breath, and laid her head back. She wasn't afraid of flying, but considered saying a prayer or something. Carli didn't question others about their faith, but sometimes she wondered about a higher presence. However, because of her life story with her birth mother, she had to admit to periodically having some angry talks with God, or whomever might be listening. If He loved everyone so much why had she been given such a raw deal? No child asks to be abandoned. Why are some people born into a perfect life, while others are forced to grovel on their own just to survive?

Once settled in their seats Del was quick to make requests of the flight attendant. "Pellegrino, please. And do you have Moroccan pour-over coffee? I'd like Eggs Benedict, not too much sauce, and asparagus, with a croissant, not English muffin, plenty of apricot preserves. Do you have veggie sausage? And keep the java flowing. How about you, Ms. Jameson?"

"Just coffee, please. Maybe a yogurt if you have it. Thank you very much."

"You don't travel much, do you, Ms. Jameson? Ask for whatever you want. They don't carry everything on board, but hey, doesn't hurt to ask, right? May I call you Carli?"

"Sure, Carli is what I prefer. I do travel a lot to horse events. We drive. Hauling the horses, you know, from show to show. Stay in small motels to keep the expenses down."

"Your life may be changing so you'd better get used to it," Del whispered so no one could hear.

"Changing how? I'm not sure I understand what all of this means. I want to think about it. You're talking about so-called family I don't know, people who have had nothing to do with me my entire life. I have no feelings for these people or understand why I should care about them or anything they may or may not own in Texas. Why am I here, Ms. Fenwick?"

"Call me Del, please, and I'll try to explain this in as clear of terms as I can from what the attorneys have uncovered, foregoing the legal jargon."

The business-like demeanor and seriousness of the attorney had Carli wondering if she should be taking notes. The entire situation seemed so surreal. She was on a plane flying to Texas of all places.

Del balanced a briefcase on her lap and continued. "Norwood Jameson, your great-grandfather, left his entire holdings to his only daughter, your grandmother Jean. Norwood's wife and Jean's mother, Lottie, your great-grandmother, was jealous of her own daughter. In a fit of rage, she left the Jameson ranch to their friend and neighbor, Russell Broderick. The unique part is what she did to Jean. Lottie turned over her only daughter's guardianship, as a minor child, to Mr. Broderick. Since Lottie didn't legally own anything, she gave up her daughter and the land that went with her. Lottie then left the United States and returned to her homeland in Europe. We lost track of her."

The words sounded strange. Grandmother. Jameson ranch. Her family's ranch? Carli could barely make any sense of it.

The flight attendant brought a tray loaded with most of Del's requests and waited as she put aside her briefcase and lowered her tray table. She also handed Carli a coffee and a bowl of yogurt covered with fresh blueberries.

A headache gradually moved from the base of Carli's skull into the top of her head. She worked her neck around and around trying to relieve the tension. None of this had anything to do with her and, honestly, she could care less but she hesitated to tell Del that. It would seem rude.

"So you see, your great-grandmother Lottie never owned the ranch legally. It had been willed to the daughter Jean, your grandmother. Their friends, the Brodericks, specifically Uncle Russell as he was known, took over the ranch and raised Jean as his own after Lottie abandoned her. He also had an only son, Fred Broderick.

"Jean married Ward Kimball and they raised an only daughter on the ranch, your mother Michelle. But Jean never changed her last name for some reason, as a tribute to her father, maybe. Your mother, Michelle, also kept the Jameson family name and passed it on to you. Your grandparents, Jean and Ward, together with the Broderick family lived on and worked the ranch their entire lives."

Carli suddenly recalled the lady with the turquoise boots and the same hazel eyes as hers. Could that have been Jean? "I think I met my grandparents once when I was around ten." She wished she could remember what had been said that day.

"That's interesting. Wonder why the Fitzgeralds never took you to see them again?" Del handed her plate to the stewardess before wrestling with her briefcase again.

Carli took a sip of coffee to soothe her headache. The question she wanted to ask hung over them like a fog. Taking a deep breath, she made herself say the words out loud. "And my mother?"

Del scribbled notes and then sipped her sparkling water before answering. "Your mother lived on the ranch until she was sixteen and then ran away. You were born in Amarillo at St. Anthony's Hospital and the nuns there handled your adoption. That's all we know."

"How did she die?"

"A drug overdose. I am truly sorry for your loss. Which brings us up to this moment. I was retained by a law firm in Amarillo to locate you in Atlanta. Billy Broderick is the only surviving heir in that family, and has applied for a loan."

"Who are the Brodericks again?" Carli looked

at the pile of paper and folders in Del's briefcase and again worried that maybe she should be taking notes. How was she ever going to remember all of this? It was like years of genealogy smacking her in the face over the course of a few minutes.

"The Brodericks raised your grandmother Jean. They were a neighboring ranch family. Upon confirming ownership of the acreage, we discovered that Billy's claim over the entire Jameson family ranch is incorrect. Your great-grandfather left everything to his daughter Jean. And since Jean's only daughter (your mother, Michelle) is dead, that leaves you. The only surviving heir of the Wild Cow Ranch."

Carli's heart skipped a beat and her head felt fuzzy. She actually owned a cattle ranch.

"Billy Broderick wants to borrow money and he is laying claim to his family's spread and your family's acreage as well. And that is why we're going to court." Del snapped her briefcase shut and stowed it underneath the seat in front of her. "Now, tell me about that beautiful horse of yours and your equine training business."

Instead of taking a quick nap, Carli found herself talking the remainder of the flight. Del turned out to be a very good listener.

Time passed quickly. The captain's voice came over the speaker. "We are descending into Rick Husband Amarillo International Airport. Please obey the seatbelt signs. Thank you for flying with us today."

Another car awaited Del and Carli, and the driver helped with their bags. As expected, Del took charge with instructions and directions to the hotel as though the local driver did not know where he was headed. He was quiet, polite, and obliging. Carli wondered if all Texas men were this courteous.

She was quiet too as she gazed out the window

at the Texas landscape—flat and dry as she had expected.

Del checked them in at the front desk of the Embassy Suites.

"Are you up for a late dinner? We could meet back at the restaurant in thirty minutes?" Del asked.

Politely begging off, Carli declined Del's invitation to eat. She wanted to unpack, unwind, maybe order room service, and call Mark to see how the horses were. She detected Del's disappointment.

"I'm sorry. You've told me so much and I'm feeling a bit overwhelmed. I need time to think."

"I understand." Del seemed sincere as she put a hand on Carli's shoulder. "Just let me know if you need anything, and if you have any questions do not hesitate to call me. Let me see your cellphone and I'll add my number. And seriously, call anytime."

Carli handed over her phone, biting her lip and avoiding Del's gaze. There was one question. Should she dare ask? Did she have the courage to ask it?

"There you go. I'll meet you down here for breakfast at eight, and then we'll leave for the courthouse." Del smiled and gathered up her briefcase and rolling bag. Carli followed her to the elevator.

They rode in silence. The doors slid open on the third floor and Del said, "I think I'm this way. Oh, almost forgot about the documents." Del balanced her briefcase on the glass credenza and fumbled through a stack of papers. Carli stepped off the elevator.

Carli cleared her throat, her heart palpitated as she drummed up the courage to speak. "There is one more question."

"Yes, ma'am? What is it?"

"In all your research about my—uh hmmm—family, in all that information you found, did...did you happen to find the name of my birth father?" Carli let out a huff of air, relieved that she finally got the question out of her mouth.

Del froze and turned to face her. "No, nothing. Besides, I think you have too much on your plate right now. That's a story for another time, and perhaps we can pursue it." She handed Carli a folder with her last name written in neat black ink on the tab. "These should explain more about the hearing tomorrow, if you feel like reading tonight. They'll for certain put you to sleep." Del made a deep, throaty chuckle at her own joke. "Have a good evening." With that, she turned and disappeared around the corner.

Carli stood stunned. The name she never thought she'd come to know might become a reality. She turned to walk in the opposite direction towards her room. Was her father's identity something she wanted to know? Why should she care about people who never cared about her? She had blocked those feelings many years ago.

Her head hurt. That's what family was good for. Heartache and pain. She wasn't sure it was worth it.

Chapter Six

After a shower and changing into a Tee-shirt and yoga pants, Carli sat on the king-sized bed, goose down pillows propped behind her. She called room service before pressing Mark's name on her cell-phone.

"Hey, how's it going?" he answered.

"You should see this place, Mark. I'm at the Embassy Suites in downtown Amarillo. I have a whole suite to myself. Comfy sofa, desk, fridge, Keurig®—the works. And First Class seat on the plane. I'm living the high life, I guess. How's Beau? And the others?"

"Oh, everyone's fine. Nothing much to report, horses munching hay, me picking up poop—the usual routine."

They both laughed.

"How are you getting along with 'Orange Top'? I don't want to be mean, but her hair reminds me of one of those troll dolls."

"Now, stop. That is a little mean. She's not so bad. Just drives me a little batty because she talks so much, and fast. And she's bossy with everyone. You should've seen her with the flight attendant. Not rude, but she certainly knows what she wants."

"What time is the hearing tomorrow?"

"Ten. Not far from here. I'm meeting Del downstairs for breakfast. But I probably won't be hungry. I hope we can wrap this up fast so I can get back home day after tomorrow."

"Don't be in a big hurry, Carli. Take your time. Read everything carefully before you sign any papers. Didn't Del say something about you'd get to tour the ranch?"

"Yeah, I suppose. I just feel so weird out here, and the plane and hotel, and cars driving us around. I miss Georgia. And Beau. By the way, what about Tiffany and her mother? Have we lost any more clients? I've been so worried about our business, not to mention my reputation."

"Well," Mark hesitated a second, "I didn't want to bring it up and burden you, but Mrs. Jones did arrange to move Rocky to another trainer. And you know she's buddy-buddy with the Wainwrights. They're probably going to take Remington. I hate to say it, but the others might move also. Once gossip starts, it's hard to pull it back. I'm sorry. You know how the horse community is. It makes me furious, but I'll make more phone calls while you're gone."

The silence on the line was palpable like a thick fog. Carli had expected the worst, but that didn't mean it was easy to hear.

"Geez, all the work we've put in on those horses and the kids. I can't believe it. Do you really think Savannah had anything to do with the drugging? I know she stole my boyfriend. Why couldn't she just take him, not my horse business, too? When I get back, I'll work harder, that's all. I'll put in more time with the clients we have left. If they start winning, that will certainly help mend our reputation."

"I admire your strength, Carli. You always face obstacles with gumption and determination. This is not the first time in your life that others have tried to hurt you, to take advantage. Our business has taken some bumps, but we've always pulled through."

Hearing a knock, Carli said, "Hang on a sec, Mark. Someone's at the door. I think it's room service."

With her ear to the cellphone, she motioned for the bellman to set the tray on the desk. She heard Mark say, "Who was that?"

"My dinner." She couldn't find her purse to give him a tip, so he turned and left. "Anyway, you were telling me about the horses. Are they all okay?"

"I wasn't going to say anything, but Beau seemed a little colicky tonight. Wouldn't eat his dinner. To tell you the truth, I think that animal misses you. But don't you go to worrying. I've been dealing with horses for something like fifteen years. They're finicky. And as strong as they are, they also have fragile systems. He'll be all right tomorrow. I'll keep a close eye on him and let you know if anything is out of whack. And Amy is just a phone call away. It's good to have a vet friend. She would do anything for you, come out any time of the day or night."

"Just something else to worry about. Please take care of my boy. I don't know what I'd do if anything ever happened to him." Carli lifted the lid from her dinner and unwrapped the napkin from around her silverware.

"Stop worrying." Mark's voice was strong. "You do that so well. Everything is fine here. Call me tomorrow and let me know how things are going."

"Will do." Carli sighed.

The chef salad was almost too pretty to eat, but Carli dug in. She removed the papers from the file folders Del had given her, and piled them on the table next to her, glancing through them as she ate. The names were there: Jean Jameson, Billy Broderick, and others; pieces of the puzzle just as Del had explained. Copies of death certificates for both her grandmother and mother. Her mother had died in Los Angeles.

Disbelief and doubt clouded Carli's mind. Why was she here? These two days seemed to be such a waste of her time. She needed to be back in Atlanta working to keep her business. This was a useless trip and she could care less about any of these people.

A thought struck her mind. She sifted through the papers again but could not find the one she wanted. Her birth certificate would have the names of her birth parents. The document was not there.

Her chest tightened and a weariness washed over her like a snuffed-out candle. Emotion was forming in the back of her throat which would soon send the tears. She swallowed hard, but it didn't work. She did not want to feel anything towards these people or have the slightest interest in anything relating to them.

"I don't care. They're all strangers to me." A tear escaped and ran down her cheek. Her brain knew she could care less, but convincing her heart would be the challenge.

Chapter Seven

The next morning Carli dressed in a straight navy-blue skirt, white blouse, heels, and carried a jacket although she wondered if the Texas weather was too hot for it. It was her usual real estate attire on the days her boss scheduled important client meetings at the office. She didn't want to spend money on another skirt because she kept telling herself Saddlebag Lane Equine Center would support both her and Mark one day, and then she could live in jeans. It had been almost seven years, but she refused to buy any new clothes. Adding mascara and lip gloss to her face, she checked to make sure that her room key was in her leather-fringed purse. It didn't go with the business casual look at all, but her independent streak refused to conform.

Carli met Del in the café. Light grays, rich wood tables, and a wall of windows offered an inviting, calm space. The nutty smell of coffee did much to lift her spirits. The breakfast buffet had everything she could ever imagine eating, but nothing looked appetizing.

She slid into the tufted booth seat across from

Del who never looked up from her portfolio. Del focused with fork poised over her plate. "The car should be here any minute. Are you ready? Did you have a chance to read over the paperwork last night?"

No good morning or hello, Del was all business. Carli tried to jog her memory on specifics, but it had been too much information. "I did try to make sense of it." She added two packets of sugar to her coffee, thinking she would need a boost for today. The first taste was as good as the aroma.

"In my mind you are the rightful heir, but let's see how the judge rules today after looking at all of the evidence," Del said before biting into an onion bagel piled high with cream cheese and blueberries. The food stacked on her plate made Carli's stomach roll. Del finished off most everything, gulped the rest of her coffee, and looked at her watch. "It's time for the car." She wore a conservative beige jacket, skirt, and heels, although her neon orange hair was certainly noticeable. By the time she had gathered up her briefcase and purse, and signed the check, the car was waiting under the portico. She glanced at Carli. "You look nice."

Carli climbed into the SUV, gazing at the buildings. Traffic was zipping around, horns beeping. Downtown Amarillo was a contrast to the flat, endless landscape she had seen from the plane window. Tall trees stretched skyward lining the congested streets and providing leafy coverage between the buildings, in various shades of greens turning to golds with the season. The well-manicured lawns held on to the last hint of summer. She had heard that the wind blows here all the time, and even on this mild fall day the treetops swayed as they drove past. They pulled into a parking space near the courthouse. Once inside, Carli couldn't help but hold her breath as she successfully passed through the metal detector. On edge and cautious, she waited for something else to happen. She followed Del.

They walked up the center aisle to the front of the courtroom. The room smelled clean, of lemon wood polish, and Carli relaxed in the peaceful quiet thinking of the countless legal cases that had found justice here.

Del shook hands with the other attorney she'd be working with who was seated at a table on one side. "This is Patrick." The older man with silver hair at his temples smiled and extended a hand towards Carli. He wore the same dark colored suit as the other attorneys across the aisle, only with a neon pink shirt and maroon tie displaying black cow skulls.

Del locked eyes with Carli and pointed to a bench behind the wooden railing and directly after the row of attorneys. Carli sat down.

"All rise for the Honorable Eleanor Wiggins-Brown," the bailiff said in a loud tone.

The judge took her place at the head of a glossy, cherry wood bench, sifted through her papers, and took a sip from a mug that read "Here Comes the Judge".

"Good morning, everyone," she announced.

The bailiff read the docket number.

"Now calling for the case of Broderick versus Jameson. And if counsel would please identify themselves for the record." Judge Brown nodded in the direction of Del.

"Yes, thank you, your honor, and good morning. Patrick Gilcrest, lead counsel for the defendant, Ms. Jameson."

"Hello, your honor. Adelphia Fenwick, also for the defendant. Seated directly behind me is Ms. Carlotta Jean Jameson."

The judge turned her attention to the other side of the courtroom where three more lawyers stood side by side at the table. Sitting behind the rail, a taller man in his mid-forties had a deep frown on his face, and, next to him, a stunningly beautiful redhead dressed in fringe-trimmed blouse, skirt, and boots. She was staring right at Carli.

When the attorney glanced over his shoulder at the couple, he motioned for them to stand. "Erick Sanders, your honor, counsel for the plaintiffs. Directly behind me is William Broderick." The other two attorneys greeted the judge and said their names, but Carli couldn't understand their monotone, soft voices.

"Good mornin', your honor, ma'am. You can call me Bill-eee." He stretched out his name in a throaty Texas twang. His team of lawyers snapped their heads around and gave him a hard look. The toothy grin faded from Billy's face. "I want to say that I hope these proceedings can be over real quick. I got some heifers I need to check. It's really unnecessary that we should have to be here at all."

Carli had missed the part about her being the defendant, and why was that woman still staring?

"As I understand it, we are here this morning to resolve a protest filed against the Last Will and Testament of Mr. Ward Kimball. You may feel this hearing is unnecessary, Mr. Broderick, but you are the one who filed the protest. Are there any other issues that either party feels should be addressed?"

Carli shuffled her weight from one foot to the other. She rarely wore heels but didn't dare sit until her attorneys did.

"Your honor, Mr. Kimball, unfortunately, passed a month ago, but not before he signed a new Will leaving all of the holdings to his granddaughter, Carlotta Jean Jameson. Counsel Fenwick was able to locate Ms. Jameson so that she could appear at the hearing today." Patrick turned and nodded his head towards Carli.

She could feel her cheeks grow warm as all eyes turned towards her. The lump in her throat caused an ache behind her eyes as she realized what had been said. A grandpa? His name was Ward and he had been alive only a month ago? She willed herself not to cry. She couldn't understand why that piece of news made her so emotional. One month. A lifetime. What did it matter?

The judge looked to the opposing counsel and asked, "Mr. Sanders? Are you ready to present?"

"Your honor, my client, Mr. Broderick, has been responsible for managing all aspects of the acreage in question, in addition to the many businesses comprising the Wild Cow Ranch operation, since he was a young man, under the tutelage of his father and grandfather before him. He was raised on that ranch and the Brodericks have occupied and worked parts of the ranch his entire life. It was the intention of Jean Jameson and her husband Ward Kimball, that the Brodericks retain part of the acreage. We have documentation showing that Jean Jameson bequeathed this property to her best friend Mary, Billy Broderick's mother, before her passing. And since the death of Billy's father one year ago, he would now like to clear title and borrow money for the funding and expansion of the cow/calf operation by acquiring additional land," Sanders explained.

"My momma said that Jean gave us part of that ranch as a gift. She wanted our family to have it. I just want what's comin' to me, darlin'—uh, Your Honor." Billy's voice echoed through the room like a cannon shot. One of his lawyer's turned to give him the evil eye again. Billy clamped his mouth shut, reluctantly, based on the deep frown that etched his face.

The court reporter raised her hand slightly and said, "Judge." She had to call out again, and this time she waved. "Judge Brown." The judge glanced down to see her nod towards the courtroom, then said, "Oh, yes. You may all be seated."

Carli kept her eyes on the backs of her attorneys and was grateful to give her aching feet a rest. She glanced over at the red-headed lady whose green eyes fixed on her like a shark's, emotionless, cold, and steely. She quickly looked away and down to her lap.

Attorney Sanders spoke for nearly twenty minutes more and produced document after document. He also announced that Carli had been abandoned by her mother, thereby negating any successorship claims. She essentially had become the daughter of her foster parents and was no longer legal kin to the Jamesons or had claim to anything of theirs. He then turned it over to his two colleagues, who each took at least twenty minutes explaining the ranch operations, and merits and character of Billy Broderick.

"Your honor," said Patrick, "the people who raised Ms. Jameson never legally adopted her. Jean and Ward devoted their lives to finding their daughter Michelle after she ran away at age sixteen, and knew she had a baby but lost track of them both. Unfortunately, the girl's guardians did not promote a relationship with any of the Jameson or Kimball family. It is ill-fated that we were finally able to locate their only grandchild after both of them passed. Regardless, Ms. Jameson is the only living heir of Jean Jameson Kimball and Ward Kimball. Our office prepared and executed the new Will last month, which Ward signed on his deathbed. All property passes to Carlotta Jean Jameson."

Billy jumped up and tore the packet he held in his lap to pieces. "I'll tell you what you can do with your Will!" He flung the strips of paper over the heads of his three attorneys. "That is my ranch. My family sweated blood and tears over that place for generations. My mother and Jean were best friends, and Jean is rolling over in her grave because her wishes are being ignored. There's a foul wind blowing in here and it's coming out of both ends of this bunch of liars."

"Mr. Broderick, I do not allow such outbursts in my courtroom." Judge Brown gave him a stern look, which he ignored.

"Jean wanted us to have the Wild Cow Ranch. Ward hated all of us. He was always jealous of my father. Even on his deathbed, Ward refused to allow Jean's wishes to be honored."

"Mr. Broderick. Sit down," said the judge. "I will not tolerate temper tantrums."

Carli froze and dared not blink. Billy and the red-headed lady were both staring at her like she was a horned devil reincarnated. Billy's face turned red, and with cold eyes he pointed a finger at her. "That little thief will not take my family's ranch from me. You will regret ever coming here today."

Carli didn't know any of these people and didn't want to be in this room.

"Bailiff! Please remove Mr. Broderick from my courtroom," Judge Brown stated her command in a hard voice tinged with irritation.

A uniformed court official walked towards the couple, swinging the gate open to step behind the wood railing. He reached out to grasp Billy's arm.

The red-headed lady shrieked.

"Don't you dare lay a hand on me!" shouted Billy, his voice booming throughout the room and bouncing off the plastered white walls. He jerked his arm from the bailiff's hand. Judge Brown gave him a furious look.

By this time, the cluster of attorneys for Billy sat motionless staring straight ahead, their backs rigid. One began writing furiously on his yellow legal pad. They never turned around.

Billy placed a silver belly Stetson on top of his over six-foot frame and strode out with purpose, his cowboy boots thudding with each step on the polished oak floor. The red-headed lady followed, but not before she shot one more hateful glance towards Carli. The double doors at the back of the room swung shut with a loud bang. Carli jumped, and she wondered if Billy had slammed the doors on purpose. It certainly made for a dramatic exit if that was his intention.

"Bailiff, Mr. Broderick is welcome to return for my final ruling if he can manage his temper and refrain from making threats. Please make sure he does not leave the building. We will adjourn for a five-minute break."

Carli let out a deep breath, realizing she had been holding it and biting her lip for a long time. Del leaned closer to Patrick, their heads bent in conversation.

Several minutes later, the double doors squeaked open. Carli did not turn around. She stared at her lap but felt the presence of Billy as he took a seat.

They all stood for the judge again.

"Please, be seated. As surviving spouse after the passing of Jean Jameson Kimball, Ward Kimball had the right to execute a new Will which supersedes his wife's Will. The provisions of Jean's Will are not in question here, Mr. Broderick, regardless of what you may think she intended to leave to your mother. The holdings in question, twenty-two thousand acres, valued at forty million dollars, shall pass to the sole surviving granddaughter. Based on the evidence presented here today, I declare the Last Will and Testament of Mr. Ward Kimball to be valid. Ms. Carlotta Jean Jameson is the sole surviving heir of the estate. Thank you all for your time and patience."

"That is just wrong," said Billy loudly as he sprung to his feet. "You're gonna regret that decision, Judge. I can rock your world and get you removed. Don't think I won't."

With a calm expression on her face, she ignored Billy, looked at the court official, and spoke only one word. "Bailiff."

He jumped into action, pulling handcuffs from

his lower back. They clicked around Billy's wrists before Carli could even blink.

"You will regret what you've done. I'll see you in jail for this," Billy said as he walked past Carli. She lifted her chin in defiance and met his stare. He was whisked quickly away out the side door. His threat echoing through the room left her heart beating fast.

Carli watched the judge exit the courtroom. Her attorneys stood and walked over to shake hands with the opposing counsel, exchanging pleasantries. She heard one mention a tee time at eight on Saturday. It was obvious they all knew each other except for Del. Patrick made introductions and Del shook hands.

Carli followed Del and Patrick into the hallway. Her emotions bubbled to the surface and she turned on Del.

"Why didn't you tell me I had a grandfather that was alive only a month ago?" Betrayed, sad, and shocked, part of her wanted to flip the whole world off and walk away from the entire mess.

"I apologize, Ms. Jameson. I thought it might be too much right now, after your horse show troubles and then hearing your mother had passed. We needed you at this hearing. That was my job. To get you here so you could put this matter behind you."

"Carli, your grandfather tried to find you." Patrick placed a hand on her shoulder. "He and I were good friends. He wanted more than anything to bring you home to Texas. He found your mother, Michelle, in Los Angeles several years ago, but she wouldn't tell him where the Fitzgeralds had moved to when they left Florida. It was as if you had vanished. Maybe it was her way of vengeance against her parents one last time? Or maybe the Fitzgeralds had been told to keep you away? There is no way to know now what was going on in Michelle's drug-fueled mind. All of the people involved are gone."

"Why would my mother do that to Jean and Ward?"

"It doesn't matter," Patrick said. "At this moment you are the owner of the Wild Cow Ranch, a twenty-two thousand-acre cow/calf operation about an hour's drive from here. How about Del and I take you out to see your place?" He punched the elevator button. "I promised your grandpa that I'd look out for you. This is my card with my private cell number. Call anytime."

Carli slipped the business card into her purse. They filed onto the elevator. So many unanswered questions. Questions she had never considered until today, and now the past had intruded into her life. She wanted no part of it.

"Del will be back in Atlanta, of course, and I'm sure she would be more than happy to help you tie up loose ends there and answer any questions you might have," said Patrick. "We both will be available to help you with this transition and move."

"Absolutely. I think you have my card," Del said.

"Move? There's not going to be any move," Carli said. "I just want to sign any papers you need and then place that ranch on the market for sale as soon as possible. I'm not leaving Georgia." How many times would she have to keep saying that?

The elevator doors slid open. She never looked back to see if Patrick and Del were following her to the front exit. Why in the world would she want to leave the beautiful green woods and lakes of Georgia for this flat, forsaken place? Even worse, she now owned a piece of this empty state made possible by some old geezer who lay in a hospital bed and thought he was doing her a favor. The sooner she could unload this headache, the better. Then she could get on with her life and work to repair her reputation in the Georgia horse community.

Family.

Never needed them before, don't need them now.

Chapter Eight

Carli and Del climbed into Patrick's Ford pickup truck. He eased into the downtown traffic and within minutes they were outside of the city.

"It's less than an hour's drive from downtown Amarillo to the ranch," he said.

Carli stared out the backseat window at the flat, treeless landscape. Del kept chattering legalese as she and Patrick discussed the case. Carli did not pay much attention, primarily because she could care less. She wasn't putting down any roots in Texas, that's for sure. Whoever the owner might be could worry about it.

Cattle grazed, some looking up from the grass they were munching. They passed a herd of red and white Herefords and what Carli knew to be Red Angus bulls in another pasture. She had always been interested in cattle breeds and cattle ranching, although she didn't know why. It was just a bunch of useless information that she'd never put to use in her lifetime. Horses were her real passion.

Patrick's pickup kicked up dust on the road when they turned off the blacktop. Nothing but grass, now light brown and rising to meet the hori-zon in the distance. Nothing of interest to see on the endless landscape. Carli bounced her knee and tried to be patient. Would they ever get there?

The road made a sharp turn around a thicket of mesquite, the wheels making a thump-de-bump as they crossed a cattle guard. They traveled downhill towards a clump of buildings with red roofs and white rock walls, shaded by towering elm and cottonwood trees. The roof of a shed by the corral was painted as a Texas flag. Once parked, Patrick rolled down his window and a couple of men approached the vehicle, and of course Del was the first to speak.

"We're here to tour the property. I am Attorney Adelphia Fenwick from Atlanta and this is my client, Ms. Carlotta Jean Jameson." They climbed out of the truck.

An older man walked closer and held out his hand. "Hello, Patrick. Good to see you again. Nice to meet you, ma'am." Crinkles formed around sky blue eyes shaded by a cowboy hat. He removed his hat and smiled at Del. His face and hands were dark and weathered from years in the sun. "Name's Buck Wallace."

"Buck's been working this ranch most of his life, so he knows every inch of the place. This is Carli, Ward's granddaughter. The judge ruled and Carli is the new owner. Can you show her around?"

At the mention of her grandfather, Buck's smile disappeared. "Yes, sir. We were told you were coming. We're sure gonna miss that old man around here." His eyes glistened with unshed tears, and then he remembered the cowboy standing behind him. "This is Lank." The kid stepped up and shook everyone's hand but Carli's. He tipped a hat in her direction but offered no greeting.

Carli reached for the old man's outstretched hand. "Thank you very much, sir. We don't want to bother anyone or take up your time."

Buck kindly held Carli's hand a few extra seconds and intently looked into her eyes. "You sure 'nuff look like your grandma. Same eyes, and it's no bother at all, ma'am. I'd be happy to show you around the place. I hear you ride. The best view, in my opinion, is from the back of a horse."

"Yes, sir, I do, as a matter of fact, but I didn't bring any jeans." Carli had to quash her excitement at the thought of riding a ranch horse, but obviously that would be impossible in a skirt.

The old man looked at Del and smiled. "You wouldn't mind if we took off across the pasture, would you? I have horses enough for everybody." He turned to Carli. "I'm sure there's something in your grandma's closet that you could wear."

My grandmother's? Carli felt strange all of a sudden.

Del mumbled something sounding like "fine" and turned her attention back to her phone. Patrick said he had emails to answer.

"Y'all can wait inside. Lank, show them to the cookhouse. And find Lola. Tell her we have guests. Follow me this way, Miss, and we'll find something for you to wear." Lank led Patrick and Del towards a two-story, metal roofed building. A second-floor balcony stretched the length of one side and towering cottonwood trees shaded the other side of the building. Carli could hear the golden leaves rustling gently. An occasional meadowlark's trill floated overhead. The quiet startled her.

Buck watched Del and, then back to Carli. "It don't appear that she would miss us one bit if we rode off for a spell. She's real involved with that phone of hers, ain't she?"

"Yes, sir, she does a lot of work on her cellphone. Thanks again. I would actually love going for a ride."

Carli followed Buck across the dirt road to a house at the end of a gravel drive. The wave of a memory flooded her mind as she got closer. She had been here before. The low roofline and the covered porch. The smell of oatmeal raisin cookies. That smiling woman in the turquoise boots who had called her "Carlotta". The hairs on her arms stood up and a chill wiggled its way up her spine. This had been her grandparents' home. She was back. But they were gone.

Snapping to reality, she realized the older man was talking. "Heard tell," Buck said, "that maybe you were the new owner of the Wild Cow. Is that the honest-to-goodness truth, ma'am?"

"Well, uh..." Carli stammered. "Actually, I guess I am."

They stepped inside. "That makes you my boss, don't it? Jean's closet is back that way. Help yourself to anything that might fit. Ward never cleared out her stuff after she died."

"You sure it's okay? Thank you."

"That was the loneliest man I ever knew after Jean passed. He worked like a man half his age every day but spent most nights on the porch in the rocker. Never went to town. Stopped going to church." His voice broke and he hung his head. He took a deep breath. "I'll meet you back at the corral," he said in a rush. The front door slammed in the sudden silence.

Carli walked down the short hall and into the bedroom. The first thing that caught her attention was a picture of herself on the dresser. She was standing on the front porch of this house with Jean and Ward. It had been taken that summer when she was ten. All three of them had big smiles and Carli held a cookie in her hand. There was another photograph of her hanging on the wall in a distressed barnwood frame, double-matted. She stepped closer. It had been taken at Chicopee Woods Agricultural Center in Gainesville, Georgia when she won the 2010 Georgia Quarter Horse All-Around award. She was riding Hot Roddin' Man, or Chevy as she had called him, the horse before she got Beau.

The picture had been blown up from a newspaper article, and it was grainy and faded. It had been hot that day she recalled. Mark was standing next to her. A handful of customers signed up after that win wanting Carli and Mark to work with them.

Why had her foster parents never brought her back here? They had taken the trouble to drive her all the way to Texas that summer, but never allowed Jean and Ward to become part of her life. Nothing made sense anymore. Maybe because a ten-year-old can never fully understand these things. The women in this family were complicated. Lottie abandoned Jean who must have raised herself. Jean's daughter Michelle rejected her mother completely, running away from home and then abandoning her own daughter, Carli. What was wrong with the crazy women in this family? The odds of Carli having a happy life were slim, and that's exactly why she stayed on her own. No complications.

Carli stepped into the closet and found neatly pressed jeans and a red Western blouse hanging right next to the door. Her heels sure wouldn't work. Searching for a switch, she flipped the light on, and the sight of turquoise boots standing in the back corner made her drop to the floor. She dug through a drawer to find socks, removed her heels, and slid one foot into a boot. It fit perfectly. Turning her ankle from one side to the next, she admired the craftmanship. The high tops had inlaid black leather with a brand and the words WILD on top and COW across the bottom.

She finished dressing and hurried out to the corral.

Carli found Buck in the saddle house—a low ceiling building next to the corral that smelled of leather and sweet alfalfa.

"Here's your set of reins and a headstall. We need to find you a saddle. You can take your pick," he said.

Both sides of the room were lined with wooden racks holding saddles and a saddle blanket sitting on top of each. She walked from one to the next noticing the unique leather work. No two were alike. She picked the one that read "Team Roping Heeler Champion".

"Funny you should pick that one." Buck rested a hand on the stitched seat. "That was your grand-ma's saddle. She was one heck of a roper. She and Ward made a great team."

The door swung open and the cowboy she saw earlier walked in.

"Lank, just in time. Carry Carli's saddle for her, would you?"

"Yes, sir." He never glanced in Carli's direction.

She followed the guys outside into the corral where a handful of horses milled around.

Buck looped his reins around the neck of a strawberry roan, the color a unique mixture of white and sorrel-colored hairs.

"He's beautiful," Carli said.

"You can ride C.P. today. He hates to think he might be left out of the fun," said Buck. A horse walked into the midst of them, bumping Carli's shoulder with his nose. Lank chuckled.

"Hello there, pretty boy." Carli slipped the head-stall on while Lank secured her saddle. She mount-ed and Lank held open the corral gate for them. As she passed, Lank handed her his dusty straw hat. To say it had been through some wrecks was an understatement. The crown had a dent, and one side was turned up higher than the other. It was a perfect fit.

Carli felt good to be in the saddle. The worries of the last few days melted away. And she was grateful for the hat the hired hand gave her to shield her from the Texas sun. Buck told her a few things about the gelding she was on. "He's gentle, laid back, obedient. Pretty too with a new copper penny sort of glisten. We call him 'C.P.'"

The old man rode next to her and gave her the rundown on the ranch operations. They started at a slow, easy walk. Carli's horse acted like he knew where they were going.

"Your Great-Grandpa Jameson acquired this place in the early forties. Built a decent cow/calf operation. Norwood's only daughter Jean was a great cattlewoman, but her heart was in the quarter horses she and Ward trained. The Brodericks tended to the cattle, and they all worked together. Nobody ever talked about who owned what."

Carli couldn't help but be curious about his life and asked, "How long have you been working on this ranch, Mr. Wallace?"

Buck stepped off to unhook a barbed wire gate. He waited until Carli and C.P. went through, and then he led his horse, fastened the gate, and got back on his horse.

"This is what we call the West Pasture, and you can call me Buck, Miss. I feel like I was almost born on this ranch. Started out part-time day workin' when I was sixteen. Never lived anywhere else. Well, I did a stint in Vietnam, but then I got back to cows and horses as fast as I could."

Carli looked over at his wrinkled, brown hands on the reins. His weathered face had somewhat of a sadness about it, maybe just when he had mentioned the war.

"Let's head to the top of that rise. You'll be able to see a lot of the ranch from up there," he said.

They fell into an easy short lope across the pasture, sometimes riding around clumps of yucca and other times her horse felt the need to jump over them. Carli coaxed C.P. to dig in up the hill and the horse naturally climbed, his strong hocks propelling them upwards.

Buck kept talking as they rode, and Carli liked hearing his stories.

"I guess you met Billy in the courtroom today?"

Buck didn't look at her but kept his attention straight ahead.

"We weren't officially introduced, but yes, I saw him."

"Billy's kind of messed up, poor guy. His daddy worked him hard, made him do double the chores than the hired help. I guess to show there was no favoritism, no free lunch, just because he was family. It was hard on Billy. He felt like his daddy didn't love him. And he's been out to prove himself ever since to be man enough to run this place."

"He did have a chip on his shoulder," said Carli, "and a bit of a temper." Closer to the truth was Billy seemed to have a hatred for her, but she didn't feel like taking Buck into her confidence yet. She really didn't know who she could trust at this point.

"Are you familiar with that story in the Bible about the prodigal son? Well, Billy wasn't the son that was lost and learned a lesson, although he did sow his wild oats, and probably still does. And he didn't run off to parts unknown. He stayed right here. The only thing was he was jealous of anyone his father paid attention to. He was like the other son in the Bible story, the ungrateful one, always questioning his father's decisions. And yes, a mighty temper. He's had such anger, even when he was a little tyke. Ya ever hear of strong-willed kids? Well, Billy was one for sure. A holy terror at times. I don't usually gossip about other people, but I just wanted you to know what you're in for. He's not happy that they found you." Buck spurred his horse around a rocky anticline. He stopped at the top of the overlook. Carli reined her horse next to his.

Buck pointed to the horizon. "You're lookin' at the Wild Cow Ranch. It's yours in any direction. Do ya ever read the Bible, Miss Carli?" Buck asked.

Their horses were blowing a little, so they settled them and looked out over the expanse. Carli saw the main house, three tin barns, and various, red-roofed houses and outbuildings. Horses were in one pen, cattle in another. They looked like black and red mice scurrying around.

The sky was a shade of bright blue she had never seen before with a scattering of cauliflower-like clouds. Carli leaned her head back and looked around in all directions. An amazing view, like a coffee table picture book. Texas was a lot nicer than she had imagined.

She looked over the acreage, the sun directly overhead shone bright patches of light green and brown. The light was blocked by the clouds turning the patches of grass a darker brown in the shade. And what a crazy question to ask her. How was she supposed to answer something like that?

She hemmed and hawed and cleared her throat. "I don't have time to read much. You know...with the horses and all...we show almost every week-end."

Buck looked at her with compassion. "You don't need to explain yourself to me, Miss Carli. We all have our own kind of faith and relationship with the good Lord. He's gotten me out of a lot of tight jams, and even saved my life a few times." Chuckling, he added, "I think anyone who rides horses knows how to pray, don't you? I mean, it's a thousand-pound animal or more against little ole us."

She grinned. She really liked him. Wanted to trust him. But there were so many unanswered questions and concerns. She wanted to know everything he could tell her about her grandparents and the Wild Cow Ranch. The words were on the tip of her tongue, but she stifled her curiosity. Knowing about them wouldn't change a thing.

It was still hot even in the fall, and Buck asked, "Want some water? We should give some to the horses, too."

"That'd be great, thanks, Mr. Wallace."

"Now I told ya, you can call me Buck," he smiled.

He spurred his horse towards a windmill. Carli heard the squeak and grind of the fan blades turning in the wind. Buck got off his horse and led him to the livestock tank that sat at the base of the mill. While his horse drank, Buck cupped his hands and held them under a stream of water that was coming from a white pipe. "This is the sweetest water you'll ever taste. Be sure to get your drink from this pipe. It's clean, being pumped straight up from below."

Carli led C.P. to the tank. He buried his nose in the water; his long slurps made her thirsty. She cupped her hands and rubbed them together, dried them on her jeans, and then filled them with more water. It was cold. Ice cold. She drank three handfuls.

Buck rested an arm across his saddle and leaned against his horse, watching her as she drank. "Regardless of whether you read the Bible or not, Miss Carli, I believe you are finally where God wants you to be. It was a lifelong dream of Jean and Ward's that you would come live with them. For whatever reason, that didn't happen. But you're here now and that's all that matters."

Carli wiped the water from her face with her shirt sleeve and turned to look at Buck. "I'm not staying, Mr. Wallace. I don't want anything to do with the Wild Cow Ranch."

Buck's eyes lowered, a deep frown etched across his face. "We'll see what the ranch has to say about that." He smiled. "Are you ready to go back?"

Carli spurred C.P. into an easy lope and followed Buck back to headquarters. She didn't admire the scenery or the picture-perfect Texas sky with its snow-white, fluffy clouds. She willed herself to not think about life on some stupid cattle ranch. God really didn't have anything to do with what she wanted. What she wanted was a successful equine business and several first-place wins under her belt. She belonged in Georgia.

Chapter Nine

As Carli and Buck rode closer to the Wild Cow Ranch headquarters, she noticed a black Dodge Ram truck parked at the cookhouse next to Patrick's pickup. Buck gigged his horse faster and C.P. followed suit. He swung out of the saddle before his horse had even stopped. Lank stepped out of the saddle house and gave a side head tilt in the direction of where he'd just been to warn Buck that someone was in there.

"Unsaddle these, will ya?" Buck asked.

Lank nodded. Carli swung a leg over her saddle and hopped to the ground. She could feel Buck's agitation but wasn't sure what it might be from.

Just then the man from the hearing, Billy Broderick, appeared at the door of the saddle house and walked abruptly between them.

"What is she doing here?" His fist clenched tight at his side as he seemed to take up the entire space of the pen.

"Just showing her around, is all." Buck didn't offer his hand in greeting.

"She has no business looking anything over. The only rightful owner around here is me, old man.

The judge may think different, but nothing has changed."

"Billy, don't forget, I worked with your daddy and granddaddy before him, and I remember when you were born, a feisty youngin' with high-pitched wailin' and a colicky disposition to match. You need to settle down."

Scarlet-faced, Billy shot a hateful glance at Buck. "You'd better watch your tongue, old man. I could easily fire you. Now do as I say and get out of my way."

"Just like you fired me last week, and then called me the next day because you needed a ride to the airport." Buck opened the corral gate. "Ms. Jameson was just leaving."

Lank led the horses through the gate and winked at Carli as he went past.

Billy surveyed the scene. He frowned and spouted off to Buck again, "Well, now hold on just a minute. I don't know if I want you two riding around my land. I want her off my property now!"

Buck tried to remain calm. "It's too late. We've already been. You're gonna have to stop this or you'll end up in jail because of that temper."

Billy had a sheepish look on his face and his eyes went down to the ground.

Carli held in her chuckle. It appeared Buck got what he wanted and wasn't afraid at all about losing his job. Her guess was this wasn't the first time Mr. Broderick and the ranch foreman had butted heads like two old bulls.

Billy clenched both hands this time, his face appearing like the top of his head might explode at any moment. Before he could open his mouth, Carli turned at the crunch of gravel. Patrick and Del walked towards the corral. Lank looped the reins over the pipe fence and hurried to open the gate for them.

"What are you doing here, Billy?" Patrick asked.

"Did you post bail already?"

"What'd I tell ya!" Buck chuckled. "So, the judge didn't take much to your temper."

"I have a right to check on my horses. I've got lots of stuff out here, too. This is my home. And yes, I was out of that jail cell in no time. I know people who owe me favors. You'd best remember that."

"You moved into town to live with Nicolette when y'all got married. The judge has ruled, Billy. There's nothing else you can do."

Billy marched over to Patrick, got close to his face, and pointed a finger. "My lawyers will appeal. I'll see you again in court. You can count on that. In the meantime, I'll be coming back to take whatever is mine." His voice turned low and mean. "I'm guessing that I won't have to move a thing though because once I prove you had it in for me and set this whole thing up with Ward, you'll be disbarred."

"Whatever you need to do, Billy, I wish you luck." Patrick took a step back out of his way.

Before Billy left, he turned and cast an angry glance at Carli. "I don't know who you are or where they found you, but I'll get to the bottom of this. Don't think I'm done. Nobody is going to steal my home. I've worked hard for this ranch and you're not going to cheat me out of it. I'd rather burn it to the ground than see you living here. You'd best watch your back."

They stood in silence and watched Billy drive off, his tires spinning on the gravel as he punched the accelerator.

Carli swallowed the lump in her throat. "That guy scares me."

"He forgot to even look at his horses," Lank said.

Carli shook hands with Buck again and told him how much she enjoyed the ride. "I guess I had better change out of these clothes."

"They look nice on you. I'm sure Jean would want you to have them. "And don't worry about

Billy. He's more bark than bite."

After she ran back to the house to get her clothes, she couldn't help but stop one more time and study the pictures on the dresser. On the way out the door she paused to look at a photograph sitting on the fireplace mantel. It was of Jean and Ward at a rodeo; she could see the look of determination on Jean's face and Ward's wide grin. Sitting on top of horses, their outstretched rope held a calf in between, one loop around the horns and Jean's loop around both back feet.

Two people, her flesh and blood. She'd never know their laugh. What was Jean's horse's name? At that moment Carli wanted to know these people more than anything in the world. Just to sit down and eat one meal or watch them at one roping event.

Her mind was conflicted. She wanted to push these people away, but at the same time, know who they were and what they really meant to her life. With a heavy sigh, Carli let the front door slam behind her. These people were never meant to be a part of her world.

She gave a wave at Buck as they drove away. She stared at the headquarters, memorizing every tree and every building. Buck had asked her if she wanted to see any of the other buildings, but she declined. Why would it matter? She'd never be back.

"Billy might be a problem," said Del.

"Yes, I'm afraid so," Patrick glanced over at her. "He's not going to take this change very well. Grandpa Ward and Billy's father, Fred, couldn't see eye to eye on anything. Ward had certain ideas for the cow operation, but Fred never did anything he was told. Did it his way with an arrogance, said everybody else around him were idiots. Sad thing was he displayed that same attitude towards his own son. Ward got tired of fighting since Jean was such good friends with Billy's mom. So, Ward turned his attention to the horses instead."

"Carli, what did you think of the place?" Del asked.

The question caught her off guard. She really didn't have any thoughts about the ranch one way or the other. Why should she care?

"I know this is a lot to absorb and it may not have sunk in yet," said Patrick, "but you are the owner. The people that work here are now your employees. You can manage the operation from Georgia, I guess, but I'd really like to encourage you to consider a lengthy visit to learn everything you can. I know that's what Jean and Ward would want."

"Are there any provisions at all for Billy to keep part of the ranch? Apparently both families lived and worked together for many years." Carli could care less about coming back. She'd just as soon him take it off her hands.

"There's nothing we could find. Billy has other property. He's running cows on a sizable spread in New Mexico and has a pig farm in south Texas. He's done alright for himself, but this is where he grew up," said Patrick. "He has big dreams for this place. Wants to turn it into a gravel pit, selling caliche and sand. He mentioned a dude ranch idea to me once with a subdivision of weekend cabins around a man-made lake. It'd be a shame to bulldoze part of it because that grass is some of the best grazing in the county."

"The man has big ideas, that's for sure, but does he know how to make them work?" asked Del.

"Not always. He's lost some money, but that never has stopped him. It's like he's always trying to measure up to his father's expectations and prove he can be successful, even though his father died a year ago now. I guess old habits take a while to get rid of," Patrick said.

Carli didn't say anything else, just listened to Patrick and Del talk. They eventually turned their conversation to other cases they were working on and Carli stopped paying attention.

A ranch. A stupid ranch in stupid Texas. What was she supposed to do now? Why should she even care? But that picture on the dresser haunted her. The photograph of her with Jean and Ward, in a faded barnwood frame with turquoise nuggets glued around the edges. She didn't recall anyone having a camera that day. It must have been her foster parents. That picture tugged at her heart, but she would never admit that out loud to anyone. Most especially to herself.

Chapter Ten

Carli's body felt like she'd just run a marathon. She closed her eyes and tried to relax on the crack-of-dawn flight back to Atlanta. It was hard though and she had a lot to think about. Her mind darted from one topic to the next.

Del remained in Texas, said she had another meeting at the same law firm regarding a different case. But she made sure Carli's seat in First Class was secured. Del was the best with details, for which Carli was thankful.

When the flight attendant came around, Carli decided to branch out a little bit by ordering scrambled eggs, but also her usual yogurt and fruit. The comfy, cool, leather seats up front were something she could get used to. Leaning back, she closed her eyes for a minute while the stewardess went for the food.

So, she'd seen the ranch. Her ranch. It still seemed like a dream she was waiting to wake up from. And she'd met Buck Wallace who was so kind. She liked him already and felt certain he'd become a real good friend, if she ever went back there. He was like the grandpa she'd never had. And that ride he took her on, there was pretty scenery here and there, but live in Texas? She just couldn't picture herself there. It was dusty, windy, and flat. And that ranch hand sure gave her some sideways glances and didn't appear too happy about her being there. Probably had never worked for a woman boss before.

Then there was the current owner, or so he thought he was—Billy Broderick. Arrogant and rude. And that scene at the courthouse, like something straight out of a B-Western. "I'll get my family's ranch back!" he had yelled at Carli. And his wife—Nicolette. Her Prada designer handbag was like a small suitcase and probably cost way more than one month of Carli's rent in Georgia.

And what about Georgia? Carli liked it there. It was green and had mountains. She had friends on the horse show circuit and her business had been progressing. The future could be bright for her and Mark, and the dreams they had to become sought-after horse trainers.

Well, except for that ridiculous disqualification and the gossip that she might've drugged her horse. Surely the truth would come out and the guilty party would be found. Another nightmare she was waiting to wake up from.

Carli blinked her eyes open as the attendant presented the breakfast tray. "Thank you so much."

The coffee was good, but suddenly Carli lost her appetite for the eggs. Maybe a little bite of fruit would do.

All around her the passengers looked to be businessmen and women, intent on their iPads. The man next to her was snoozing. With no one to talk to, it was back to her own thoughts as she thumbed through the in-flight gift catalog.

What was that deal with Josh and Savannah? She suddenly realized that Josh hadn't crossed her mind in almost three days. Except for last night in the Texas hotel after she had gone to sleep. Around midnight, her phone chirped annoyingly with a one-word text from Josh: "Sorry."

Awake the rest of the night, thoughts and worry spun around her brain. She would not reply, or speak to him ever again, she vowed to herself. That seemed to be her typical luck with men and people in general. They were users and then they just walked away, like her mother.

That was another piece of this whole nightmare—her mother. Dead. Carli decided she wouldn't think about that...at least not now. She had to figure out her own life; no one else would do it for her. She was in this alone, which wasn't anything unusual.

"Would you like a refill?" the attendant asked as she was making her rounds. "We'll be landing pretty soon."

"No, thanks." Carli snuggled in the blanket the stewardess had brought earlier.

She looked forward to getting back to her cozy little home, and to seeing Beau of course. She loved that horse. All her favorite things were there. In Georgia. Not Texas.

When the plane landed, the pilot announced there would be a delay deboarding but that soon people could use their cellphones. Carli was planning to text Mark who would meet her at the curb. She only had a small carry-on piece so no need to go to baggage claim.

Carli waited patiently through the lines and crowds, finally working her way to the exit.

Mark gave her a sideways hug when they met. "Hey, there! World traveler. How was the Big D? Oh, that's right, you went to the Big A—Amarillo, not Dallas. Now you're back in the other Big A. How was it? Lots of cowboys and horses? Nice boots! Is that your brand?"

Sometimes, Carli thought, he was bubbly like a girl. But she liked that he was happy to see her. He was about the only family she had.

The drive to Athens from the airport was an hour and forty-five minutes so they had plenty of time to catch up. And besides, she had only been gone a few days. But a lot can happen in a few days, it seemed.

"How's Beau?"

"Beau's just fine. I think he missed you."

Carli smiled. She could hardly wait to see her horse. "And the others? Did y'all have a good weekend?"

"About that, the customer horses...well, they're gone. Tiffany's mother arranged for hers to be picked up yesterday. And Dana and Margie left also. They're all going to Peachtree Stables. The last two will leave this afternoon."

"You're kidding! What did they say? Why didn't they call me if they had a problem?"

"They're just skittish. You know how people gossip. They figured they needed to distance themselves and they saw their opportunity when you were away."

Carli wanted to scream. Or cry. She was so hurt, especially after all the months of hard work she had put in on her clients' horses.

"I can't believe this." Carli looked down at her hands, then out the window. She would not cry though. "What do I do now? What about our business?"

"I hate to even say it," Mark started, "but you do have that Texas ranch to straighten out. Tell me about the hearing. You didn't call or text."

"There's not much to tell really. My grandfather signed his Last Will only a month ago on his death-bed and left everything to me. I own a cattle ranch with real live cows and ranch horses."

"That's amazing. Maybe you should stay there awhile until things settle down, get the lay of the land, and sell it as quick as you can. We could sure use an injection of cash for Saddlebag Equine Center when you sell the Texas place." Mark laughed a little.

"You're right, I'm going to unload that ranch as quick as I can. I don't know about going back though," she said. "It's such a dusty, flat, deserted kind of place. My life is here. Although maybe my life is drying up in Georgia, for now at least. I guess I could leave for a while until things blow over. It is business, like you said."

Carli began thinking of the possibilities. What if she stayed in Texas for a few weeks? What could it hurt? She'd have to take a leave from her job and start packing. Never in a million years did she ever think something like this would happen. Her life had been so simple before. She had a plan and that had meant staying in Georgia and winning the All-Around for this year. She and Beau had worked so hard. Why would she want to leave her life here? But could she manage the sale from Georgia, even with the help of Del and Patrick?

Mark glanced over at her while she stared out the open window. She could feel his eyes watching her. "I missed you, Carli. We can get through this together. You know I'll always be here for you."

As Carli and Mark pulled into her place, a pickup and trailer were parked by the stalls.

"It's Holly's rig," said Mark.

Carli jumped out of the truck and hurried over to greet them inside the barn. Holly and her father were putting a headstall on her horse, Pepper.

"Hey, Holly. Don't we have a lesson scheduled for today?" Carli stepped inside the stall.

The girl glanced over her shoulder and gave Carli a half grin, but then a worried frown. Her father walked right past them, never saying a word. He unlatched the trailer door. "Bring Pepper over here, Holly."

"Where are you going? What about your lesson?"

Carli followed them out to their vehicle. Holly's family owned several horses, and her wealthy dad was well connected in the Georgia Quarter Horse Association. He was past president and had served on the board for many years.

"There will be no more lessons here. We're leaving and we won't be back," Holly's father said.

"But why? I know people were gossiping at the show. It's all a big mistake. Someone is lying and trying to ruin me."

"Carli, I don't know if you purposely drugged your own horse or not. But I have my daughter's hard work and reputation to think about." The man's face was red, and his voice was climbing. "We trusted you with our daughter's future. We want her to go far, win at the Quarter Horse Congress and the World. And that will take a reputable, number one trainer. We also heard about your romantic troubles. I don't want my daughter around that kind of behavior. Now, get out of our way."

"We're doing everything we can to find out what happened. Carli's innocent." Mark blocked his way.

"It doesn't matter what happened. It's over, Carli. I don't want to see you anywhere near my daughter. I doubt if anyone in this town will want you around their children or their horses for that matter. I think you're done here. Now, I said, get out of our way!"

Carli opened her mouth to apologize again but froze. Her throat closed and the words were lost behind unshed tears. His tirade washed over her. No one in this town will want you near their children. Could it be true? All because she was disqualified from one class, and because of some silly romance problems?

"There is no need for that kind of outburst," said Mark. But it was too late. He stood next to Carli as they watched Holly and her father drive away.

"He's right. Word will keep spreading. Things are

messed up here. And I never imagined that episode with Josh and Savannah was public knowledge, but of course someone must've seen or heard about it. Probably one of Savannah's friends or one of the girls who competed in the same class. Apparently, I must have been the topic of conversation for the entire horse center that day. And maybe Savannah is spreading other gossip about me. Why would Holly's father be so upset and say those things? Well, this is just great!"

Carli spun around and marched back to her house, forgetting about Beau. With each deliberate step, her grandmother's turquoise boots crunched the gravel. She wanted to cry or scream or punch something. She could hear Mark hurrying along behind.

"This is all just a big misunderstanding, Carli. Let me make a few phone calls."

"That's all you ever do. Make a few phone calls. Answer a few emails." She spun around at her back door. "I need to think. Just go home, Mark."

"We can fix this, Carli. Just give me some time."

"It's too late. You can't fix this, Mark, and besides it's not your job to fix my troubles." She dug the keys out of her purse and unlocked the door. Mark stepped up on the step behind her. She turned and put her hand on his chest. "I need to be alone."

Hurt reflected in his eyes, but Carli didn't care. Stepping inside, she let the door slam in his stunned face. She dumped her purse and keys on the kitchen table and dropped onto the couch. Now what? She couldn't get the hurt look on Holly's face out of her mind. She had been one of Carli's favorites, and Carli counted her as a good friend.

Anger and frustration bubbled up in her chest, almost smothering her. Like she couldn't catch her breath. Sounds of Mark at the backdoor again echoed, probably unloading her luggage out of his truck. She glanced out the window to the sound of tires on gravel, thankful that Mark heeded her request to leave.

A part of her felt sad for being so rude to him, but another part just needed quiet for a few minutes. Maybe he was right. She could visit Texas for several weeks, stay in Jean and Ward's house, and keep that attorney Patrick on track to sell the ranch. With her in Georgia, they'd never get anything done. She needed to be there to secure a realtor as quickly as possible and make sure they found a buyer. If she were in Texas, she could definitely speed that whole process along.

Ticking off a mental To-Do list, she needed to talk to her boss and ask for the time off, get the laundry done, house cleaned, and pack her bags. She'd be back in Georgia by Halloween but could stay longer if needed. Carli smiled to herself as an idea formed in her head. Beau was going, too.

Wandering numbly out to the barn, Carli soon stood in Beau's stall and hugged his neck.

"Just you and me now, Boy. Like it's always been. Seems like everyone is against me. Can't seem to do anything right. Stupid Texas. Who in their right mind would live in such a place?"

Carli had made up her mind. She was going to Texas and taking Beau with her.

Chapter Eleven

Exactly one week later in the dark of the predawn, Carli loaded last minute gear into the trailer. Most had been packed the night before. She had kept waffling about her decision, but Mark had encouraged her to go. He helped her box up some things from her house that she wanted to take. They spent one afternoon cleaning the house and barn and loading the horse trailer.

This was really happening. Her boss had given her a month's leave of absence and she had notified Del about her decision. Del had promised to relay the message to Patrick and Buck.

It was a little bittersweet for Carli as she looked at the "art" displayed around her house—magazine pages really. She took her cowgirl muse off the wall, carefully smoothed between cardboard. When she got to Texas, this picture would remind her that she could face anything.

Mark was in the barn sweeping when she brought him a glass of iced tea, sweet of course. "I'll check on your place while you're gone, Carli. After you wrap things up in Texas you'll be back before you know it. Nothing to worry about."

"If you say so," she said. "I just don't like how

everything is changing. I'm gonna miss my little place. But I'll be back, two weeks tops."

"When the sale of the ranch closes, we can start planning the expansion of our equine center. Have you ever thought about a horse sanctuary? By the time you get back all this gossip baloney will be old news." Mark stopped sweeping and propped an elbow on the broom handle. "Now the only thing I'm concerned about is your route. You realize it's about eighteen hours from Athens to that ranch outside of Amarillo. I wish you'd let me drive you. I could fly back. I hate to think of you and Beau alone on the road. What if you break down?"

"I won't break down. We had the truck serviced and the tires on it and the trailer are all in good condition. I'll stop half-way, drive for about eight or nine hours, then pull off for a while at a rest stop. You and I have done long hauls like this before. I can handle it. I'll take the smaller trailer and leave you the larger one. Beau and I will make it just fine."

A frown etched Mark's face. "That's just it, Carli. I was with you on those trips. This'll just be you and the horse."

"You said Arkansas was half-way, right? Well, I called the Larsons. Remember them from the Big A show? Nice folks. They're an hour outside of Little Rock. I plan to stay there overnight."

"You're so stubborn, Carli. Always doing things yourself, your way. Just be sure to call me along the way, keep me posted. I don't want to worry the whole time."

"Me stubborn? You're kind of like a nag, Mark." They both smiled.

Carli made one more pass through her house. She grabbed the thermos of coffee and loaded sand- wiches she had made the night before into a cooler. Along with chips, chocolate, and some apples, she felt sure she wouldn't have to stop except for gas and bathroom breaks. Beau would be fine with his hay and water and wouldn't have to get off the trailer. Pulling off the interstate half-way would give him a chance to rest from balancing on his four legs, stopping and starting in whatever traffic they'd come across. She had invested in a padded trailer liner which should make it easier on him.

Mark led Beau to the trailer, shipping boots on, and hooked his halter in place to the wall. Beau was used to this routine from all the horse shows they had hauled him to, but Carli noticed a little sleepiness in his eyes.

"Looks like Beau would've liked to have stayed in his bed a while longer this morning."

"Me, too," Mark mumbled as he sipped his coffee.

"Well, I guess this is it," Carli said.

Mark went through the checklist again, and she replied, "Yep, got it" to everything.

"I'm ready, Mark. You're a good packer. We've done this so many times for horse shows. I just want to get on the road before the sun comes up and the Atlanta speed demons awake."

"All right. Be safe. Put your phone in the holder. Got your GPS ready?"

"Yes, yes, and yes. Now just give me a hug and let's get this show on the road."

He stepped close and wrapped both arms around her for a tight, warm squeeze. In Carli's mind he held on a little longer than seemed comfortable. It was all business between them, and they had never crossed the line into something more, until now. When he released her, he gazed into her eyes.

"Call me periodically. It's a long drive."

"Mark, take care. Thanks for holding down the fort here. I know you'll do great. And thanks for everything. I'll call you. I really appreciate all you've done for me."

And with that, Carli climbed up into her truck, accelerated slowly out of the drive, and out of her life in Georgia.

***

After driving for a little over two hours, reaching Birmingham, Carli decided to pull into a rest stop for just a few minutes. They were making good time. The Atlanta traffic had not been as bad as expected. She got out of the truck, walked around to Beau's window, and opened it.

"How're you doin', good boy?"

She petted his cheek and felt the side of his neck for any unusual heat, but he was cool at this time of morning. She offered him water, but he only took a few sips, which was okay for a trip like this.

Carli knew that horses needed about a fifteen-minute rest for every four to six hours of a long haul. The trailer should be stopped and parked. This wasn't an official stop though; Carli just wanted to check on him. Maybe in Meridian, Mississippi, they'd stop for twenty minutes or so. Carli could have a pit stop, Beau could stand quietly, and she'd see if he wanted a longer drink of water. He was munching now on what was in his hay net and she'd replenish it soon if need be.

So far, so good. This road trip wouldn't be so bad. Mark had worried for nothing. But it's nice to have a friend who cares about me.

She telephoned the Larsons on her next stop and they were looking forward to her visit. When she reached Little Rock that afternoon, she went through a mental checklist: gas up the truck, stretch and potty break for her, give Beau a drink, and hay if he wanted, and clean out the trailer from his confined bathroom breaks. She pulled into a roadside park with trees, a broken picnic table, and one semi taking up half the lot. She tied Beau to the side of the trailer and mucked it out, discreetly spreading manure around the trees at the back edge of the grass, away from people. Nature's fertilizer. Then she called Mark and put his mind at ease that all was going well.

Carli had switched to soda and ate some chocolate for the caffeine. No time for healthy eating on long road trips. Maybe in Texas. Her head hurt and her eyes felt dry from not blinking much as she kept focused on the road. She probably had that "deer in the headlights" look from the extended driving, but had to keep going, she told herself. Just keep plugging and tomorrow she'd be back in Texas on the ranch, her ranch. She still couldn't wrap her mind around that.

Sirius radio helped her stay alert and she'd listened to just about every style of music she could find. On a whim she changed it to a Classic Country station to relieve the boredom. George Strait came on singing "All My Ex's Live in Texas". His next song was, "I Can Still Make Cheyenne". It was about a "rodeo man" who called his girlfriend from the road and she told him not to bother and come home; she had found someone else who didn't rodeo. A lot of the country songs were tear-jerkers about messed up relationships. She liked all kinds of music—jazz, classical, Western. Vince Gill and Amy Grant too, although she wasn't sure what label to put on their kind of music. Christian Country? But you couldn't get more Texas than George Strait. Listening to him while her truck ate away the miles made her think of cows and cowboys and ranch horses. She couldn't help but feel a little excitement at the new experiences to come, leaving her troubles with horse showing and her equine center business back in Georgia. At least for now.

She decided she would keep everything about the ranch on a professional level. Quick in, get the lay of the land, and unload it as fast as she could. No time for relationships. She didn't need to know any of those people.

Then George sang a song called "Run" that some-how touched Carli. Maybe it was his voice, maybe the words. It caught her off guard. Is that what she had been doing all her life, running? Definitely not running to someone. There wasn't anyone to run to, but she had always wanted to be part of a big family. The thought that someone might be waiting for her somewhere teased her thoughts sometimes, but how would she ever know where to find them? She had never had a serious relationship and it was her own fault. She guarded her heart carefully.

Buck's words that the Wild Cow Ranch was where God wanted her to be was just ridiculous. Like the universe had some master plan for Carli Jameson. She controlled her choices and decided her direction. No one else.

A tree-lined drive led to the Larsons' place, and they came out on the porch to greet her. No surprise they had heard about her troubles. She knew them from the horse show circuit for many years. After she got Beau settled in his stall, she ate fast and ex-cused herself due to exhaustion. She didn't want to rehash the suspected drugging issue and she wasn't ready to share news about her inheritance either. Just said she was visiting friends in Texas.

The next day was much the same as the day be-fore. Long hours on the interstate split up by short stops, junk food for her, hay and water for Beau, and occasionally she let him out of the trailer to stretch his legs. However, she didn't let him graze on the roadside park grass; she was never sure about the county's use of fertilizer. The radio kept playing and she kept driving west.

The GPS said straight ahead on I-40 and only two more hours of driving. And just then, as she was almost to Amarillo, the most beautiful sunset filled the wide, open sky in front of her. She looked to the right and the left and forgot all about being tired. For miles it seemed, there were pink and peach colors, deep rust and reds, deep blues. She slowed, opened the window, filled her lungs with a deep breath, and took it all in. She felt so small and insignificant under that vast expanse.

Tomorrow would be a brand-new day, her very first day on her own ranch. She could hardly believe it.

Chapter Twelve

Carli exited the interstate, checked her GPS to make sure she remembered the road to the ranch. Still another hour of blacktop and dirt to drive after nearly twenty hours on the road from Atlanta, except for her stopover at the Larsons. Everything looked different in the dark from when she had last visited the ranch with Del. Carli steered her truck and trailer up the gravel drive and under the sign that read "Wild Cow Ranch". This would be her new home for the next several weeks, but instead of feeling like the owner, she felt a little like an intruder into a world where she would never belong.

Headquarters was quiet and no one was around, so she found her way to the barn. When she turned off the truck, she could almost hear Beau let out a sigh. They both were exhausted.

An outside floodlight around the barn helped her to see what she had to do. She walked around to the back of the trailer and unlatched the doors behind Beau, then stepped up inside next to him and unhooked the chain to his halter, laying a lead line over his back. When ready, she took the pin out of the butt bar and made sure it was out of the way.

With a little click of her tongue and a slight touch on his rump, she said, "Back, back" and he complied easily. He was always so good about loading and unloading.

"C'mon, boy, let's get you to bed," she said as she led him towards the barn.

Carli could've sworn she heard faint guitar music as she approached the barn. It was nice, but she must really be out of it from driving. Maybe her ears were ringing from too much George Strait.

Inside the door, she flipped on all the lights and the other horses whinnied. "This isn't a late-night snack time. I just brought you a new roommate."

She saw an empty stall and headed Beau in that direction when suddenly the music stopped, and a man's voice startled her a little. "Stop right there. Who the heck are you and what do ya think you're doing with that horse?"

Carli looked over Beau's back at a dark-haired man standing in the doorway to the saddle house. She couldn't remember if this was the same cowboy she'd met before. She ignored his question. "Who are you?"

"Lank Torres and I'm askin' the questions. Step into the light so I can see ya."

The name sounded familiar. Maybe it was the same ranch hand she had met before. Carli led Beau into the empty stall and ignored the questions until she had taken off his halter. Beau started sniffing and pawing the ground of his new quarters.

"Stop right there. I've already called the sheriff."

"You told me to step into the light. So, which is it? Stop or move?"

They both stepped into the light from a flood-lamp.

"Do I know ya?"

"Well, seeing as how I'm your new boss, Lank Torres, my horse needs hay. You can bring that now. Where is Buck? I met him last week. Foreman, right? He knew I was coming." Carli walked closer to the cowboy. He gazed back at her with arrogant blue/gray eyes and a smirk on his face. She could get lost in those eyes, so deliberately turned her attention away but not before she noticed the white Tee-shirt that stretched over a broad chest. Blue gym shorts hung below his knees and he had on a pair of lime green Crocs™. This is the guy who watches over Grandpa Ward's cows?

"Buck is the foreman; you got that right. He went to Wednesday night services and then headed over to New Mexico to look at some hay grazer."

"A real nice man and seems very competent. When is he coming back?" Carli asked.

"Who are you again?" Lank crossed his arms over that broad chest and stood his ground.

Ignoring his question, she said, "Mr. Torres, do you think you could help me unload a few things from my trailer? I'd like to get my horse settled. I'll give him grain in the morning. I don't need most of the boxes unloaded tonight, that can wait. But if someone could show me to a spare bedroom, I'd love to turn in soon. It was a really long drive and my head still feels like I'm spinning from the road." Carli turned and walked towards her rig.

"No."

She spun around and stared at him. "What do you mean 'no'?"

Lank pulled his phone from a pocket and punched in a call with his thumbs. "Yeah, this is Lank Torres over at the Wild Cow Ranch and I have a situation here. Did you get my message to the sheriff? I got me a trespasser."

In the time it took him to drawl out the sentence in that low Texas twang, she could have had her truck unloaded.

"Wait just a minute." She had no idea what possessed her, but she suddenly lunged and took the phone from his hand.

"Hey!" he shouted and stepped back. "What are you doing?"

She didn't miss the fact that he had taken a step back. Good. All bark, and no bite. "I'll give you your phone back if you'll call Buck."

"Fine."

"Is it a deal?"

"Give it to me." He dialed the number. "Hello, Buck. This is Lank. Do you know some gal named Cara? No? Never heard of her?"

"Carli. My name is Car-r-r-li." What a stupid moron. She tapped her boot toe with frustration. Poor Beau. He must be starving. "Give me that." Carli took his phone again. "Hello, Buck? This is Carli Jameson. We met several weeks ago." Heat rose to her face as she listened to the voice on the other end of the line. She wouldn't be surprised if steam came out of the top of her head next. She glared at Lank. "This isn't Buck? Your name is Colton?"

Lank's face turned into a huge grin and he let out a belly laugh which made her even madder. "Buck doesn't carry a cellphone."

Carli stomped around Lank, went to her trailer where she broke off several flakes of alfalfa to stuff into the feeder in Beau's stall. She left the gate open so that he could get to the water tank on the other side of the corral. By this time several of the other horses in the next pen stood at the rail, curious to watch and sniff their new bunk mate.

Lank watched her in silence.

Carli tried to unhitch her trailer but couldn't see that well in the dark and the light from her cellphone was useless. Instead she found her overnight bag. "Is the house unlocked?"

"I've got the key right here," said Lank.

They stood staring at each other. Carli fumed. The nerve of that guy, questioning her. "Well? Are you going to let me in?"

Headlights cast a beam on their faces as a vehicle

turned into the headquarters. A sheriff's cruiser pulled to a stop next to Carli's rig. A deputy stepped out, straightened his hat, and rested a hand on his sidearm.

"Lank. How are you this evening?"

Lank hurried over to the gate. "Sheriff Anderson, I'm good. Thanks for coming out. I don't know who this lady is, but she acts like she owns the place."

"Where's Buck?"

"He's gone to look over some hay grazer. Should be back tomorrow."

Carli walked closer to the two men. The deputy tipped his hat. "Good evening, Ms. Jameson. I heard that you'd be visiting us."

The look on Lank's face made Carli stifle a giggle. He looked at her, back to the deputy, and back to her. "You know her?"

"She's Ward's granddaughter. You sure do look a lot like your grandmother Jean. Has anybody ever told you that? Same pretty eyes."

Carli smiled. "I'm trying to get this knucklehead cowboy to unlock my grandparents' house for me."

"What's the problem, Lank?" The smile on the deputy's face disappeared as he used his official law enforcement voice to ask the question. "Why are you making the lady stand here in the dark? I bet she's had a long drive from Georgia."

Carli couldn't hold in her giggle any longer.

Lank was speechless, still with that dumbfounded look on his face. "Why didn't you tell me you were Ward's granddaughter? I didn't recognize you in sweatpants and Tee shirt."

Carli followed the men across the compound. The sheriff aimed his Maglite at the door so Lank could see to unlock it. He swung the door open, flipped on the entry hall light, and stepped back, but didn't say a word.

"Good night, ma'am," said the sheriff. "Welcome home."

Carli gave him a bright smile and then glared at Lank before closing the front door behind them. She was exhausted and had no idea which bedroom she should use. Pulling off her shoes, she sank down with a sigh onto the oversized leather couch in the living room. Sliding a blanket from the back of the couch over her shoulders, she nestled her head into a pillow. As Carli relaxed, her aching muscles released some of their stress. Her mind drifted off to sleep and she could still hear the sheriff's words: "Welcome home."

Chapter Thirteen

Carli stepped out of her grandparents' ranch house and stopped to survey Wild Cow Ranch Headquarters. There were trees, lots of trees, which she hadn't really noticed during her first visit. Cottonwoods, elms, and perfectly shaped pear held on to the last bit of fall color. The October air had a slight chill despite the sunshine.

She walked towards the two-story cookhouse and stepped into the smell of pancakes and bacon. Several tables and chairs took up part of the cement floor. On one end of the room a rock fireplace rose to the twenty-foot ceiling, and on the other end an oak staircase gently wound up to a second-floor balcony. The metal tiled ceiling gave the modern building an Old West charm. Windows with no curtains and burnished wood chandeliers lit the space up like an airplane runway. Carli squinted and blinked from the bright glare.

"Welcome to the Wild Cow, Miss Carli. Sit here." A tiny woman with silky black hair and dark eyes greeted her with a bright smile, set down her mug, stood, and disappeared behind a set of swinging doors. Carli was certain she'd be without her usual breakfast, but it was long past lunch, and her empty stomach would be happy with anything.

She sat down at the same table, not sure what to do next. Behind her sliding oak doors hung on an iron rail. They were closed. She glanced up to the balcony and noticed four doors, must be bedrooms. Not one for chit chat, the silence felt awkward for some reason. Before she could think of what to say, the woman appeared again.

"I'm Lola, Buck's best half. It's good to finally meet you." She placed a plate of food and a sizable mug in front of Carli. "It's almost lunch, but we didn't want to disturb your rest and I saved some breakfast for you. Do you use cream or sugar in your coffee?"

Carli had to admit the smells from the steaming mug made her heart happy. A neat pile of blueberries balanced on top of the pancakes and next to that, bacon fried to perfection. "Nice to meet you too, and black is fine. Thank you."

Lola sat again and watched Carli eat. "If you'll let me know some of your favorites, I'll add them to my grocery list. Breakfast is early, around six-thirty. Lunch is always straight up noon, but the men come and go depending on their work, and then the evening meal is hit or miss with leftovers or the café in town unless we're working cattle. Then I fix three squares a day. This building is also the bunkhouse with a few spare rooms. Buck and I live upstairs."

The door opened; the jingling of spurs followed. Carli glanced over her shoulder. Lank was talking to Buck but stopped the minute he saw her.

"Have a seat, boys." Lola disappeared behind the swinging door.

Buck sat on one side of Carli, closest to Lola, and Lank was on the other side.

"It sure is good to have you here, young lady." Buck patted her back. "That looks good. I hope we're having some of that too. How was the drive?"

"Long," Carli answered between bites. "I hope Beau is okay. I need to get out there and see him."

"He's fine. Checked on him myself this morning. Gave him a scratch between the ears. Sure is a nice-looking animal. How does he feel about cows?"

"I don't think he's ever seen a cow, except maybe from afar at a horse show when they had those events." Carli had never had the opportunity to ride him up close around cows.

Lola returned with iced tea and soon after emerged from the kitchen again with two plates of smothered steak, mashed potatoes, and salad.

"Let's bless it," said Buck. "Dear Father, thank you for this day and for sending Miss Carli to us. Bless this food to our bodies and bless the hands that prepared it. Amen."

The prayer happened so fast Carli had just stuffed a bite of the fluffiest pancake she had ever tasted into her mouth and then forgot to bow her head. She felt her cheeks warm with embarrassment. She'd be better prepared next time.

The men ate in silence. Whatever Lank had been saying when they arrived was not going to be continued with Carli sitting there. She could feel Lola's eyes watching her.

"Do you like the pancakes?" Lola asked.

"Yes, ma'am." She took another big bite so she wouldn't have to say anything else.

"Lank, why don't you help Carli unpack her pickup truck and get settled in?"

Carli looked up from her plate. Lank avoided her glance.

"He thought Carli was a burglar. Called the sheriff on her." Buck looked at Lola and they both laughed.

Lank managed a grin. "I honestly didn't know who she was."

"How could you not know? She was here only a

few weeks ago." Buck gave him a look of disbelief and shook his head. "I just hate that you bothered the sheriff for nothing."

"I really appreciate the offer about unpacking, but I need to tend to my horse. I can manage by myself."

"Lank, get Carli unloaded and then take a look at the mill that's down in the East Pasture." Buck leaned closer to Lola and gave her a peck on the cheek. "Thanks for lunch, hon."

Carli thanked Lola and followed the men outside and saw Beau standing next to the pipe fence, watching her walk towards him.

"Hey there, fella." She scratched his ears and then walked to her trailer to find his vitamins and supplements.

"What's all that for?" Lank asked.

"Nutrition supplements for my horse. It makes his coat shiny and helps his joints. What brand do you feed your horse?"

"God's brand."

"I've never heard of that. What's in it?"

"Grass."

"What do you mean, grass? What kind of grass?"

"Texas pasture grass."

"Are you making fun of me?"

"Honest truth, Ms. Jameson. We feed our ranch horses the pasture grass you see all around here. It's a special mix of rain, dirt, and Texas sunshine. Grown special by God." Lank was grinning at her. Carli fumed. She really wanted to wipe that smirk off his face.

"Where is the tack room that I can use?"

She mixed up Beau's feed, but now felt silly doing it. And then followed Lank with the rest of her tack to a little tin building set in the middle of the corral.

"We use this building as a spare for guests. Buck may want me to make room for your stuff in the big room. I'll ask him. What in the world is this tiny thing?" Lank held up her English saddle with one hand.

"It's my saddle."

"You can't ride that around here. You'll be laughed right out of the county."

Carli ignored him and arranged her tack on the pegs along the wall. She made a note to herself to locate a broom.

"That should do it," said Carli. "Thanks for your help. Where should I park my trailer?"

"You can back it up over behind the bunkhouse, in line with the others."

Carli unhitched and drove her truck back to her grandparents' house. There were vehicles already under the carport, a bright red SUV, and an old truck, so she parked at the front door. She didn't see Lank anywhere and was glad. Seemed she couldn't breathe normally when he was around. He made her nerves more jittery than usual.

The first order of business was to decide where she could put her belongings, even though she didn't bring much with her from Georgia. She wandered through the house. It was as if her grandparents were only gone for a few days and would be back any minute. The laundry room was well-stocked, bathrooms clean, cabinets full of neatly folded towels, plenty of toilet paper, shampoo, soap. There was not an empty closet in the place though.

She assumed the bedroom at the front of the house might be for guests because of the sparse decorations. The nightstand and dresser drawers were empty and there were not as many knick-knacks. The mustiness tickled her nose and she almost felt a sneeze brewing. This room would be perfect for the next several weeks. She brought her suitcase in from the empty hall and filled up several dresser drawers. Spinning around on her heel she surveyed the walls. The perfect spot for her cowgirl muse would be directly in front of the bed. Carefully removing a prairie grass landscape, she hung her framed magazine page on the nail and took a step back to admire it.

Discovering that the bed had no sheets, she went in search of a set. They smelled old and musty too, so she figured out how to start the washer. Pondering whether to ride Beau or not, Carli decided they both could use a rest after their long trip. Sheets or not, she crawled on top of the bed. If her grandparents had still been alive and she lived with them, would this have been her room? They had really lived here. With pictures of her on their walls. This ranch that she now owned. Life sure takes some crazy turns sometimes. Maybe she should ride Beau but before she could make herself put a weary foot on the floor, she smiled remembering the taste of those pancakes and drifted off.

Chapter Fourteen

Carli woke from her nap with a start to pounding on the front door. Her eyes opened and for a minute had no idea where she was. The room did not look familiar.

"Carli! It's me, Buck. You're sleeping the day away. Is everything okay?"

"Good grief!" She ran to open the front door. "I can't believe I slept that long. Yes, I'm fine. Just tired. How are you?"

"As good as can be expected for these old bones, thanks to the Good Lord. I guess it beats the alternative as they say." His laugh was becoming a welcome sound to Carli's ears. She smiled and rubbed the sleep from her eyes.

"I came by to tell you that I've cleaned out a spot in the main tack room if you want to move your stuff over. That little tin building where Lank had you put your things is really dirty. I apologize."

"Thanks very much, Buck." Carli stepped back from the front door. "Please, come in. I feel funny saying that because I'm the intruder."

"You should never feel that way. This is your place, just found a few years later than we had hoped is all. Have you settled in? The master bedroom at the back of the house has a bathroom attached so you don't have to go down the hall. Billy's wife, Nicolette did most of the decorating. You can always change it however you want to though."

Redecorate? Why in the world would she want to do that? "I won't be staying that long. The smaller bedroom is fine. Thanks for your help."

"There should be some food in the kitchen. I haven't cleaned out anything since Ward went to the hospital over a month ago. But if you don't find what you want, get yerself something at the cookhouse. Lola is one heck of a cook. Just let her know what you like. But beware, she might recruit you for the next yoga class."

"Your wife teaches yoga? I might just be a willing recruit. And no need to go to any trouble on my account. I don't want to bother anyone. I can manage for myself. That's what I'm used to." Carli stepped out onto the porch and leaned against the door jamb.

"Whatever you say, Miss Carli, but you feel free to rearrange anything you'd like. Make this place comfortable. And welcome to the Wild Cow Ranch. It's good to have you home."

Carli's heart jumped at the sound of that word again. Home. This wasn't her home, but if everybody thought that they might be easier to get along with.

"We're putting out salt block and checking mills today. I better get back at it." Buck tipped his hat.

"I'd like to walk out to the corral with you if that's the direction you're headed. Give me just a minute." Carli went back inside, yanked on her boots, and grabbed a cap.

Carli and Buck walked in silence to the corral. Lank stood in the pen with his arms draped on the top rail of a corral and one boot propped on the bottom rail. He was watching a cowboy lunge a young colt. "See you in a few, Colton." He bounded over the rail in one easy stride when he saw them and climbed in Buck's truck without saying a word. So that was the mysterious voice at the other end of the line, when she had thought she was talking to Buck. She still didn't think it was funny. Carli turned her attention to Beau.

He paid her no mind, instead sniffing noses with the horse in the next pen. She decided they both could use some exercise, so she jogged back to the house and changed into her riding gear. By the time she made it back, Lank was in the barn, saddling a horse.

Lank surveyed her from head to toe, eyeing her tight-fitting English breeches and her to-the-knee, black leather boots. Not exactly cowgirl wear.

"Where are you going?" she asked.

"We found a dead momma, eaten by a pack of coyotes. Her calf is missing, so I'm going to sweep the pasture and bring her orphan baby back, if the coyotes didn't get it too."

"I want to go. Just give me a second to saddle Beau." She hurried into the tack room.

Lank called out after her, "It's no place for..."

"For what? For a woman? For me?" Carli stopped and met his eyes as she carried her gear over to Beau. "Well, I'm the ranch owner and I want to see every aspect of my business. I'm going."

"I was gonna say that it's no place for that kinda saddle and what do you call those skinny pants? You sure git riled up easy." He gave her the once-over again before swinging a leg over his saddle.

She dropped the bridle over Beau's head.

"You sure that show horse of yours won't get spooked out there, Ms. Jameson?"

"Beau will be just fine. He's pretty laid back."

With Lank in the lead, Carli pulled her ball cap tightly down on her forehead and urged Beau into a canter. They didn't need to race but wouldn't be dawdling either. She told herself she probably should be wearing a helmet. Anything can happen on horseback. She'd known people to fall off, hit their heads, and die. Although some bull riders wore helmets. But this wasn't bull riding. What she knew about cattle ranches and ranch horses was practically zero, but she'd never let them know it.

She followed and Lank occasionally glanced back over his shoulder to make sure she was behind him. She always looked away when he looked back. Good grief. She acted like a junior high school girl with a crush.

Soon they came upon Buck standing at an adult cow's body, or what was left of it, a carcass really. Carli had never seen bones stripped that clean before. The spine lay off to one side, the skull was laying a short distance away, with other leg bones scattered about. Carli certainly wasn't going to let these men see the shock and sadness she felt inside.

Lank spurred his horse and made a circular pattern around and around, back, and forth. Carli nudged Beau to follow.

"The momma must have been sick or injured, otherwise she would have fought off the coyotes. It's dangerous when the coyotes pack up like this. She was one of the last to drop a calf. Hopefully, it's still bedded down where the momma put it."

They crisscrossed the pasture, Lank sometimes riding around clumps of yucca. They rode down into a washout, the bottom filled with thickets of bushes.

"Wild sand plums," said Lank. "I see something."

Lank edged into the brush and a solid black calf came flying out in front of him. Beau jerked his head in a start and backed up, even did a little buck to show his desire to flee, but Carli held him in place.

While she tried to get Beau to move, Lank came flying out of the plum brush with his rope swinging over his head. He laid a nice loop over the calf's head, and his horse came to an abrupt stop. Beau was at attention watching the commotion.

"No ear tag. A little bull calf born maybe a week ago, but I think he'll make it." He leaped off his horse and slid a gloved hand down the rope. When he got to the wiggling calf, he wrapped his arms around the head, laid him on his side, and had the little guy's feet tied up in no time. "Let's go get the trailer," he said as he unlooped his rope from around the calf's neck.

They loped back to headquarters and left their horses tied at the rail. Without any instruction, Carli kept a close eye on Lank and followed him across the compound. She wasn't sure if he wanted her to go or not. They jumped into the truck, hitched on to a trailer, and headed back out to the pasture. Carli helped Lank lift the calf and place him in the back. His weight surprised her.

"He's solid muscle," she said as she held his back while Lank lifted him by four bound feet.

"He already weighs around sixty pounds. I'll put him in a stall. He doesn't look too much worse for the wear, a little stunted though. We'll fix him a bottle and he'll bounce back. No telling how long he's been hiding in the bushes, staying right where his momma put him."

Carli dismounted and led Beau inside the barn, unsaddled him, and put him in his stall. She could rinse him off later. He wasn't hot. But right now, she was excited and concerned about the baby bull. He was all black except for a tuft of white right in the middle of his forehead. He sure was a pretty little thing.

"I can feed him. Show me what to do."

Lank measured powder from a large sack stored in a metal trash can and added water in what looked like an oversized baby bottle. He shook the bottle to mix the contents and handed it to Carli.

"Since this little guy's lost his Mom, we've got

to take over for her. There's actually a name for an abandoned calf—'Maverick'. There was a man around 1861 in early Texas, Samuel Maverick—a rancher, lawyer, and one of the largest landowners. The legend goes he never branded or earmarked his cattle, refusing to register a brand, instead laying claim to anything with slick ears, although his neighbors branded theirs. He thought they should be free and independent. As they roamed the state, his herd multiplied and grew into the thousands. Anytime an unbranded cow was seen, people would say, 'There goes a maverick,' and the name stuck. Mavericks are spunky. It's like they know they're on their own and they need to be tough to make it. Strong, wiry, and untamed like the land where they live.

"Here," Lank handed her the baby bottle and held the back end of the little bull for her. "Give it a go. He's probably pretty hungry."

Carli held the bottle towards the bull calf. He hesitated. Untrusting of these humans that watched him. Lank pushed him closer to the bottle, urging him to sniff the milk. He squirted some on his fingers and rubbed the milk on the calf's nose. "It's not momma, but he's so hungry I'm hoping he'll take to it."

He started to suckle. He bumped the bottle with incredible strength, causing Carli to back against the metal wall of the barn.

"He likes it. We'll call him Maverick," Carli said.

"He needs a bottle twice a day and we'll give him a little grain too. He's younger than the others, but I think he'll make it."

They were holding the bull together and watched him down the bottle in no time.

"I want to take care of him," Carli said. "Is that alright with you?"

"You're the boss, Ms. Jameson. And honestly, I'm glad to have one chore taken off my list." Lank laughed.

When Lank stood to walk out of the stall and had his back to Carli, she scratched the calf's head, and he jumped back like something big was coming after him. "Don't be such a scaredy cat," she said. It surprised her, but she loved him so much already.

Overwhelmed by the connection she felt to this animal, it seemed they had so much in common already, each on their own in the big world. Untamed. Wiry. Alone. Skeptical of everyone. They had to be strong to survive. She'd help Maverick survive. She'd be his family.

Chapter Fifteen

In between fretting over Maverick and riding Beau, the days quickly slid into a week. Carli tagged along with Buck as he went about running the ranch; he seemed happy to explain how the operation worked. She had learned the pasture names and met several of the local dayworkers who helped on occasion. She realized she hadn't given a second thought to Mark. The limited cell service made it difficult to check on things back in Georgia every day as she had originally planned. Carli made a mental note that she would drive into town this evening for a stronger signal and call Mark. Part of her felt bad about dumping the Georgia responsibilities all on him, but then again, she'd never had more fun in her life than now being in Texas.

It seemed to Carli that "little" Maverick looked forward to her appearances. He soon got over his skittishness and greeted her eagerly at the gate. He attacked his bottle with gusto. She didn't want to be silly though. After all, he was an animal, a hungry one, and she was just the person who brought him a bottle twice a day. But she thought there was more to it than that. He wasn't around his cow momma for very long before she was killed by coyotes, so Carli liked to believe that he was bonding with her—imprinting, she knew that term from horses. She wasn't sure if that happened with cows. With horses, the foal takes in the aroma of its human. The human gently blows breath into the animal's nose and touches every part of its body thus establishing trust.

Speaking of smell, Carli noticed cow manure on her jeans—must've gotten there when Maverick jostled her around in the stall trying to get a hold of his bottle. He was growing fast and wasn't exactly a baby anymore.

She didn't care much about the manure. She could rinse it off once she was done feeding him and got outside the barn.

But before she could do that, she heard a somewhat unfamiliar, but at the same time familiar, high-pitched female voice.

"Billy, come along. They said she was in here with a cow, doing something. My goodness, it smells. Yuck. Are you coming, Billy?"

"You go on. I'm looking at the horses."

Carli heard the voices and got to her feet in Maverick's stall, then panicked for a minute but there was no place to hide. She swung the gate open halfway and stepped through it as she brushed shavings off her jeans the best she could. The manure would have to wait.

She stopped short to keep from plowing into a red-haired woman wearing high-heeled, black boots pulled over skin-tight, denim leggings. An off-white lacy, see-through flowing blouse revealed a buxom figure. Her nails were filed to a point and painted blood red. "Hellooo. We came to see you."

As she faced Carli in the corral, she lowered her black designer sunglasses onto the middle of her nose. "You're Carlotta Jameson, is that correct? I saw you in court."

"Yes, I am," Carli said.

"I am Nicolette, Billy Broderick's wife. We're still newlyweds. Been married almost a year." She giggled and turned a flirty glance in his direction. Her slim, delicate fingers braced under her nose as she looked down to the manure on Carli's jeans.

"Oh, sorry. I'm a bit of a mess. I was feeding a bottle calf. He's a little maverick bull."

"A what?" Nicolette frowned.

"Oh, it's an orphan baby. Lost his momma. He's cute. Want to see him?"

Billy appeared at her side. "Nicolette has never shown much interest in the cattle business."

"Uh huh. Well, no. Anyway, I'm here to be neighborly. We may have all gotten off on the wrong foot, so to speak, with this legal business. There's no reason we can't settle Ward's estate on a cordial basis. I'm just leaving it up to Billy's lawyers. God knows, he pays them enough. But enough of that. I want to invite you to my sorority tea, at our home, this Saturday at two. Normally, these teas are for legitimate members, women from prominent families of our community, but we're having a membership drive and I bring a guest occasionally. I thought you might like to meet some of your neighbors. You do have something to wear, don't you? A dress preferably."

Carli found herself shocked and speechless. Didn't this woman and Billy hate her? Why was she now being invited to a tea? It didn't make any sense. But she didn't want to be rude. All the reasons why she didn't want to go ran through her mind, but the words stuck in her throat and she couldn't think of one excuse. She should probably go so she could find out what they had up their sleeves. It was her suspicious nature. She'd been that way all her life. Truly, she just wished they had the money to take the ranch off her hands. That would be the simplest solution.

"Okay," she managed to squeak out as she shook her head before she could think about it too much. "I'll just need the address."

Without any expression, Nicolette pushed her sunglasses back to cover her eyes. "Talk to Lola. She knows where we live."

And then she walked gingerly out of the barn, sidestepping dirt clods and any other unsavory pieces of animal waste along her way.

Billy had left without acknowledging Carli and was already waiting in his truck.

Carli walked to the pipe fence to watch Nicolette leave. With a deadpan expression on his face, Billy stared at her. Carli suddenly felt cold, but knew it wasn't from the air temperature.

Just then Buck walked up followed by Lank who was leading a ranch horse to the barn.

"What was that all about? Was that Billy?" Buck asked.

"It was odd. Nicolette invited me to a ladies' tea. I said okay."

"Those two are always up to something." Buck frowned. "They're pretty upset about being run off this place. I always like to give folks a second chance. The Good Book tells me to forgive after all. But I knew Billy's daddy and he didn't exactly raise Billy with a lot of love. That young man developed a mean streak just like his pa's."

Carli glanced at Lank who remained quiet as he suddenly appeared leading a horse.

"Well, I'll be polite. It'll give me a chance to get to know them better. I really don't want to make waves or cause any trouble, plus I'll get to meet some other women who live around here." And then to Lank, she said, "What're you doing with that horse?"

"I gotta doctor it some. He's a little touchy on his left leg. Maybe a rock in his hoof or a sore ankle."

Carli just nodded and looked towards Buck.

"I just fed Maverick. He's getting pretty big."

Buck turned to Lank. "Let's run him through the chute. I'll go get the medicine bag."

"Yes, sir."

Lank fixed a bottle and held it out for Maverick. Even though Carli had just fed him, the calf's ears perked at the sight of more food, but Lank kept backing up not letting the calf get a taste. The calf followed until they were in a narrow alley, enclosed on both sides by sheet metal. Lank allowed the calf to pass and pushed him from behind through an opening and into a chute. "You can go around that way and stand by Buck."

Carli climbed over the pipe fence. Buck operated a few levers and the chute closed tight around Maverick. His head fit perfectly through the opening at the end.

Buck filled shot needles. "We vaccinate against black leg, which is a horrible disease caused by a virus."

Lank stepped up to Maverick's head and clipped a dangle tag on his left ear. "With Carli's help I bet we can lay him on his side."

Buck swung into the saddle of his waiting horse and formed a loop with his rope. "Carli, I need you to put one knee on his neck and hold his front leg back when we get him on the ground. Can you do that?"

"Sure," said Carli. "I'm ready."

"Okay, let him out," Buck said.

Lank worked more levers, the end doors opened with a clank, and Maverick gave a crow hop out of the chute. He looked to Carli, his food source, just as the coil of rope circled around his back feet. Buck urged his horse backward dragging the calf for several feet until he landed on his side.

"Now, Carli," Lank sprang forward and grabbed the two hind feet as Carli settled on his neck. Before Lank could remove the rope from the back feet, Buck was at Carli's side to show her how to grip his front leg. Poor little Maverick. So trusting, and now they were ganging up and holding him down.

Buck took a knife from his pocket.

"What are you doing?" Carli asked.

"We're making him a steer." Lank worked to undo the rope around his back feet, stretched taut by the horse at the other end.

"You're cutting him?" Carli's voice raised as she frowned at him.

"That's what we do." Buck walked closer and leaned down. "We use only registered bulls for breeding, and we castrate the herd bulls. He'll grow a lot more and then he'll make a great beef steak next year."

"Steak! No one's touching him and no one's cutting off any...you know what. You're not doing it. And that's an order. He's as gentle as a lamb. And he's my responsibility. He's not going to be served up on some platter." Anger rose in her chest and she felt her breath come fast. She looked from Buck to Lank.

"We raise premium stock that produces beef, Carli. That's what we do. We grow food just as if we grew a field of potatoes. This is a cow/calf operation." Buck stood and looked at her with a dumbfounded expression.

Lank watched her with sparkling eyes, his lips pursed together. She noticed he had trouble stifling the grin on his face.

"You think I'm crazy, don't you?" Carli glared at him and then stood up. When she did, Maverick found purchase on the ground with his front hoofs and slid out of Lank's hands. The calf ran straight for the horse at the other end of the rope, which until now had been standing patiently. Calf and horse took off for the other end of the pen. The horse spinning and tugging. The calf spinning and tugging in the opposite direction.

"Whoa. Whoa," shouted Buck. He ran towards his horse.

Lank sprang up from the ground in seconds and grabbed for the rope, finally lunging himself across Maverick's back. They both landed in the dirt. Buck stepped in to remove the rope from the back hooves.

"I guess we're not making him a steer today." Buck was breathing hard as he coiled his rope.

Carli glared at them, hands on her hips.

"Yes, ma'am. You're the boss." Lank complied with a smirk as he rolled off the calf. Maverick gave a swift kick before he stood up, catching Lank right on the shin. "Thanks Mav, I felt that one. Just be sure to warn everyone to stay clear when he grows up. You'll have a thousand-pound pet on your hands. Then you'll wish you had castrated him and shipped him in the fall."

Maverick sauntered over to the water trough making a sucking sound as he took long drinks. Poor baby. That had been a traumatic experience.

Carli made a "humpff" sound and glared back at Lank. She would never regret saving Maverick from disfigurement. She spun on her boot heels and tromped towards the house growing angrier with every step. What was it about that guy that got under her skin?

Chapter Sixteen

After Carli had dusted herself off, changed into clean jeans, and washed her face, she wandered back over to the cookhouse. Still aggravated at the men for what they were going to do to Maverick.

Inside, Lola was in the kitchen fixing lunch. "Hamburger, Carli? Or maybe a chicken salad sandwich?"

"Uhmmm, I didn't have any breakfast really, so how about just coffee? Sure, Lola, I could eat maybe just a half of a sandwich. Thank you very much."

Lola grinned wide, delighted to serve Carli, and scurried around the table setting a plate down in front of her with a full sandwich on it. She then added silverware, a napkin, a glass of iced tea, fruit and cottage cheese, tortilla chips with guacamole and salsa, and was about to cut a piece of pecan pie when Carli put up her hands to stop her.

"Whoa, Lola, I only want a half of a sandwich. I can't eat all this. Thanks anyway. I appreciate it."

Lola looked downcast. "But, Miss Carli, you should eat. You have to keep up your strength to stay on top of the outside work that goes on around here."

"It is a busy place, that's for sure. I'm just fine,

Lola, thank you. By the way, do you know where I can buy a dress? I've been invited to a sorority tea, they called it, and I don't really have a dress with me."

"There are many nice shops in town with ladies' dresses. We have a Chico's. And the mall is great too. Dillard's or JCPenney's. I'd love to take you shopping. Who invited you?"

"Nicolette. Out of the blue actually. I'll be fine. I hate to take up your time. I'm sure I could find those stores on my own." She could plug the names into the map on her phone once she got a good signal.

"The sorority tea and membership drive she hosts every year. They're a service organization and raise money for community projects. I was invited too, but I'm not going this year."

"Wish you could go. I'd at least know one friendly face." Carli bit into her sandwich and her eyes widened in surprise. It was the best chicken salad she had ever tasted.

Buck and Lank came through the door and sat at the table.

Catching the tail end of Carli's conversation, Buck asked, "What are you girls planning?"

"Carli needs to do some shopping this afternoon in Amarillo." Lola piled the table with grilled hamburger patties, vegetables, and poured the men glasses of tea.

"Lank has to go as soon as we finish eating to get some supplies we need. You can ride together." Buck grinned at her before taking a bite.

"Oh, no, that's okay. I'm sure he has plenty of work to do. I don't know how long I'll be and don't want to be any trouble."

Lank took a seat and grabbed a hamburger for his plate. "It's no trouble, really. I'll be leaving in about twenty minutes if you want a ride. No problem. Where ya headed in town?"

Carli dabbed the corners of her mouth with

a napkin. She didn't want to announce that she needed to buy a dress. Pushing back her chair, she stood, thanked Lola, and, without looking at Lank, quietly said as she passed by, "I'll grab my wallet. Be outside soon." She carried her dishes into the kitchen as she had seen the men do after every meal.

Carli chided herself as she walked back to her house. It seemed as though there was a conspiracy to match her and Lank together, and she allowed it to happen. Every. Single. Time. She wasn't quite sure why she had agreed to ride with Lank. She could just have easily driven herself to town to shop, but guessed it was good to conserve on gas. That's what people did around here—consolidated their trips since town was miles away.

They rode in silence for the hour into the city. Lank turned the volume up high on his playlist, which surprisingly wasn't all country music. Carli enjoyed the mix from pop rock, jazz tunes, rap, and a little bit of George Strait too. Occasionally he would tap his phone in the middle of one song and another would begin to play, which annoyed her.

"What is that?" she asked, yelling above the noise.

"Red Dirt Country," Lank replied.

The singer's voice was soulful and deep, the words different from anything she'd ever heard before.

"We need to pick up vet supplies and then I need to buy socks at the Western store. So which store are you headed to?"

"I guess I can look at the Western store." They wandered into Cavender's and parted ways at the front entrance, Lank heading to the boots and Carli going in the opposite direction towards the women's section. After trying on about five or six different dresses she settled on a pale blue dress that draped across her chest and wrapped at the waist into a knot.

Carli thought if she was back in Georgia, she

might wear pumps with the dress, but the saleslady advised, "You need dressy white or tan boots and a concho belt with that."

Following the saleslady through the boot aisle, Carli noticed some dressy options. She wondered if her grandmother's turquoise boots would work but decided on a tan pair with light beige stitching. A belt to match with tan leather and silver conchos would make the outfit. The boots were more than her budget usually allowed but she was in Texas and she owned a ranch. So why not dress the part?

The saleslady carried her purchases to the front counter. Lank appeared at her side with a stack of white socks but his attention was on the girl behind the register. "Hey darlin', how ya been? It's been a long time. How're your folks?"

"Oh, Lank! I've missed you!" She gave him a big, wide smile and a blush marked her cheeks.

"I'm great, Mandy. Good to see you, too." He answered with a wide grin as big as hers. They stood there motionless as they stared at each other.

Carli cleared her throat and pulled her credit card from her wallet. "How much do I owe you?"

The girl placed the tan boots in a box and rang up her other items. "You can swipe your card." She spoke without looking at Carli, instead flashing another flirty grin in Lank's direction.

Carli waited patiently while Lank paid for his purchases. Mandy came out from behind the counter to give him a big hug and then draped her arms around his neck. He pulled her closer. Carli felt her cheeks grow warm at their display of affection.

Lank watched her climb into the truck. "Where are you going that you need a new dress and new boots? Is there a dance somewhere I don't know about?"

"No, I am not going to a dance. If you must know, I'm going to Nicolette's tea. Her sorority or something."

He mentioned, "My mom used to go to that."

"Really? She's not a member any longer?"

"She passed away from cancer last year." Lank cranked up the radio before Carli could respond.

She wondered if his father was still living. Carli finally got the nerve to ask about Mandy and yelled over the music. "Is that girl at the store an old girlfriend?"

"Not really. We went out a couple times. I guess she had a thing for me. I knew her folks. She's really young."

"And pretty, too," Carli said.

On the drive back to the ranch, they made stilted small talk. And Carli once again thought she should've made this shopping trip on her own. It always seemed to become a mistake to involve other people in her life. This Lank guy was a prime example—he was bugging her. And to see him flirting with the girl in the boot store bugged her too, but why should she care? He was like all the rest of them. She should just stick to Beau and Maverick and forget about men. Get back to business, she told herself.

They rode the rest of the way to the ranch in silence.

Chapter Seventeen

Saturday. The day of Nicolette's tea came too fast for Carli. She regretted accepting the invitation but appreciated the gesture and was curious about the man who had grown up knowing her grandparents. Walking out of her house to tend to Maverick and Beau, she was surprised to see the cookhouse lawn covered with women doing yoga stretches. She was always up for any kind of stress-relieving activity.

The mid-morning sun felt nice on her bare arms. A gentle breeze rustled the cottonwood leaves, still mostly green but showing only a hint of orange with a promise of the changing season.

"Come join us," Lola called out.

Carli laughed and thought how silly to be doing yoga in the middle of a cattle ranch, but then the activity suited Lola. She joined the back of the group and spent a pleasant time stretching and bending. Afterwards, Lola introduced her to the group, so many names she would never remember but genuine smiles and friendly faces. They seemed like nice ladies.

She hurried through her chores, and then needed another shower. Carli felt strange and pretty in her blue dress and tan boots, something she'd never wear at home. Pinning part of her hair up in back, she let the rest fall softly on her shoulders. Silver earrings finished off the outfit, and she was ready to go.

She would drive herself rather than ask anyone to take her and planned to quietly slip out unnoticed. That didn't seem to work though. As she walked out the front door to her truck, she felt the glance of the ranch hand. Lank stopped working on the faucet next to her house to watch her. She looked over at him, but then quickly turned away.

Buck walked across the compound and waved a greeting. "Lookin' mighty fine, Miss Carli. Do you know where you're goin'? Have directions? One of us could give you a ride if you want."

"No, Buck, thank you. I've got the directions. It's only about a half hour away. I'll be back in a while. Probably won't stay very long."

"Okay, Carli. Just call if you need anything."

"Thanks, Buck. I appreciate it."

***

Billy and Nicolette Broderick lived on the edge of the small town of Dixon, their home a showplace with white brick and pale-yellow trim. A circular drive lined with perfectly trimmed oaks, and bumper to bumper with cars and trucks.

As Carli parked her vehicle on the street, she watched groups of women walk into the house. They giggled and admired each other's outfits. Some wore spike heels while others wore cowgirl boots adorned with bling. Their fingers, wrists, necks, and ears were dazzling with gold, silver, turquoise, and diamonds.

She almost drove away but then remembered her boss and the real estate business. If she wanted to sell the ranch, it made sense that she should utilize every networking opportunity available. She understood the value of making connections with people.

Carli already felt out of place, but was determined to go in. She carried a bag of muffins that Lola had baked for the occasion.

Nicolette was stationed at the front door, greeting all the women as they entered. She smiled widely showing off her dazzling, snow white teeth, and hugged and laughed with each of them. A cloud plume engulfed her face as she took a drag from her vape device. Compliments were exchanged about hair and fashion choices. Carli stood in line behind a group of girls.

"Where did you get that delightful vape pen?" one of the guests asked.

"I bejeweled it myself," Nicolette laughed. "How do you like it?" The pink and purple glass sparkled in the light from the front door.

They tittered and hugged and tittered some more.

Carli was almost to the point of turning around and leaving when Nicolette saw her and smiled. She stepped in and extended her muffin bag. Nicolette dropped her smile and said in a loud voice as she tossed the bag on a table behind her, "Oh, my dear, this event is catered. It's not a potluck." Turning to other laughing women, she said, "Ain't that sweet? Bless her heart. This is Ward and Jean's granddaughter, y'all. She's from Georgia."

Carli looked down, muttered, "Sorry, but Lola made them special for you."

"Make yourself at home," said Nicolette with a sweeping gesture of her arm.

The home displayed the most expensive and the best—full and big and over the top. Bronze horse statues, opulent vases with complex designs, and sofa-sized oil paintings of cattle, which Carli felt sure were originals, filled every room.

Wandering through a formal living room, a family room with one wall covered by a large television, Carli walked under a wide arch into the sunroom.

The brightness and large plants drew her in. Chairs had been set up in rows. She took an empty seat towards the back. The windows were tinted to block the Texas sun, and of course it was air conditioned. Ceiling fans spun slowly. Carli admired the plants that lined one wall, hanging baskets overflowing with pink blossoms, and vases of fresh flowers.

One lady approached Carli. "Ward and Jean were so important to this community. I'm wondering just where you came from and what you're going to do with their ranch."

"It's for sale," said Carli.

Another lady joined their conversation. "We are so thrilled at the lakefront community that Billy is developing. Are you involved with that?"

"No, she's selling the ranch," the first lady said.

They both stared at her, but before they could say anything else Nicolette walked to the front of the large family room where a podium and microphone had been set up. Carli joined the group of ladies who stood at the arch. All available seating was occupied in the large room. Nicolette tapped a small, wooden gavel and said, "Ladies, ladies. Let's all find our seats and come to order now. We need to conduct just a little bit of business, and then we can adjourn and partake of all the goodies that are waiting for you in the dining room. Billy, the love of my life, gave me carte blanche budget on the menu." At that, she flashed her huge, glittering ring and everyone laughed and applauded.

Nicolette tapped the gavel again and continued.

"Now, ladies, as you all well know, we are working extremely hard to establish our very own local chapter of a community service sorority. Some of you may already belong to another chapter, but my dears, the closest one is in Amarillo, for heaven's sake, almost one hour away! Who wants to drive for that long when we can make a difference right here in our own community? And frankly, we'd like to make some of our own decisions regarding events we'd like to hold."

Nicolette flashed her bright smile, tossed her red mane back, and everyone applauded again.

"It has come to my attention that there may be some among us who are...well, imposters, if you will. I think they are called "posers". A person trying to pose as something, or someone, they are clearly not. They come here from the outside to our great state of Texas and they want to slide in, fit in, I guess is what they're trying to do. They buy up property or obtain it in devious ways and try to impose themselves on the local community," she said, looking straight at Carli. Several other women glanced in Carli's direction.

"I think we need to be made aware of what's happening in our very midst so we can be on our guard and know what to look for. And, certainly, pray to the Good Lord above that they will not infiltrate our time-honored traditions, our historical organizations, the very land and community that our forefathers, and mothers, fought so hard to preserve."

Again, Nicolette's words were met with thunderous applause. She was skilled at manipulating a crowd.

"I am truly honored that you have bestowed upon me the office of president. Now we will hear reports from the other officers, and then we can eat."

Carli sat patiently until the end of Nicolette's speech, but she got angrier the longer she stayed. After a few more minutes for the treasurer's report, she decided she could slip out without anyone noticing. The women got up from their chairs, chatting with animated smiles and fake giggles as they made their way to the tables of food and drink in the next room.

Perfect time to make my exit. Her blood boiled.

Did they all think she was the poser? I'm not staying after Nicolette's direct attack. And all those women are staring at me.

As she was making her way through the crowd, Nicolette blocked her path. "Leaving so soon, Carlotta? Won't you stay for refreshments? Or perhaps you'd like to take your little bag of muffins home with you?"

Three women who huddled at Nicolette's elbow all chuckled and fake-smiled at Carli.

"No, Nicolette. You can keep the muffins. Thank you but I've suddenly lost my appetite. Besides, I need to get back to my ranch. I have actual work there that needs to be done. And yes, I did live in Georgia for some years, but I have recently discovered that my ancestors are all from Texas, and I was born here. I guess that makes me a Texan, one hundred percent. My great-grandparents started the Wild Cow Ranch. By the way, I heard something about your family being from back East. Is that true? So, you're actually from New Jersey. You're a Jersey girl?" Carli raised her voice on that last bit, to make sure the news carried throughout the room.

Nicolette's face turned scarlet and she pursed her lips. Her three shadows covered their mouths to conceal their giggles and disappeared into the family room.

Nicolette leaned closer to Carli's face. "We know what you are."

"Why did you ask me here?" Carli asked.

"As they say, keep your friends close and your enemies closer." Nicolette stared at her with pure hatred reflected on that beautiful, angelic face. Before she could form an answer, Carli scanned the crowded room. She smiled. Gossip would travel as quick as a prairie fire through brittle dry grass in July within the small community.

As she walked through the entry hall, she heard Nicolette frantically attempting to quell the talk before it spread. "Now, ladies, that is just a big fat lie. I don't know why that Georgia girl would want to make that up about me. You know, she literally came here and stole that ranch from my Billy. I just invited her here today to simply be neighborly. And look at how she repays me. Now don't y'all worry about her. Let's go eat our sliders and have some Bloody Marys."

Driving back to the Wild Cow Ranch, Carli couldn't stop her eyes from filling with tears. She told herself it was from anger at the way Nicolette had deceived her. This had been a setup, pure and simple. A subtle and very public way to tell her to mind her place. But she was hurt and felt so naïve.

Buy a new outfit. What a dope I am. She really had thought that maybe she'd make some new friends at the luncheon.

She had to smile when she thought of the look on Nicolette's face when she revealed that she was a true Texan. During the hearing prep, Carli remembered Del mentioning that Nicolette's family was from New Jersey. She never intended to insult her. But she never intended to stay and run the ranch either. True, she felt some pride knowing her family had such a rich legacy, but a move like this was too complicated. And then Carli remembered what one of the ladies at the luncheon had said, something about a lakeside community. Was Billy Broderick planning to divide up her family's land into a housing development? As she drove through the headquarters, she had to admit the idea of that was disturbing.

Carli skidded to a stop in the gravel and a cloud of dust swirled around as she slammed the pickup's door and stomped inside. In her room she yanked off her tan boots and threw them with a crash against a corner wall, then removed the blue dress and flung it over a chair. She felt more like herself once she was in jeans and a Tee-shirt.

After she had changed clothes, she wandered over to the cookhouse to find Lola. That woman always managed to lift her spirits with her bubbly energy.

Lola and Lank were seated at one of the tables. "Miss Carli, are you back so soon? Come see Lank's cut. A black horse bucked him off."

Carli didn't really want to see anyone right now but stepped inside anyway and walked closer.

She saw blood trickling from a wound on Lank's forehead, and Lola dabbing it with a wet cloth. Even with a torn shirt and bloody dirt on his face he was ridiculously handsome. One more thing that annoyed her about him.

"You okay?" Carli asked. "Need stitches?"

"Gosh, no. I've had worse happen to me than this little scratch. You look a little worse for the wear, though. Have you been crying? I guess those women can be pretty rough, huh?"

He smiled just a little, which made her all the angrier. And how was he able to identify her moods so easily? Add that to the list too.

"No, my eyes are not red from crying. Just a little dust out there, that's all. This whole place is like one big dust bowl. It's so darn dry."

Lank looked at her like she was idle-brained. "This is Texas. There's gonna be dust and wind. Lots of wind. Which means things are gonna get covered up with it. It's a never-ending battle."

Lola stopped her doctoring for a minute to look at Carli. "I'm sorry you didn't have a nice time at the ladies' tea party."

"It wasn't really a tea party. More like a club meeting of which I was the outcast." And the more she thought about what Nicolette had said, the more steamed she got.

But rather than yell at Lank, the one person who always seemed to enjoy teasing her, she thought it would be best if she did chores. Why she always felt so aggravated at him, she couldn't explain. And speaking of men, she had forgotten to call Mark when she was in town. He must be royally upset with her.

It was almost time to feed Maverick, so she headed to the barn. "Hope your head is alright," she managed to say to Lank before giving him a weak smile.

Maybe she could be alone at the barn. Dealing with people is such a pain. She knew she'd feel better after talking with Beau and Maverick.

Maverick was hungry as usual and crowded her to get at the bottle. It had been more than a week now feeding him the milk replacer and it was time to start him on solids. She had brought him a flake of hay along with sweet cow cake to boost his appetite, and, along with the bottle, he scarfed everything up. That little bull was a good eater.

After he finished and was content, she leaned against the railing in his stall and, as usual, Maverick wandered over to stick his wet nose against her wanting to be petted.

"Maverick, it's just you and me and Beau. The only ones I can truly depend on. Those witches wanted to string me up today. I don't know that I belong here. Maybe I should just take Beau and go back to Georgia. And of course, I'd have to take you too. At least there I had a few friends and knew what I was doing at horse shows, except for that scheming Savannah. Here, everything is so different, and the people are different. I don't know that I'll ever fit in."

She was furious with herself. She had always maintained a tough exterior, not getting too close. Her clients were only business, but their leaving had hurt her more than she'd like to admit. The old man who had left her his Texas ranch was a stranger, yet she felt some connection. But the ambush at the tea party had really cut deep. She would never let anyone know. What a fool to think she might work out a deal with Billy and Nicolette, but now she knew that would be impossible.

And then the tears fell as she scratched Maverick between his ears, which made her even angrier at herself. She never wanted anyone to see her cry but felt a release like she needed to get it all out. So much had changed in such a short time.

"Miss Carli." It was Buck's voice and she heard him undo the gate latch and close it again. He walked up beside them in the corral.

"I don't mean to intrude. I just wanted to check on you. Lola said the tea party was a little rough. Could I tell you a little story?"

"Sure. I'm always up for one of your stories." She wiped her cheek and looked away from him towards Maverick.

"I don't know what Nicolette may have said, but I want to tell you that you do belong here. I knew your grandmother well, as you know, and saw your mother from time to time. They weren't perfect by no means, but they were Texas women, strong and independent. They tried to help people and do the right thing even if they weren't always a success at it. And then there are people like Nicolette. When you look at her, you're not looking at anything real. She becomes whatever suits the occasion or plan."

Carli looked up at him and frowned. "I may have started a war, I'm not sure."

"Oh, boy," Buck said. "The war was actually started before you even got here. But, ya know what, Carli? None of that matters really. I think it's all the way people treat one another. It's obvious to all of us that you're a kind person and you're trying to learn the ropes around here. You know I'm a church-goin' man. I've learned over the years about the kind of people that God likes and others that get his dander up. Well, I mean He does love all His creatures, even that Maverick bull, even people like Nicolette. But I think He'd rather us love one another, help each other, and do good instead of being jealous or greedy or all those other things. Make sense?"

"Sure, Buck. But I don't know about the God thing so much. He and I haven't always seen eye-to-eye. Besides, what does that have to do with my staying here or going back to Georgia? I'm not sure I really belong in Texas."

"That's what I'm tryin' to say, Carli. You do belong. This is your family's ranch and they've worked, lived, laughed, and loved right here. Now it's yours. We need you. We'll help you, Carli. I'll help you hang on to this place and make it work, if that's what you want. Just open your mind and heart to the possibilities. God will reveal his plan for you. Heck, I'll even invite you to my church, if you think you'd like to go." He winked at her.

"I'll think on what you said," she smiled at the kind old guy and petted Maverick on the top of his head. "Hey, ya know what? I think this fella's too big for the baby bottle."

Buck smiled. "Yes, Miss Carli, and he's gonna get even bigger."

Carli wondered if there really was a plan for her. Heaven knows the plans she makes for herself seem to never work out. And more importantly, what was she going to do with a bull in Georgia? She thought about her friend, Mark. He had always been part of her plans, but where did he fit in now?

Chapter Eighteen

Carli drove into the little town of Dixon early the next morning hoping to find something for breakfast. She barely noticed any of the other businesses once her eyes spotted the coffee shop—B&R Beanery and Buns. She knew she had found her new happy place as soon as the smell of roasting beans assaulted her senses. As she sipped on her latte, she listened to Mark on the other end of the line. She was thankful for a good signal.

"Not much to report on the drugging front," he said. "Frank has it on the top of his list to find any loopholes for you, but I have to be honest. It doesn't look good. How are things in Texas?"

"This is a whole different world. Lots of dust, lots of work. I've been busy but having fun. I had no idea a cow/calf operation involved so much. I haven't talked to the attorneys this week, but I'm hoping to get this thing on the market as soon as possible."

"When are you coming home?" The second time Mark asked the question, the first being the minute he answered the phone.

"It's hard for me to answer that right now."

"You know you have an obligation here, too. Although we don't have any boarding horses right now, we can build this thing back up. I hope you're not jumping ship."

Carli bristled at the comment. "I never said that I was out of the equine center. Where did you get that idea? I have to settle my family's holdings first. You were the one who encouraged me to come to Texas for several weeks, remember? Now you're accusing me of abandoning you?"

"That's not what I meant, but it's been almost three weeks."

Carli took another long sip to calm her anger. The silence at the other end of the line did not help. Before she made it any worse, she decided to just hang up. "I've got to go, Mark. I'll call again when I can."

"Carli, I'm sorry. We need to talk about our future."

"Bye, Mark." Carli disconnected the call and took her time finishing her coffee. Why did she feel this pressure from him? He'd never been that way before. They had always sailed along just fine, with no real business plan. Things were easy with him, but now he's trying to pin her down to a date as to when she'll be back in Georgia so they can plan out a future for their equine center. Funny how she hadn't thought of Mark or their business the entire week.

Carli drove back to the ranch and the minute she reached headquarters her spirits lifted. Grateful for a new day, she felt better about herself and being in Texas after Buck's talk with her in Maverick's stall the day before. The cool October air gave her energy, and she knew Beau would have some too, so she needed to work him.

Wearing light-colored breeches, tall English boots, and a dark green Polar Fleece, she headed to the barn before Lola could stop her for breakfast. If she kept eating everything Lola placed in front of her, these riding breeches would be a chore to put on.

Reaching Beau's stall, she quietly said, "Hey, boy, how ya doing this morning? Ready to ride?"

She brushed his coat of that Texas dirt and worked her fingers through his tail to pick out the shavings, although his tail had been braided and put in a sock the night before. Saddle pad, English saddle, front jumping boots, rear skid boots, crop, helmet—and she was ready to lead him out of the barn.

"Mornin', Ms. Jameson," said Lank. "That shirt matches your eyes." He ducked his head and continued brushing a solid black horse.

She stopped suddenly to look in his direction. He had noticed her eyes? She decided to ignore his comment.

"Is that the horse that caused your wreck yesterday?" she asked.

"Yep. I'm going to work some kinks out of him."

She asked, "I'd like to set up some jumps in that large pen. Can you help me?" Earlier in the week during her wanderings about the ranch, she found a pile of jumps in an old shed. She couldn't believe what she was seeing. No sense in wasting a good opportunity to keep Beau in shape.

"Sure," he said. "Ya know, this is your ranch. We'll set up anything you want. I'll find Buck to help."

Lank and Buck hauled the jumps around as Carli directed.

Lank looked up at her atop Beau and displayed a mischievous smirk. "Is that required garb for jumping?"

Something about him always perturbed her, but she couldn't quite put her finger on what it was. Maybe because he always seemed so sure of himself. Cocky, in an arrogant and extremely annoying way.

"Where do you want that last jump, ma'am?" Lank asked.

"Over there," she pointed, "about three feet off the rail. By the way, why would this ranch have jumps anyway?"

"Nicolette fancied herself an English rider. Got all the latest clothes, best tack that Billy's money could buy. Paid almost half a mill for a papered horse. Funny thing though, she never rode it. Not once. It was all for show, I guess. To impress her friends."

Buck walked closer to Carli. "Is this how you want it?" Just like Buck had said, nothing was real about that woman. Carli moved Beau with her legs into a walk and said, "Yes, sir. That looks perfect. We'd better get to work. Thanks."

"You kids have fun." Buck jumped into his feeder truck and drove away.

"Hey," Lank said. "Would you mind if I rode Blackie in here with you? He's actually pretty quiet, it was just a fluke yesterday, so he won't bother Beau or anything."

"Well..." she said, a bit perturbed, "...I guess so, sure, just don't get in our way." Carli cherished the time she and Beau spent riding. It was her solace and sanctuary. She didn't like the idea of someone intruding on that private time.

"Yes, ma'am," he saluted.

After walking Beau around the pen on the rail and spending a good bit of time posting to his trot, Carli asked him to canter and expertly guided him over the jumps. He tucked his feet nicely and sailed over them with ease. Lank, who was spending time walking the black horse slowly, stopping, turning, and backing up, always looked over when Carli flew over a jump. As Carli finished a jump, Lank rode in beside her. "You have great form. I'm impressed."

Carli was surprised. That was the first time he had actually paid her a compliment.

When they both came to a resting point and were walking their horses around the pen, Lank came up next to Carli and said, "You know, I can do that, too. Jumping, I mean."

"You're kidding. Cowboys don't ride in English saddles. And they sure don't go over jumps."

"That's where you're wrong. Sometimes a cowboy has to ask his horse to jump a stream or a log that's blocking their path. Many cow ponies do more dressage movements on the ranch than some English horses. They can turn on a dime the minute a cow breaks ranks and head in the opposite direction after him. Sometimes my horse will go around a yucca and other times he sails right over. I never get much warning as to what he'll decide." They both laughed.

"Dressage? Now you are kidding me. How do you know about dressage?"

"I'll tell you about that some other day," Lank said. "For now, I'll make you a bet. If I can ride Beau and take him over those jumps as good as you just did, then you have to ride Blackie here. I'll tell you what to do. Whaddiya say? Are you up for the challenge? Or are ya chicken?"

He smiled that annoying grin again. Carli didn't have to think for very long about the challenge.

"Chicken? Why would I be chicken about riding your horse? Piece of cake. I'm just a bit worried that you'll mess up my Beau. Don't you dare be rough or injure him. And take those spurs off."

"Fine. You hold Blackie by the gate while I hop on Beau. Don't worry. I'll be gentle with your little baby." To make good on the bet, he removed his spurs and handed them to her.

Again, the smirk but this time he added a wink. Carli hated the way her heart lurched.

Lank had to lower the stirrups on Carli's English saddle to accommodate his longer legs, and it was a little difficult fitting his cowboy boots into the slender, silver stirrup irons.

"Are those stirrups going to work for you?" Carli watched him struggling to barely put his toe tips on the irons. Riding depended on the seat and calf muscles anyway, not the feet.

He reached down to pat Beau's neck and proceeded to walk and then trot. Posting up and down, forward and back, was a bit tricky but Lank seemed to be doing alright. Carli was impressed with his skills, but she'd never admit it. She wondered if cowboys sometimes posted out on the range if they were at a faster trot or needed to lean forward and out of the saddle a bit.

After a few canters around the pen, Lank and Beau seemed to feel comfortable with each other.

Lining Beau up to face the center of the rail that was placed at almost three feet, Lank headed for the first jump. Up and over, no problem. It was coming down that gave Lank a jostle. In fact, it looked as though he almost came unseated. Now Carli was the one to smirk, but she was polite enough to cover her mouth with her hand and stifle a giggle.

Lank regained his balance and called over to her. "I'm gonna try that again."

This time he sat back but also gave Beau his head to get over the jump unencumbered. They landed lighter without Lank flopping all over the place. Carli was indeed impressed.

After a few more jumps, they came to a halt and Lank said, "Okay, pretty good, right? I have to admit. This is a nice horse. You ready to ride Blackie? Let's see whatcha got."

Lank walked the horse around the perimeter of the pen to cool him off.

"Get used to him," Lank instructed Carli about Blackie. "Walk him around. When you're ready, click your tongue and ask him for a slow trot. You can sit a trot, can't you?" He smiled.

Carli looked at him, rolled her eyes, and the

corner of her lips tightened together in a perturbed pout.

She completed all the tasks Lank called out to her: walk, slow trot, reverse, back up, relaxed canter or lope as the Westerners called it. As she was almost done, she thought she'd try something. She took a breath, settled herself and collected Blackie, then tapped her right heel against his side while lifting the reins to her left. Lank watched as the horse's front feet crossed in front of each other to perform a nice side pass. Then she leaned back, again put her right heel firmly into the horse's right side, this time draping the split reins in one of her hands over the horse's neck and guided him around to the left in a complete circle while his left hock remained planted firmly on the ground. A 360. Then, finishing the circle and coming to a halt, she put her left heel to his side and draped the reins to the right to perform the circle in the opposite direction.

"You know your way around a horse. You're just showing off," Lank smiled. "See, I told ya our ranch horses can do the same as dressage horses."

"I actually knew that," Carli said. "I was just teasing you before. I used to train with an old Georgia cowboy who taught me the basics. Horses are horses. You just have to know how to move their bodies around. They learn through repetition. You can teach almost any of them to do what you want. Just takes patience."

"So, you were kinda hoodwinking me before saying that ranch horses were just like bumps on a log, right?"

"Well, do I win the bet? And what do I win?"

"I'd say it's a draw. I did a pretty darn good job over those jumps, wouldn't ya say?"

"I guess you did okay, but I really had the better form, don't you think?" She was about to dismount when he spoke, so she waited.

"Yeah, your form is better than mine and your britches fit way better," he said under his breath, but Carli heard it. She felt her cheeks warm. He walked over to her as she sat on the black horse and placed his hand on her boot.

"What are you doing?"

"Well, one more challenge. Let's see if you can do some of those maneuvers with your feet out of the stirrups. That'll show if you're a real horsewoman."

He tugged one calf, then walked around to the other, and took the other foot out of the stirrup. She felt a tingle zap through her body at his touch but did her best to ignore it.

"There, let your feet dangle. Now walk him around, trot, and lope. Then try the 360s, all with your feet out of the stirrups."

Carli rode Blackie around the pen and performed every task asked of her and felt quite comfortable with her legs long and free, although perfectly in place hugging his sides but not too tight.

As the icing on the cake, and again, probably to show off a little, Carli lined Blackie up and sailed over a jump before Lank could say anything.

She was pleased with herself and the horse until he stopped abruptly upon landing causing her to lose her balance. She hit the ground with a thud and tumbled into a roll.

Lank ran over and touched her shoulder. "Are you okay?" He reached out and carefully lifted her to her feet.

"Darn. Yeah, I'm okay. Just misjudged the landing and him stopping like that."

Lank brushed off the sand from the back of her shirt and gently stroked at her hair. "You've got some dirt in your hair too."

She backed away a little and looked up at him, concerned at their nearness but couldn't help noticing that real concern showed in his blue-gray eyes. She was surprised that she didn't mind him standing so close. And, for once, he wasn't being a smart aleck.

Lank gathered up Blackie's reins and as he and Carli walked towards the gate he again brushed at the dirt on her shoulder. She winced a little and uttered, "Ooh."

"I think you're gonna be a little sore. You smacked that ground hard. Better ice it soon. And it might hurt worse tomorrow."

"I'm fine. It's not the first time I've come off and I'm sure it won't be the last."

"Well, we don't need the new owner getting hurt so you'd best be careful."

She saw extra worry in his eyes that she hadn't seen before, and it perplexed her.

"By the way, did I tell you what the winner of the bet gets?" Lank called out, running to catch up as she walked across the gravel road towards the house.

"No, as a matter of fact, you didn't. And I thought you said it was a draw." Carli stopped and turned to face him.

"Yeah, it was. We both did a good job. That is until the dirt came up to meet ya. But I won't count off too much for that. So, since we both won the challenge, there's a dance at the Olsen's ranch this Friday. It's a celebration and sendoff for their daughter who's going into the military. Want to go with me?"

Carli was caught off guard, unsure as what to say. She didn't feel like being in a crowd, plus she'd be nervous going with Lank.

"Lots of food and fun. Plus, you'd meet your neighbors. What do you say?"

"Is this a date?" Carli hesitated.

"Do you want it to be?" Lank offered her that silly grin, the one she could not figure out and could not get out of her mind.

"I guess so," she said, and then wished she could take it back. She did not need to complicate things even more by getting involved in a relationship with one of her employees. What could possibly go wrong?

Chapter Nineteen

Carli had to admit she was a bit nervous about going to the dance with Lank. Fixed her lipstick about three times, her hair again and again, and changed her dress. She only had two—the new blue wrap-style she had worn to Nicolette's luncheon and the black one she had packed in Georgia "just in case". She wanted to wear her grandmother's turquoise boots instead of the new tan ones, so black it would be. Those boots calmed her. She felt more connected to the people and this place when she wore them.

A knock at the front door resulted in Lola calling out from the entry. "Can I come in? I've got something for you."

"I'm in the bedroom." Carli took one more glance in the mirror and turned to see Lola holding a turquoise squash blossom necklace between her hands.

"This'll look really nice with that black dress."

"That's a beautiful piece, but I couldn't wear your jewelry. I'll be fine. Plain suits me better."

Lola's eyebrows formed a stern little V-frown. "Plain is never okay. You need some pizzazz. Please, it'll make me happy."

Carli wasn't used to this kind of camaraderie from another woman; it was almost like a sister, girlfriend, or...a mother. Her heart warmed from the attention, but she couldn't help but feel a little awkward.

"Thank you, Lola. I'd be honored to wear it."

"Good. I'll tell you the story about it sometime. You look pretty. How are you holding up?"

Carli adjusted the necklace and checked the mirror for the tenth time. "I thought my butterfly-filled stomach was settling down, but I imagine they'll all gawk at me. A misplaced Georgia girl in Texas is how I feel."

"They will see the beautiful girl that you are. With their mouths open, they won't be able to say anything. The guys are on the porch waiting for us."

Lola smiled like a proud mom sending her daughter off to the prom. As the two exited the bedroom, Lola hung back watching. She was right.

A hard knock and Lank stepped inside before Carli could tell him to come in. Lank's mouth fell open slightly as he gazed at her and removed his hat. Then he mustered a few words, "Wow, you look great."

Buck echoed the same, "Carli, you're like a vision. Just lovely."

Carli's face warmed. "Oh, stop. It's just a dress. You're used to seeing me in jeans all the time." It was rare that a roomful of people turned their attention towards her.

Lola joined them and she and Buck proceeded to give the obligatory mini speech about driving carefully, having a good time, and not staying out too, too late.

"She can't help herself. She mothers all of us equally," Lank said as he laid an arm around Lola's shoulders and she gave him a squeeze back. Carli noticed that everyone seemed to be so comfortable with each other and hugs were common. She was not used to that close invasion of her personal space.

"Y'all know that I'm nearly thirty years old and I'm also your boss, right?" Carli smiled. They all laughed. She had said it to be funny and it got a laugh, but the moment it passed from her lips the words did not ring true. She knew they were pretending to like her, with fake smiles on their faces. She would always be the outsider, never the one truly in charge. Her grandfather had not done her any favors, that's for sure.

Lola mentioned she and Buck would also be heading for the Olsen's party soon. All the neighboring ranches were invited and would join in the sendoff for their daughter.

Lank's hand touched the small of Carli's back as he opened the door for her, and they headed to his vehicle. She jumped at the unexpected touch but could not deny the tingle and those butterflies that returned to her stomach as she climbed up into his pickup truck. What was she doing? And why in the world had she agreed to go to a dance with him? Wasn't he the smirking hired help and she the boss lady? The feelings and memories of Josh were still raw.

It wasn't a very long ride to the Olsen's ranch, so they didn't have time for much conversation. Carli watched the road ahead or gazed out the window, but from her peripheral view she noticed Lank surveying her legs and all of her. When she turned to look over at him, he returned her stare with a big toothy grin each time.

"Are we calling this a date? You should probably call me Carli instead of Ms. Jameson."

Lank laughed. "Carli it is then. Those new boots?"

"No, old ones. My grandmother's."

"That's cool you're her size."

"I can wear most of the clothes in her closet, although Western attire is not much in demand for the type of horse shows I participate in. She has some fancy things."

"Jean was one heck of a roper. I remember watching her when I was little. She and your grandpa made a great team and they turned out some nice horses too. That was their passion."

They passed under a rock and wrought iron entrance which sported a huge O with part of a triangle over it. "Here we are," said Lank. "The Rafter O Ranch."

As they pulled up, Carli took in all the decorations around the main house—lots of red, white, and blue streamers and rosettes on the columns, American flags everywhere. She saw a plume of smoke rising from the back.

Lank steered his pickup truck through a gate into a grassy pasture and parked at the end of a line of cars. "They've got the smoker going. Good, I'm starved."

He seemed to always be starving, she thought. But where did all that food go since he looked so fit, so strong, and those tan muscled arms. Lank opened her door and helped her out of the truck. Again, his warm hand was on her back.

Their boots crunched on the dry grass as they walked towards the main house. She made herself focus on the crowd of people that had already gathered. His nearness consumed her thoughts. Stop looking at him.

As they walked in together, Carli noticed others watching them. She liked being part of a couple again even it was just for one evening. Walking next to Lank seemed like the most natural place to be but she was still conflicted. She stayed guarded, never letting anyone close. The easy-going friendliness of these people kept her edgy and prickly, but she tried not to let it show.

There was a big crowd in attendance to wish the Olsens' daughter well as she was about to enter the military. A sea of cowboy hats filled the front room. Carli had never seen so much turquoise jewelry in one place before, except for the outdoor craft markets. She almost took off Lola's necklace and left it in the truck but had changed her mind at the last minute at the risk of hurting Lola's feelings. For once she fit right in. Most important was to celebrate, and the décor bore witness to the purpose. All ages were there—from toddlers to the very old. This was the land of family, friendship, and patriotism. Red, white, and blue was everywhere, from the fresh flowers in the foyer to the mantel which sported an arrangement of red carnations and flags—Texas and American, too many to count.

Lank introduced Carli to the Olsen family, three girls and two boys.

Carli felt genuinely welcomed and eased into conversation with Mrs. Olsen and her daughter who explained all about where she would do basic training, what study and work programs she was planning to enroll in, and possible deployment locations in the future.

Lank was close by talking with Mr. Olsen and some of the boys when suddenly a high-pitched, female voice interrupted. "Lank! I was hoping you'd be here!"

The girl from the boot store grasped Lank's bicep and with her other hand touched the lapel of his Western-detailed jacket. Lank's face formed into that lazy grin that was beginning to seriously irritate Carli, as he looked from her to the girl, then said, "Mandy, good to see ya."

The butterflies came back to Carli's stomach. Or were they buzzing bees now? She felt she was being attacked. Other people watched Lank and Mandy, some smiling politely, others glancing sympathetically at Carli. She felt on display, exposed, as though she were standing there in her underwear in a dream. She wanted to run and hide. Why should it bother her so much? They weren't an item. This was a first date. They hadn't known each other for that long. Why should she care? But she did.

Hoping Lank would ditch the girl and come back to her, Carli instead watched as Mandy pulled him out the back door where men stood around the smoker. Through a window Carli saw Mandy reach into a cooler for a beer, then hand one to Lank.

"Well, this is just great," Carli mumbled to herself. Abandoned in a roomful of strangers. She scanned the crowd but did not see Buck and Lola anywhere.

Mrs. Olsen stood nearby witnessing the whole scene and remarked to Carli, "Mandy and Lank used to date some a while back. I'm sure they're just catching up. Would you like some food, Carli?"

"No, thank you. I'm fine." Carli sulked. Hadn't Lank told her they just went out a few times, and now it seems they were a couple. For how long, she wondered, and then Carli reminded herself that she didn't care. She could not understand why she cared about what these people thought, about Lank ditching her for his ex-girlfriend, or about her desire to make a good impression. This was not her life. She didn't really belong here.

The eldest Olsen son gave Carli a friendly smile and came up beside her.

"Hey. You're the new owner of the Wild Cow, ain't ya? I'm Nathan Olsen. You can call me Nate."

"Yes. I'm Carli Jameson. Nice place you have here."

She smiled into his clean-shaven face with laughing brown eyes. He tipped his hat when he shook her hand. The tall, young cowboy was probably Carli's age, but it was hard to tell.

"You want a beer?" he asked. "I've got some in a cooler right over here."

"I'm not much of a beer drinker. Do you have any wine?"

"I can get ya some, no problem. Follow me. Or my mom makes the best sweet tea you'll ever find anywhere. It's really good mixed with lemonade. And you probably should meet some of your neighbors." He led her through a flagstone patio shaded with oak trees. Sparkling lights draped from the branches. The smell of smoked meats made her mouth water. The tables were full, and people milled around. As they passed, Nathan introduced her to so many people her head was swimming. Soon becoming officially known as "Ward and Jean's granddaughter", a story about one or the both usually followed the introduction. A few people remarked that she looked just like her mother, Michelle, or her grandmother.

They made their way inside to the dining room. The sideboard was covered with every kind of beverage you could think of, and nearby a rusted, antique metal box retrofitted inside with a cooler to hold ice.

Soon, Carli found herself laughing at something Nathan had said. She enjoyed the conversation and friendly, relaxed atmosphere. Instead of Georgia horse talk, there were plenty of ranch horse stories that kept her entertained. She couldn't help but feel a kinship with people who loved horses as much as she did. Not exactly what she had thought the evening would be, but she willed herself to go with the flow. She could be upset with Lank later.

The Olsen cowboy talked a lot—about his love of bronc riding, his sister going into the military, growing up in a house with five kids, his family's ancestry, and their sense of patriotic duty. At one point he did take a breath long enough to ask about Carli's background and how she got to be the new owner of her ranch, to which she answered as honestly but as briefly as she could.

Her ears perked when he began talking about the cattle business and the generations of Olsens who had worked their ranch. Once again Carli was reminded that she had a lot to learn. She wanted to learn. And that was the surprising part. Never in a million years could she ever imagine finding herself with a desire to know anything about Texas cattle. Maybe she was in the right place for the time being, but she doubted it had anything to do with Divine Intervention or a Higher Power. She would not be staying long. Georgia was where she belonged.

She finally caught a glimpse of Lank heading her way, without the girl. Not sure why she did it, but suddenly Carli put her hand on Nathan's forearm and laughed out loud.

"You're really sweet. Thanks so much for the wine."

Lank came up to them, nodded to Nathan and extended his hand. "How ya doin', man?" They shook.

Then he placed his hand on Carli's back and said, "You want to go outside and get some food?"

"Seems like you've already been outside, Lank. I was just going to go find something with…uh, uh." Her mind went blank. She didn't remember his name, if he had said it before. That played well.

Lank glared at the other cowboy. He kept his hand on Carli's back even though she was trying to move away a little.

"How many glasses of wine have you had? I'm guessing you haven't eaten all day."

"I know you're not my momma because she's dead. Are you the scorekeeper or something? Not that it's any of your business, but this is number two. I think." Carli noticed the pain cross Lank's eyes and wished she hadn't mentioned anything about dead mommas. She looked to Nathan and let out a high-pitched giggle. Feeling a little lightheaded, her balance wavered some. When the cowboy reached to steady her, Lank moved between them and said, "I've got this, Olsen."

Carli lowered her eyes and quietly said, "I just stood up too fast. And you're right, I haven't eaten anything since breakfast. Maybe the wine is making me a little woozy." She sat down again.

"I should get you home," Lank said.

"She needs some food in her stomach. Come this way. My name is Nathan, by the way." He chuckled.

Just then Mandy came up, all bright eyed and giggly. She grabbed Lank's hand and said, "Now, ya gotta dance with me, Lank. This is our song, dontcha remember?" The whine of a fiddle drifted in from outside through the open French doors.

"No, I really can't, Mandy. I'm sorry. We're leaving."

Carli got up from the couch and said, "Go. Go, Lank. It's your song. Go for a dance."

"But, Carli..." he said.

As she watched Mandy pulling him away, Carli surveyed the young girl's lipstick-red boots and too-short yellow dress. It was all topped off with long, platinum blonde hair. The bleached kind.

Carli felt sick. In more ways than one. But she turned towards Nathan and grasped his outstretched hand.

Once Lank and Mandy were out of sight, Carli asked him, "Do you think you could give me a ride home? I don't feel so great." The smell of smoked meats suddenly made Carli nauseated.

"You promise you won't throw up in my new truck?" He smiled to show he was kidding, but Carli knew part of him was dead serious.

"I won't throw up. I don't even have any food in me. So, no worries in that department."

"I wish you wouldn't go. We're having a great time talking." Nathan pleaded but Carli shook her head. He was very sweet, but the crowd and noise were overwhelming.

Carli put her sunglasses on as the sun hadn't completely gone down yet, but mostly she just wanted to shield her eyes from the world.

During the drive, a question kept nagging at Carli but they were almost to the Wild Cow Ranch before she found the nerve to ask it. "I need to ask you something."

"Sure. What's that?" Nathan steered the truck across the cattle guard that led to headquarters.

"Did your mother send you over to talk to me?"

"Yes, she did. She asked me to introduce you around since Lank fell short on the task. I was the one that decided to stay."

"You're not just saying that?"

Pulling up to the Wild Cow Ranch...her ranch, she reminded herself...Nathan turned in the seat to face her. "We should go out sometime."

"Thanks very much for the ride and for being a gentleman. Please give my thanks to your parents and my apologies for ducking out early."

"Don't let Lank upset you. He's there for the fun. Has a string of girlfriends in five counties. I'll be seeing you again, I hope."

He opened the passenger door and held her elbow to help her down. They walked in silence to the porch. Just before she unlocked her door, she turned to face him. "As for going out, I won't be here much longer. It was nice meeting you. Good night, Nate."

"Good night, Carli."

She turned to wave goodbye before stepping inside, and then collapsed on the leather couch. After spending her entire life without knowing any of these people, the memories of her family kept hovering over her like a haze. She couldn't see clear, couldn't breathe sometimes, and wanted to escape, but something held her here. So many stories about people who were growing more and more real to her. The thought of being a part of something special, something bigger like a cattle operation, making a difference in the community, and relying on neighbors. Working alongside family. She wanted to belong, yet she'd never felt more alone.

Chapter Twenty

The next morning Carli didn't join the others at the cookhouse. She hoped to avoid Lank for as long as possible. Instead, she went to the barn and saddled Beau. This time she wore jeans and put a Western saddle on him. When in Rome. Her over one hundred pound "baby" Maverick stood in a corral munching hay.

Beau raised his head and greeted her with a nicker.

"Hey, boy, it's just you and me again." She loved brushing her chestnut gelding and having alone time with him. Seemed like any worries she had, at least for a while, just evaporated through the brush, onto his shiny coat, and away into thin air.

The mellow time was abruptly interrupted.

"Morning, Carli. Can we talk?" Lank looked through the bars of Beau's stall at her brushing him. "Where did you run off to last night?"

Her neck prickled with annoyance. Glancing over her shoulder, she pursed her lips and gave him a perturbed stare. Granted it had been rude of her to leave without letting her date know, but then again, she was still stinging from the notion that she had been ditched.

"What's there to talk about? I'm about to go for a ride anyway."

"Look, I'm really sorry about last night. It wasn't my fault. Mandy was pulling me in every direction. Next thing I know, you had left with Nathan."

"Well, if it hadn't have been for him, I would've had to walk home. Since you abandoned me. Some date."

"You're the one who said go dance with her."

"It means nothing. I hope you had a good time." She rubbed Beau's hind end none too gently. He turned his head to look back at her.

"Carli, please. I can't say 'sorry' enough. That's not how I wanted the evening to go. We just got off on the wrong foot from the beginning. Let me make it up to you." He leaned against the railing with both arms propped on the top pipe. His eyes never left her face, and his expression did seem to show remorse.

She walked closer, meeting his gaze. "You don't have to make it up to me. I understand you have a history with her. I should have never accepted your invitation. I'm your boss, you're the hired help, and I won't be here that much longer. No harm, no foul. Let's forget about it."

After finishing up with Beau, she slid the stall door all the way open, led Beau out, and mounted.

Looking down at Lank, she said, "Isn't there work you should be doing?"

Trotting out of the compound, Carli felt his eyes on her. Buck was cleaning a saddle and looked up when she rode past. He called out to her, but she didn't answer.

Then at a canter she and Beau rode up the hill. The air was cool, and she was glad she had thrown on a medium-weight jacket. She knew she should have worn a helmet, but no one around here did. Stained, dusty cowboy hats or ballcaps seemed to be the accepted attire.

Following a cattle trail, she slowed Beau to a walk. Watching for rocks and on guard for snakes, Carli was lost in thought about Lank, the ranch, why she was here. Her whole life had been turned upside down. And who could she trust? Seemed like at every turn her heart was getting bruised, even stomped on.

She did like Lola and Buck. They had never done anything to hurt her. That turquoise and silver squash blossom necklace that Lola had let her borrow last night was so pretty. Lola said there was a story about it. And Buck. Like a loving grandpa she never had, or never knew. He was always looking out for her. They were nice, but probably because they wanted to keep their jobs.

She passed a windmill, the blades squeaking as they turned in the gentle breeze. The hoof-beaten trail then curved into the dry creek bed and wove through a plum thicket. The water had cut deep, the sides of the dirt bank rising above her head. Beau's plodding feet and occasional snorts were the only sounds along with an occasional meadowlark. The problems that burdened her mind seemed like a universe away.

Beau's ears suddenly twitched back and forth, and he did a little sidestepping jig on the path jamming her leg into the prickly plum thicket. Gripping the reins Carli looked around for the cause. Then she saw it. A light brownish coyote ambled along the creek bed in their direction. He seemed just as surprised to see her as she was him. He bolted into the shade of a bush. Beau spun in one direction, and then another.

Her horse reared at the scent unseating Carli but luckily, she landed on her feet like a gymnast, knees bent, then stood upright. She held tightly to Beau's reins the whole time even though spiked branches stabbed her back.

Buck appeared at the top of the rise. "You all right?"

"Yeah, I think so. Where'd you come from?"

"Decided to check on you. Since you're not used to the terrain and the area, I wanted to make sure you made it back to headquarters alright."

"Thanks, glad you were here. I hate to think what could have happened."

"Can you get back up on Beau?"

"Sure. These Western saddles make it easy with the big stirrups. Like a step." She smiled at him.

"Let's get you home then."

"Do we have that many coyotes?" It didn't escape Carli's attention that she had used the word "we". It slipped out, like it was the most natural thing in the world.

As they walked their horses back to the ranch, Buck launched into one of his talks or sermons as Carli was starting to think of them. But she didn't mind. His steady, deep, "grandpa voice" was comforting. She wanted to lean into it and forget her troubles.

"Coyotes are a big problem. Too many newborn calves are lost to them. We offer a bounty to hunters, but we don't use traps or any kind of inhumane devices. There are a few poachers who trespass to hunt deer and antelope. Your grandpa never allowed any hunting around ranch headquarters."

"That coyote came out of nowhere. He was bigger than I expected them to be."

Buck changed the topic of conversation suddenly. "Did you have fun at the party?"

"Yes, I met so many people. Wish I could have jotted down all the stories I heard about Jean and Ward."

"They would have been so proud of you. You'll discover we have some fine neighbors, and some not-so-good people. For the most part, it's a great community. Hard-working, salt-of-the-earth families. We have to learn to steer clear of the bad. I think sometimes God nudges us to help the bad or troubled ones. That doesn't mean we have to get up close to them or have them hurt us. Sometimes it means we help them from afar, like praying for them, but not being their bosom buddy. Make sense?"

"I understand what you're trying to say, Buck. But what about when others hurt? What do we do with that?"

"I'm sure you've had a lot of hurt from others during your young life. Maybe you've learned to not trust anyone?"

Carli looked away. The sky caught her attention for a minute. It was an endless blue, a shade she had never noticed before. A hawk with wings wide-spread, glided overhead on a wind draft.

"And Lank last night. I hear you arrived together and then you left with one of the Olsen boys. You were looking forward to a nice evening and then things turned out opposite."

"Exactly. He left me. Alone. Nate was nice enough to give me a ride."

"Like others in your past have done. Left you. Like they always do?"

Carli turned her head sharply towards him and almost felt tears starting to form. He could sure hit a nerve. Anger or sadness, she wasn't sure. Was she that obvious? They probably thought she was a total head case.

"I don't want to talk about that. Besides, I never knew my father. He could've been anyone. I hear Michelle played the field a lot." Carli's cheeks warmed after she blurted the comment about her mother. As religious as Buck is, it's not the sort of thing she should have said.

Buck didn't broach that subject. Instead, he said, "Carli, someday you might want to talk to someone about the hurt you carry inside. It can eat away at ya. I know from experience. My pa was around, but he wasn't very nice. A real stickler for every little thing I did. Nothing ever seemed to match up to his standards, no matter how hard I tried to please him. That can be tough on a kid. And I carried it into my teens and young adult years. I even hated him for a lot of years."

He took a purple bandana out of a pocket and wiped his brow and neck, then placed both hands on the saddle horn. Carli looked over at him a little sheepishly, compassionately, interested in his story.

"I had so much bitterness towards my pa for years. It felt like a heavy weight I was carrying around on my shoulders. Then I met Lola. She loved me unconditionally. Never picked at me for things she might've thought I was doing wrong. Unlike my pa. She grew up in a religious household. Together we learned about our Heavenly Father. He's not like any earthly father. He always welcomes us with open arms, no judgment. Always forgives. Always loves."

Carli was glad to see headquarters up ahead. They'd be there in a few minutes. Instead of a nice, peaceful ride, the morning had turned intense. Never wanting to be rude, she had listened lately to his religious talks, but knew it wasn't for her. He was just a kind old man.

"Thanks for rescuing us, Buck. I'm gonna get Beau unsaddled. Then I've got to check on things in Georgia and do some paperwork."

"All right, Carli. Maybe you could have supper with Lola and me later."

"I don't know, Buck. I've got a lot to do. I'll see you around, okay?"

"Carli. Stop worrying so much. If you let Him, God will work it all out. I need to ride through the new bulls. You have a good day." Buck spurred his horse towards the trap, a smaller pasture located behind her house.

She let Beau drink his fill at the trough, unsaddled him, and hung up her tack. As she turned to leave, she noticed Lank standing near Maverick, watching him intently. She walked closer.

Without looking in her direction, Lank said, "I think he's sick."

Carli placed a hand on Maverick's head. He turned to her and bumped her leg, indicating he was ready for a bottle but not with as much enthusiasm as he usually showed. "How can you tell?"

"He's wheezy when he takes in a breath. Look at his eyes, and you can feel that he has a fever."

His sides did feel hot and his eyes were glassy, and buggy. "Will he be alright?"

"Sometimes these dogie calves survive, something they don't. We'll give him a dose of antibiotics and see how he's doing over the next two days."

Tears pricked the back of her eyes. Why would she even allow herself to get attached to some stupid cow anyway? No matter her choices relating to people or animals, it seemed she always made the wrong one.

Chapter Twenty-One

Vehicle lights and the roar of an engine woke Carli from a deep sleep. She punched her phone. Six in the morning. Hearing voices, she padded over to the window to see several pickups with livestock trailers parked near the corral. One cowboy was unloading his horse in the predawn darkness. The glow emanating from the barn did not offer much visibility. Every light in the cookhouse was on, and she noticed several men standing in a clump on the covered porch.

Her warm bed beckoned, but curiosity got the better of her. She grabbed the jeans from yesterday, a Western shirt and vest, stopping at the back door long enough to jam her feet into boots before scurrying across the road to the cookhouse. She walked into bright, blinding warmth and the smell of fresh baked bread.

"Good morning," Buck greeted her at the door and gave her a hug.

Lola stuck her head out from the kitchen. "Good morning, Carli. It's time for fall weaning."

"I see it's time for something." She surveyed the dining hall. Several men sat at tables sipping from mugs while others stood waiting patiently at the coffee pot.

"I completely forgot to tell you we start fall weaning this week. I'll introduce you to everybody. These are the local dayworkers who help us now and then," Buck said.

Carli wandered into the kitchen to find Lola whisking a large skillet full of eggs. More scrambled eggs than she'd ever seen in her life.

"Stir these, would you?" Lola grabbed potholders and opened the oven to remove a pan of fluffy, golden biscuits which she sat on the bar that opened to the dining room. She came back for a second pan.

"What's going on today?" Carli asked as she kept mixing the yellow mush that was slowly forming into something edible. The thought of putting food into her mouth this early made her queasy, although the smells were heavenly.

"Buck should have told you. The guys will drive all the momma cows and their calves to headquarters. We need to doctor any sick ones, make sure the mommas are pregnant, and then the calves are separated into another pasture to be weaned off their mother's milk."

"Want to ride with us?" Lank walked up behind her and she swiveled to look at him. Still perturbed about the party, but she wanted to learn.

"Keep stirring," said Lola.

"I guess. Where are you riding to?"

"We'll start at the far end of the South Pasture and work our way towards headquarters. It's going to be a brisk morning. You'll need a heavier coat. Our horses are eating now; you might want to give Beau something before we load up."

Lola interrupted. "Here, take my canvas jacket. It'll keep you warm. Gloves are in the pocket."

Carli thrust the spatula towards Lank and tugged on Lola's coat, not before her eyes fired darts at the spur-wearing jerk. She hurried out to the barn and Beau met her at the trough. Tossing a little grain into his feeder, she gave him a pat on the neck. "I'll be right back, sweet boy."

***

"Here's our new boss lady," Buck said as she came back inside. "Let's bless it." He prayed for a safe week with no injuries, and right after the 'Amen', the guys lined up to fill their plates.

When Carli grabbed a mug, a cowboy blocked her way to the coffee pot. Turning around to find her behind him, Nathan Olsen smiled wide. "Good morning."

"Hello again. Nate. See, I remembered." Carli giggled. "What are you doing here?" She liked his kind eyes and rugged good looks.

"Neighboring. I work at the Wild Cow for a few days, and then Lank and Buck will help us at the Rafter O next week. You probably met most of these guys the other night at our house." He swept his hand over the room.

With mug in hand, Carli followed Nate around the dining room. He called out names and she shook hands. If she had met any of them before, their faces had escaped her memory. Some were her age and younger, while others had weathered faces and sweat-stained hats from long days in the sun and saddle. This group of dayworkers wore wild rags, vests, chaps, with gloves tucked into the front of their belts. They looked completely different from the party crowd at the Olsen's ranch the other night.

"You can ride with me," Nathan offered.

Carli smiled, filled her mug, and joined Nathan at his table.

"Time to head out. You're with me." Lank suddenly appeared at her side just as she stuffed the last bite of a biscuit with sausage into her mouth.

She only drank a half cup, not wanting to get off her horse in case Mother Nature called when out on the ride.

The men ate fast in silence. Spurs jangled as they stacked their plates on a cart and tossed their silverware into a wreck pan of soapy water before grabbing hats and coats that hung on hooks by the front door. Carli did the same, glanced back at Nathan, deciding not to argue the point of who she would be riding with, and then followed Lank to the corral.

The air had a bite to it making her thankful for Lola's heavy Carhartt® jacket and gloves. Beau gave her a quizzical side glance as he munched the last of his breakfast, but within minutes he sported a Western saddle. "We have work to do, boy," she whispered.

Lank walked past her leading Blackie, and Carli followed. She loaded Beau into the back of a livestock trailer that was already full. Lank held open the door and she squeezed into the back seat of a double cab pickup with the other cowhands.

They rode in silence across white caliche-covered roads and then turned onto bumpy pasture roads, two dirt lanes separated by clumps of vegetation that grew in the middle. The vehicle rolled to a stop and they all piled out. Carli unloaded Beau first, mounted, and waited for Lank. The cowboys gathered in a circle facing Buck. No one spoke.

Impatience tugged at her, but she kept silent.

"Is everyone here?" Buck looked over the group. "Lank, you take five guys with you and cover the east fence. The rest can go with Nathan towards the west. I'll take the middle. Let's git 'em to the mill near the gate that goes into Middle South. Carli, you come with me."

"She's with me," Lank insisted again.

Buck glanced at Lank with a deep frown. Carli's cheeks warmed from Lank's persistence, but she didn't argue. She cued Beau into an easy lope behind the others as they took off down the fence line. One guy stopped, and the group kept moving to the next rise where another cowboy stopped. This continued until the only two left were Carli and Lank. They stayed next to the fence line. She was keen to pay attention to every instruction.

"Keep an eye out for the guy next to us, and don't cross in front of him or over his path. As we maintain sight of each other, we sweep the pasture for the cows and push them towards headquarters."

"I don't think Buck wants me here." Carli said as she gave Beau more rein. He followed behind the other horse.

"Why would you think that?"

"The way he frowned at you at the mention of my name."

Lank laughed. "Buck's the ranch foreman and he doesn't like being crossed. I said you could go with me and he didn't like that after he'd told you to go with him. There's got to be one man in charge, and on this ranch, Buck's that man. Unless the owner says different."

That may be the story that Lank told her, but Carli still felt like an intruder. Everyone was so nice, but was it all fake? Did they talk behind her back? How could they even care about what she wanted? She didn't even know what she wanted. They sure got the short end of the stick when Ward made out his Will.

The morning passed quickly as she and Lank snaked through the pasture. Carli felt small under the big sky and the brown grass that stretched out before them for miles. She took deep gulps of the fall air. Her nose tingled from the scent of a weed she didn't recognize and the early morning chill. The trill of an occasional meadowlark broke the silence.

No cows yet, and she worried about Beau and

what he would do if they came across any. They rode in silence until she saw a black animal with a white spot on his right shoulder calmly grazing against the fence. As they got closer, she noticed how huge he was.

Lank reined over next to her and keeping his voice low said, "That's Spot and he may be difficult."

"He's enormous," Carli said.

"That's how big your Maverick will be one day."

Carli heard what he said but didn't believe him. That bull was massive.

"Get on now," said Lank as he edged his horse closer to the grazing animal.

"Why is he here by himself?" Carli stopped Beau, not sure where they might be needed. Beau's ears were like perked triangles at the sight of the bull. His nostrils took in the strange scent.

"He's done his job. All the cows are pregnant, and he probably just needs a moment of peace away from the girls."

They both laughed.

Suddenly the bull turned his attention towards Carli and Beau. Spot raised his head as if to sniff the air, and then tucked his head and pawed the ground. He charged.

Lank quickly steered Blackie into his path, to cut him off before he reached Carli. Beau pranced a little and raised his head, unsure about the threat. Blackie was fearless. Using his chest, he bumped the bull's nose and deflected his track. The bull stopped, pawed the ground, raised his head, and charged again. Aiming right for Carli and Beau.

Carli froze.

Beau didn't move. He stood his ground, snorted a little air from his nostrils, and then swung his rump around just as the bull passed.

"Run with him, don't chase him," said Lank as Carli reined Beau alongside the largest animal she had ever laid eyes on.

The bull spun towards her.

"Don't jam into his head." She backed Beau off a bit, and they kept a steady pace until they reached the others.

"Move on, Spot," Lank shouted as Blackie tried to head the bull off in the right direction again.

Spot turned and ran right between Beau and Blackie, taking off towards the back side of the pasture. For a big animal, he sure was fast.

The cowboy that rode next to them appeared at the top of the hill. He watched for a minute and then started his horse into a run. He cut the bull off and turned him back towards Carli and Lank. They fell into place on either side of him.

"Get on now, bull!" Lank yelled. "He knows where we want him. We do this dance every year."

Sure enough, Spot broke into a run heading right towards the rest of the herd. The three riders followed him.

The stubborn bull joined the rest of the herd without any more trouble. It took three cowboys to wrangle one bull. Carli reined Beau towards the back as they pushed the bunch up the hill towards a set of working pens. She watched the cowboys over the backs of the cows, learning how they positioned their horses to keep the bunch moving.

Carli listened to the bawls and moans of the cattle coming from just over the next rise. She could hear them long before they came into sight at the top of the hill.

"I think that horse of yours may have given up jumping to become a cow horse," Lank said.

"You may be right. I think he was kinda angry at that bull." Carli patted Beau's neck. "You did good, boy." She smiled and her heart swelled with pride like a mother with her kid who'd just won a gold star at school.

Riding with the cattle, coming face-to-face with the bull—it was all so exhilarating for Carli, not at all like riding in a show ring trying to look the perfect part. Her heart was nearly beating out of her chest. She loved every minute of it. And was so proud of her horse.

As she rode along with the herd, she had to admit this kind of life was addictive. Working from the back of a horse filled her soul. Joy swept over her like a warm blanket.

What if she stayed? What about that cowboy, Lank? Yeah, she was attracted. But also miffed after the Olsen's party. And Nathan Olsen? He was kinda nice, too.

But a darkness fell across her heart as she recalled the years spent without these people in her life. They could have tried harder to find her. Carli had more important things to think about than cowboys and a cattle ranch. The best thing she could do was take the money and run as fast as she could back to Georgia.

Chapter Twenty-Two

Before riding into the corral behind the other dayworkers, Carli turned Beau to look at the scene behind her. The grass of the Wild Cow Ranch stretched for as far as she could see and for a short minute, Carli thought about Georgia and how it was so full of trees. Pines, cedars, live oaks. So much lush greenery. And hills. Even mountains. Maybe not as high as in the western United States, but Georgia could boast of one mountain around forty-seven hundred feet. She loved the greenery and the smoke, as it was called, that clung mysteriously to the mountains.

Here, the flat pasture stretched up to meet the sky. The view broken only by an electric line that stretched out of sight. White wind turbines dotted the far horizon standing like otherworldly giants. Remembering the scenery from her beautiful Georgia sent a wave of homesickness through her until she had to pay attention to the chaos in front of her.

Nathan held back from the bunch and reined his horse beside Carli. "How'd it go this morning?"

"Beau met his first bull. He's taking to ranch life

just fine." Carli laughed. "I think."

"I'm glad to hear it. What about his rider?"

"It takes some getting used to, that's for sure. But I won't be here much longer." She had no idea why she felt the need to add that last little bit. Maybe because she was missing Georgia and the trees. No complications. No involvement. That was her motto. She had to keep reminding herself.

"I'm sorry to hear that," said Nathan. "If you want more riding time, you should join us at the Rafter O next week for our weaning roundup."

Carli snapped her head around and looked at him in surprise. She felt her cheeks warm. "I'll see how this week goes first. There are some things I need to take care of, ranch business."

Lots of things. She had done nothing since she'd been here but ride Beau and eat Lola's delicious cooking. First thing in the morning she needed to call the Amarillo attorney and find a real estate agent. In the meantime, she settled in her saddle and enjoyed the ride. The noise of the cows made it impossible to talk to Nathan, so they rode along side by side into the pens.

Carli couldn't explain the joy she felt after the early morning ride. The camaraderie of being connected to something. Riding alongside a group of people who all worked in unison towards a common goal. She had never felt that she was really a part of anything like that before in her life. Always on her own.

The dust, the loud bawls from the cattle, and the skills of the dayworkers kept her enthralled. And Beau had really surprised her. The horse had heart, that's for sure. She knew he would do anything she asked in arena competitions, but she never realized he would face down a feisty bull too.

The cows were crowded together and then two bulls decided to face off at that moment. The herd squeezed around them, bawling, their calves trying to stay at their momma's side in the bedlam, but that didn't deter the bulls from fighting. The men edged closer from behind encircling the herd until finally every cow was through another gate into a sorting pen.

Beau watched the whole production. After the bull incident, Carli felt confident he wouldn't bolt or go ballistic like some young, inexperienced horse might. But all this was still new to him, so she'd stay on guard and watch for any skittishness. Through her seat and legs, she could feel he was on the alert, listening and looking at gates slamming, cowboys yelling, and sometimes a cow bolting from one spot to another.

That's when the real ranch work began. Carli stayed on Beau near the back of a pen with a few others while several of the cow hands stripped the calves from their mommas. Their horses were amazing to watch, like dancers, each knowing their part and executing it fluidly. Calves went into one pen and momma cows were turned into another.

The bulls were separated into a third pen.

At that minute Carli glanced over to see a tall cowboy wearing a silver belly Stetson, arms propped on the top rail. Billy Broderick.

After the sorting was done, Buck rode over to him. They exchanged words, but over the noise Carli couldn't hear what was said. Billy looked directly at her, and then unlatched the gate to walk in her direction.

"I just want you to tell your lawyer that I'm laying claim to this here calf crop. I've worked this herd all year long while your grandpa was laid up sick for most of it, and these are mine. I'm not backing down."

"You know I have no control over the outcome. The only thing we can do is let the attorneys work it out."

"Make it easy on yerself, little gal. Go back to Georgia."

"I have nothing against you, Mr. Broderick. And me going back to Georgia doesn't change the fact that my Grandpa Ward left me his ranch. I didn't ask for any of this."

"I have my doubts you're even his kin. If you stay, things are gonna be mighty hard so you'd better git ready." The last part he yelled so everybody could hear.

"Is that a threat?" Carli couldn't believe she was even talking to this idiot. The gall of him to confront her like this, in front of the hired day workers. She was mortified and furious. Tensed and clenching her jaw, she refused to say anything more to him.

Buck rode up and Billy suddenly turned and walked towards his pickup. Carli could clearly see Nicolette watching from the passenger seat. Her face set in stone, eyes hidden behind designer sunglasses. Billy slammed the vehicle door a little too hard, and she could see his mouth working, his face red. Nicolette took a draw from her glittery vape pen, never turning her head toward him. Billy spun out, his tires throwing rocks as he left.

"Don't mind him too much, Carli. He's always been a hot head," Buck said.

"I'm sorry you're in the middle of such a bad situation," said Carli. Buck always appeared so calm. He was caught between two owners in this mess.

"I have a job to do and I'll stay at it, until someone tells me otherwise. The Good Lord has a way of working things out. He tells us not to worry about anything, to bring our requests to Him. That's all He asks of us—just talk to Him." In a louder voice for all to hear, Buck yelled, "Let's move." He swung his arm over his head.

The cowhands rode into the momma cows and pushed them into a tight group, through a gate, and into a separate trap.

"We're taking them up the hill and then we'll

preg-test them in the morning," Buck explained.

"Here we go again," Carli said to Beau. He seemed eager to get back to his new job. By the time they rode back to headquarters, it was lunch time. Carli tied Beau to the fence rail next to the other horses and followed the group to the cookhouse. Lunch was more relaxed and after two plates of enchilada casserole, Carli was stuffed beyond reason and realized every muscle ached. There were a few comments about Beau and his first encounter with a black Angus bull, so apparently Lank had been talking about her. After the morning's ride, she felt a new kind of respect coming from the men. They were more at ease with her. She had held her own.

"Thanks for lunch, ma'am."

"Great lunch, Lola."

Every cowboy filed past the kitchen door and expressed thanks to Lola before grabbing his hat from the tall rack that stood by the front door.

"I'll see you in the morning, Carli," Nathan said as he walked past her.

**

Carli unsaddled, turned Beau out into an empty corral, and he immediately rolled in the dirt, his coat shining dark with sweat. Plodding to the water trough, he slurped a long and well-deserved drink.

"Pretty hard work this morning, huh, boy?" Carli laughed.

"Let's haul some bulls," Lank called out from the pickup. "Hop in."

Carli climbed in and watched Lank carefully back up the long trailer to a gate.

"Where are we taking them?" Carli asked.

"The bulls are pulled from the herd every fall. They winter in their own pasture until spring, and then we'll put them back. Babies will come beginning in March or later. Newborn calves born in winter snows are too hard on them, and us." He laughed.

Several mounted cowboys pushed the lumbering bulls down the alley and up into the trailer. Their weight and movement made the pickup shake and the trailer rattle.

The ride to the bull pasture was slow and bumpy, as Lank maneuvered the pickup and long trailer over a few washouts in the road, a shallow water crossing, and back up the other side on sand. The tires spun, but they finally made it.

As they pulled into ranch headquarters, Lank said, "You may want to give Beau a rest tomorrow. You can ride one of the ranch horses."

Carli knew Beau might need a day off and she had already decided to volunteer for dish washing duty, spending the morning with Lola. The thought of riding again was appealing though. How different would it be on a ranch horse, one that knew the ropes, no pun intended. She had to admit all of Beau's strangeness about cattle and the charging bull and her own worry over him had made her stressed a little too.

"Okay, sure. I'd like to ride," she said.

As Lank eased the pickup next to the fuel tank, Carli noticed a familiar vehicle with Georgia license plates parked in between the others at the cookhouse. She gasped.

"What is it?" Lank asked.

"Mark," was her only reply.

Chapter Twenty-Three

"Mark! What are you doing in Texas?" Carli hurried across the compound towards her friend.

"Well, hello to you, too," Mark said with a smile.

"I'm surprised, is all. Welcome to the ranch."

The whole time Mark kept his eyes on Lank.

"Oh, where are my manners? Mark, this is Lank Torres. He works here. Lank, this is Mark Copeland, my business partner from Georgia."

"And friend," Mark added.

"Of course. And my good friend."

Lank shook his hand. "Good to meet ya, man. Welcome to the Wild Cow."

"How is our girl Carli doing?"

"A real cattle ranch owner in the making. She's doing great, loves it here in Texas."

"We sure do need her back in Georgia."

The two men eyed each other suspiciously. Carli looked from one to the other, couldn't quite read what was going on, but it seemed to be a stand-off. Mark's abrasive behavior had her puzzled, and why were they talking above her?

"Y'all do know I'm standing right here. Why didn't you tell me you were coming, Mark? We would've picked you up at the airport. Oh, right, you drove."

"I did try to tell you. I've texted, emailed, left phone messages over the last few days, ever since our last telephone conversation, but never heard back from you."

Lank stepped closer to her side. "Is there anything you need from me, boss?"

Carli shook her head and then turned to Mark. "I'm sorry. The cell service is not the greatest out here and I've just been so busy trying to get acclimated to the ranch and have had some legal issues to sort out. Is everything okay in Georgia?"

"Yeah, everything's fine. I'm doing okay training a few horses and involved in my investments business. Your house is still standing in case you wondered." He chuckled a little. "I drive by from time to time to check on it for you."

"Yeah, I miss my little place," Carli said.

Mark pointed to the main house. "Well, looks like you've done okay for yourself. I guess you're getting it all sorted out, huh, Miss Ranch Owner?"

"It's not like that, Mark. It's a working ranch and I'm learning how to run it. And like I said, I'm trying to sort out some legal stuff, too. So anyways, why did you pop in like this? And you drove all that way?" Carli suddenly remembered his pickup truck parked in front of her cookhouse. Why would he take two days to drive out here?

"I hope you don't mind that I just 'popped in' as you say. At the last minute I thought you might need an extra hand to load up some of your inheritance. When are you coming back?"

"You keep asking me that. I don't know." Carli bristled.

Mark glanced at Lank, and then to Carli asked, "Do you think we could talk somewhere in private?"

"Sure. Let's go across the road to my grandparents' house."

"That'd be good. You don't mind if I stay a few days, do you?"

"Of course not. I have a spare room. You can stay as long as you want." Carli stopped and turned to face him. "It really is good seeing you."

Mark smiled. "I've missed you."

Lank seemed way too interested in their conversation, but Carli led Mark across the road without saying anything more to her hired hand.

As they settled into comfy chairs, Mark cleared his throat, seemingly nervous about what it was he had to tell her. Carli decided to give him a moment to gather his thoughts. "I'll make coffee."

She found grinds in the fridge, started it brewing, and then opened every cabinet door until she discovered mugs. Mark liked sugar and she liked cream on occasion, but black would have to do. She really needed to do some grocery shopping.

Mark took a sip of his coffee. "There is something I need to tell you." He hesitated again.

"Try one of these cranberry muffins. Lola does the cooking for the ranch." Carli settled into her chair again. "What is it? You've driven all this way. Just tell me."

"People are still gossiping about the horse show. Some say you left town because of it."

"Well, people are gonna talk, aren't they?"

"There's more bad news." Mark took several sips of his coffee before continuing. He stared at the muffins for a minute but never took one.

Carli was losing patience with him. "We've been friends for years, Mark. What's wrong? Just tell me." This nervous hesitation was so unlike him.

Mark took a deep breath. "You need to be in Georgia. Help me rebuild our business. We need to get you back on the circuit, and on a horse that can't lose. The time to start training is now."

Carli sat back in her chair. She didn't feel the urgency to return. But felt pressure from Mark and couldn't make any sense of it.

A knock at the door interrupted her thoughts

before she could reply to Mark. "Come in," she called out.

"Everything okay in here?" Lank entered the room.

"This is a private conversation, cowboy." Mark's face turned a deeper shade of red.

"Lank, it's okay. We're just talking." Carli stared at Mark. She had never seen this kind of rude behavior from him.

"I wanted to check if you need me to exercise and feed Beau. I'm doing chores now. It's no trouble."

The intensity hanging in the room was broken and whatever it was that Mark had to say could wait. "Thanks, Lank." She turned to her friend. "Stay a while, Mark, if you want. We can figure this stuff out. Right now, I've got to go to the barn."

After she showed Mark which room to put his bag in, she told him they would eat at the cookhouse and then she'd give him the grand tour.

While Mark settled in, Carli headed to the barn to find Lank.

"There you are. I wanted to talk to you."

"What about? You guys looked pretty cozy in there."

Carli pulled him into the tack room away from earshot of anyone who might be working in the barn, namely Buck.

"Mark showing up here is as surprising to me as it was to you. He's a good guy and we've been friends for a long time. We used to ride and show a lot together. We had, have, a business partnership but he also helped coach me and Beau. I owe him a lot for all his hard work and loyalty. We're business partners."

"If you say so." Lank was pouting just a little.

Carli put her hands on her head in frustration. "It's just that I have a completely different life there. I don't know what to do. I'm torn between both places."

He let out a sigh of resignation and said, "I can see that he's a friend and important to you. When's he leaving?"

"I told him he could stay awhile. We need to sort out some issues with our business. It's complicated."

"He thinks of you as more than a friend, you know. And I sure as shootin' won't be lettin' the two of you alone in a room as long as I can help it."

"That is the most ridiculous thing I've ever heard. You do realize we're not dating. And besides, I'm your boss. You can just turn off that Texas cowboy charm. It won't work with me." She stared at Lank for a minute. He returned the stare with a smirk that made her stomach flutter and annoyed her at the same time.

Strange how this cowhand whom she had just met was so easy to talk to. She always told him things she'd never told anyone. With Mark, they'd been friends and business colleagues for years, but face to face seemed so awkward, even more so that he was here now. It made no sense.

Carli gave Beau a pat on the nose, leaving Lank to his work. As she walked back to the house, she couldn't help but frown. She'd been looking forward to riding this week, maybe going over to Nathan Olsen's ranch to help with their weaning. What did he call it? Neighboring? However, with Mark here, it might seem rude if she got up early and rode off across the pasture. Now she might have to keep Mark occupied. Maybe it would only be for a couple of days, unless they had an extra ranch horse. How ridiculous that she owned a ranch and had no idea which horses belonged to her.

Back at the house, she pulled up a chair next to Mark at the dining room table where he had set up his laptop. Next to that, an open briefcase of files and papers.

"I have other news. I feel a little awkward talking about this, but Savannah and Josh are getting married."

Of all the things he could have told her, that was not something she ever expected to hear. Surprisingly, it didn't upset her very much. In fact, she suddenly realized that Josh hadn't crossed her mind at all since coming to Texas. Her last boyfriend incident had made her more cautious, with an overwhelming desire to guard her heart even more. It hadn't been easy with those dreamy eyes Lank cast her way and the all-American good looks of Nate Olsen.

"After that news, I think we need to stretch our legs and then food. I'd like to show you around the place and then we'll find something for dinner in the cookhouse. We can talk more later."

"Lead the way," Mark said, standing up suddenly from his chair. He seemed relieved their talk was over, at least for now.

They explored the ranch headquarters. Carli showed him the tack room, the shop, the cookhouse where Lola showered him with enchiladas and homemade salsa hot enough to burn your mouth into next week. A few of the cowboys hired to help with weaning were staying in the rooms upstairs, so dinner conversation was pleasant. Carli laughed at their stories and Mark heard all about Beau's encounter with a bull named Spot.

"I enjoyed that. You've made some great friends here," Mark said as they walked backed to the house.

"They are really nice people," Carli said, but what she wanted to tell him was that she felt like such an outsider. She had never shared personal feelings with Mark before. They always kept it on a professional level.

"How long have we known each other? Something like seven, eight years?" He held the door open for her.

"Yeah, I guess so." Carli plopped onto the leather couch and stretched her feet out on the ottoman.

Mark sat on the couch next to her.

"Since I first met you, I always felt a special connection. We've been close friends ... worked the horses, hauled them all over the place, showed together, won, lost. Always had fun, always had each other's backs. Right?"

"We've worked great together, Mark."

"I want to say something else. It's been on my mind forever and I'll go crazy if I don't get this off my chest. It's the main reason I drove all the way to Texas. Let me just spit it out. I want more than just working together. I want to be with you. I love you, Carli. Always have. And I hope you feel the same about me. I've missed you so much since you've been here in Texas. Tried to put it out of my mind, but I just couldn't. I had to come here face to face and talk with you." Mark spoke in one big rush without a breather, as though he'd been holding in his feelings for a long time.

Carli's mouth opened to reply, but nothing came out. She had no idea Mark felt this way about her. Sure, he was a great guy, a true friend, but she never had any romantic feelings towards him. Did she lead him on in some way? She couldn't find the words to say anything at the moment, so she stood up and walked to the window.

Mark followed. She was facing away from him, looking out at a group of ranch hands sitting on the front porch of the cookhouse talking and laughing. She searched the bunch for Lank, but he wasn't with them. Behind her, Mark put both of his hands on her arms and turned her around to face him.

"Carli, I love you." And with that, he leaned in to kiss her.

His lips were warm. A nice kiss as far as kisses go, but not earth shattering. Again, she was shocked and gently pushed him away.

"Mark, you're my family. I really care about you, but not like that. As a very dear friend. I thought you knew that. I love you, but I'm not in love with you."

He pulled her into a tight hug as if he thought she might change her mind, but she only felt trapped.

"It's that ranch hand, isn't it? I saw the way he looked at you when I first arrived." Sadness etched his face.

She pushed him back. He dropped his arms. "We went to a neighbor's party together, but he's one of my employees. You're a good guy, Mark. And I've treasured our friendship. In a town where I didn't know anyone, you were the one person I could always count on. I hope I never led you to think it was anything more than a special friendship. You know I haven't had family in my life. You were my family in many ways."

"Will you think about a future with me? Come back to Georgia."

Carli walked into the kitchen and he followed. "We definitely need to work out future plans for the equine center, but I can't deal with that right now. I have to tend to the Wild Cow Ranch."

"I don't want to be just friends." Mark raised his voice this time.

Carli turned to the coffee maker, anything to keep her busy so she could avoid his pleading eyes. "I always want you to be in my life. Do you think we can still be friends? You have really made things complicated."

"I only want you to be happy. And if you're happy with that guy Lank, you're wrong. We have too much history to throw it all away."

"I don't know if it's Lank. I'm just getting over Josh, and you drop this on me while I'm learning about a family I never knew I had? It's just too much right now, Mark." She fought back the tears as she measured the coffee.

"You have to know I'm right. We're meant for each other. No one has been there for you except me. Do you realize how many hours I've spent trying to get that horse show gossip to stop? To tell people the truth about your character." Mark leaned against the counter as the stream of liquid ran into the pot, breaking the silence that permeated the room.

Carli calmed her anger, grinding her teeth before she answered. "I really appreciate your efforts, but it would also help you. If we could clear the air, we could get more clients and build our business back."

"What do you want, Carli? I'll do anything." He stood and walked closer, his hands clinched into fists at his side.

She turned from searching for clean mugs to face him. "I need you to stop pressuring me to come back. I've got to deal with this legal situation. My grandfather left me a working ranch with cattle and employees and important decisions that must be made. I have no choice, Mark."

"You're saying I'm not important? You have a life in Georgia and a business, a job. You have obligations to me. You can't turn your back on all we've built."

"I'm not turning my back on anything. This is temporary until the ranch sells. You know that." She drew in a slow, steady breath because she had never yelled at Mark before. They had never argued about anything. Ever. His intensity scared her.

"The important thing is to remain friends, and then we can work out the equine center issues when I get back. I know one day you'll find a girl who's worthy of you and head over heels in love with you. You deserve that. I treasure your friendship, Mark."

Anger and hurt glinted from his eyes. "I'm not sure we can be friends when I want something more. I'll be gone in the morning." He turned on his heels and disappeared in the hall, the slam of the bedroom door echoing in the empty house.

Carli poured herself a cup of coffee and made a

face when she took the first sip. She must buy some cream. Only a moment before, she might've been a sobbing mess, but now a calmness settled on her. The Wild Cow Ranch needed her now and that was the right thing to do. This was only temporary. Mark seemed to be in a frenzy for no reason, although his confession of love certainly threw a kink into their business relationship. He'd calm down once she got back to Georgia.

In the meantime, Carli decided on a halt to noticing any and all men in her life. Getting involved with someone right now was not what she needed or wanted. She and Mark had an equine center to run, nothing more. Nathan Olsen was a neighbor. Their paths would never cross again once she went back home to Georgia. And Lank. Those dreamy eyes and that slow, deliberate way he smiled at her was something she'd just have to ignore. She was his employer for goodness sake.

Love. Who needs it?

Chapter Twenty-Four

Bright lights and rattling livestock trailers awakened Carli for the second morning and this time she was prepared for riding. Mark's truck was gone. She never heard him leave and it made her sad that they parted on difficult terms. She pushed Georgia out of her mind and focused on another day of fall weaning work. She had a lot to learn.

Lank had C.P. saddled for her, the horse she had ridden the first time she visited the ranch. The minute her seat hit the saddle and her legs nudged C.P., all the worry and troubles in her life faded away. The rest of the week went by in a blur. Riding every morning to move livestock from one place to another, weighing the calves, and watching the vet preg-check every momma. The auction rep came to video this year's calf crop, and a date was set for the sale, which reminded her she needed to contact the attorney. If Billy claimed the proceeds from the calves this year, how could the ranch survive?

Every night she fell into bed exhausted, but it was fun work, satisfying work. She enjoyed being a part of something. It was a week of riding, roping, sorting, bawling calves searching for their mommas, but by Friday everyone had quieted down.

The calves buried their heads in fresh hay just across the fence line from the mommas. The cows stayed by the barbed wire for several days, but soon wandered away in search of grass that looked appetizing to them. Buck had said they wouldn't have to start caking cows yet, a supplemental food, until the first cold front or snow.

After lunch on Friday, everyone loaded up their horses and gear and headed for home. A few would be back for shipping in December and the rest would be back in the spring for branding. Carli dried the dishes for Lola, and then told her she'd need to buy a few groceries. She was in desperate need of creamer.

"You should run into Dixon," Lola said.

"Great lunch, Lola. Thank you." Lank strolled into the kitchen catching the tail end of their conversation and leaned on the counter. "Where are you going?"

"Carli needs a few groceries. I told her to drive into Dixon instead of going all the way to Amarillo."

"I'll take you," offered Lank. "Let me help everyone get loaded and rolling, and then I'll meet you at your place."

"I should try to reach Patrick first, and then I'll be ready." Carli felt like Lank was hovering, but maybe he was just being nice. She was glad to have someone go with her.

Nathan poked his head into the kitchen. "Thank you, Lola. And I'll see you next week at our place." He pointed a finger at Carli and smiled.

"Sure thing." She was looking forward to it. That meant another week in Texas, but since she had yet to sign any papers about the ranch she'd probably have to be here anyway.

If she stood by the second tree near the corrals, Carli got a decent cellphone signal. She placed the call to the attorney in Amarillo, Patrick, to ask about retaining a real estate agent. She also asked about Billy's claim to the calf money.

"We need that money to make payroll, utilities, buy cake and mineral block for the winter." Carli may not know much about cow/calf operations, but she did understand business and cash flow. The entire ranch relied on the calves selling at auction and shipping at the end of the year.

"I understand your situation Carli, but, considering Billy's claim, it may not be the ideal time to sell your inheritance. I can only advise you though. You have the freedom to make the final decision," Patrick said.

"If I don't sell, how am I supposed to run a ranch in Texas from my house in Georgia? You may not believe me, but I do take my obligations very seriously. Ward—uhmm, Grandfather, has laid a lot on my shoulders." Truth be told, a total stranger dumped her with a mountain of aggravation, but she realized that many in the local community relied on the Wild Cow Ranch to thrive.

"Find a real estate agent as soon as you can," Carli said.

Patrick answered her with legal jargon that didn't make much sense but said he would proceed after the paperwork was finalized.

Tires crunched gravel as Lank rolled to a stop. "Are you ready?"

She climbed up into his pickup. "I need to get my purse and list from the house."

He drove into her drive, she bounded up the front steps and thought about changing her dusty jeans and boots. It seemed only right since they were going into town.

"Should I change?" She poked her head into the pickup before climbing back in.

"Are you kidding? You haven't seen Dixon yet, have you?" Lank laughed.

Instead of taking the route towards the larger

city of Amarillo, Lank turned the opposite way. They crossed a cattle guard and bounced over a wide creek bed, which ran dry this time of year.

"That there is Antelope Peak. Apaches and then Comanches used it to guide them." Lank pointed to a pinnacle of dirt rising from the surrounding landscape. "If you ever get lost, get to the highest place you can and look for this peak. You'll know that ranch headquarters is directly south from there. When you see the hay barn which sits on the hill right behind your house, you'll know you're close."

"What's up there?" Carli snapped a pic with her cellphone, thinking she might send it to Mark but then remembered their friendship was strained at best.

"It was a sacred place for the tribes that wintered here, but any artifacts are gone. Now the neighbors ride dirt bikes over the summit. Wish I could've found an arrowhead or two."

They turned onto a narrow-paved, farm-to-market road that stretched to the horizon and divided pastures of endless grass. No trees in sight with nothing to stop the wind. Once again, she felt so isolated, like she and Lank were the only people in the world. They did not meet another vehicle, and Carli kept her eyes on a clump of buildings and trees as they got closer, but it took forever before they reached them.

"Welcome to the town of Dixon," Lank announced as he slowed and then stopped. They watched an old man and his collie walk across the street, his feet shuffled and his back stooped. He raised one arm in a half-wave but never looked their way. "First stop, the gas station."

Except it was not a working station. Lank pulled in front of a refurbished brick building with old pumps and a tanker truck shining with new paint. Lank opened his door and so Carli did the same.

They peered into the windows. Like stepping back in time, everything was arranged just as it had been years ago, as though someone had shut the door and intended to return in a few minutes.

"When was this built?" Carli asked.

"1920s, I think."

"This is really neat."

"Let's get your groceries."

They got back in the pickup and Lank drove three more blocks to a white stucco building. Long and narrow, it stretched all the way to the back alley. The picture window display was covered in posters and flyers, the cement just deep enough for parking. Faded silver letters on the glass door read Jack's Grocery. A bell jingled when Lank held the door open for her.

"Hey, Jack," Lank called out to the man sitting on a stool behind the counter. They talked in hushed tones.

The floor was wide wooden planks, some of them squeaked with each step. Carli grabbed a hand basket, and wandered the aisles of canned goods, cereal, boxed dinners. Some items were dusty, like they'd been there for years. Refrigeration units covered one wall from front to back. The back corner had household goods, more like a hardware store. She made a note to come back when she had more time.

Carli found creamer for her coffee, thank goodness, and pasta, bread and turkey for sandwiches, a few basic spices. No yogurt, which she could live without for a few more weeks, and she finally found the laundry soap. Lola's cooking was certainly delicious, but sometimes she just wanted to be alone. And her jeans were getting tight.

She piled everything on the counter next to the oldest cash register she had ever seen.

"Find everything you need, ma'am?" an old man asked.

"Actually, I need some tomato sauce," Carli said. She wouldn't mention it to Lank, but the thought had crossed her mind that she might make spaghetti and invite Nathan over one night. Then she remembered the promise she had made to herself: no men, no complications.

"If it ain't on the shelf, I don't have it," Jack grumped. Obviously, he wasn't going to make the effort to find it either.

He didn't take credit cards, so Carli dug in her purse for cash and Lank had to spot her a five. Jack put her groceries in a dented, cardboard box labeled "Borax" on the side. He studied Carli, his steady gaze making her uncomfortable. He frowned. "Ward was a good man. I liked him."

"Now let's go find that sauce," said Lank and he steered into the street, drove one block, and parked in front of a brick building, Roy's Grocery. Carli looked at him with questions on her tongue, but he had already hopped out and was holding the door open for her.

They walked into a store that couldn't have been any more different than the one they had just left. Bright and modern, they were greeted with a friendly and very loud hello. "How can I help you folks? Lank. Long time, no see." The man behind the counter laughed, and, not surprisingly, he looked a lot like the man across the street.

"This is Roy. Jack's brother," said Lank, as if he were reading her mind. "We need some tomato sauce."

"Right this way," said the man. Carli followed him up the aisle.

"I couldn't help but notice that you shopped across the street first."

Carli felt confusion but answered. "Yes, but he didn't have any sauce."

"I guarantee he won't order any either. Has he dusted yet?" He held out the can to her.

Unsure how to answer, Carli looked to Lank for help, but he had the widest grin on his face, looking like he could barely hold in the laughter. His shoulders were shaking but no sound was coming out.

They followed Roy back to the cash register. "Is there anything else I can do for you?"

"Do you take cards?"

"We sure do, but the place across the road does not. You just remember that next time you need anything. You're Ward's granddaughter, aren't you? Heard you was in town." He rang up her purchase on a modern modem, which she signed with her finger, and they were out the door.

"You enjoyed that way too much." Carli turned to Lank who couldn't hold in his laughter any longer. "You set me up on purpose."

"Yeah, I guess I did but it sure was funny." Lank laughed some more and then turned to look at her. "Are you hungry?"

She hated to admit it, but she was. The physical exertion of riding all week had zapped her energy and she couldn't get enough fuel to keep going.

"I'm buying," said Lank. As they drove, he pointed out places of interest. "We even have a coffee shop, B&R Beanery and Buns, if you like those fancy drinks."

"As a matter of fact, I discovered B&R before. And I do like those fancy drinks as you call them. Have you tried one?" Carli added.

"I take mine straight and strong enough to float a horseshoe, like it should be."

Carli laughed. He kept doing that. Making her laugh at the most unexpected times.

They turned off the main street lined with storefronts, aptly named Main as Carli noticed on the road sign, into a neighborhood with older brick homes. Most of them two-story, surrounded by large elm trees and flower beds now dormant, long driveways, and leaf-speckled lawns. Lank parked on a side street, next to a white house on the corner. Columns surrounded the first floor where a covered porch wrapped around three sides.

"This way." Lank led her through a side yard and onto the back porch. He yanked on the screen door and they went inside.

Carli found herself standing in someone's kitchen. A kitchen filled with the most heavenly smells she had ever encountered. Every burner on the white stove had a pot on it. Dishes were stacked in the sink. A small island held bags of flour and sugar, and assorted spices.

"This is Mozelle's Place, and this is Mozelle." Lank opened his arms wide as a short, dark-skinned lady stepped into his hug. Her hair was covered in a bright pink scarf and her lime green cooking apron reached all the way to the floor. The apron read, "All this AND I can cook."

"Where you been, boy? Haven't seen you in several weeks."

"We've been working cows. Weaning time."

"And this must be Ward's granddaughter. Heard you was in town."

Carli smiled, but couldn't say anything because so many questions were jumbling her mind at once. Why were they standing in this lady's kitchen?

"What'll it be, kids? Chicken or pig?"

"It's pig for me." Lank turned to look at Carli.

"I guess chicken?" Her comment came out weak, more as a question rather than an order. What was Lank up to now?

Lank gave Mozelle a ten-dollar bill, and then he grabbed Carli's hand and led her into the living room where several small tables and chairs were set up. They sat at a rusted patio table that had seen better days. The chairs were mismatched, one wooden with turquoise paint partially peeled off, and the other a metal chair painted bright red.

Within minutes Mozelle appeared carrying two

plates. In front of Lank, she set a pile of barbecued ribs with red beans, coleslaw, and French fries. In front of Carli she placed fried chicken with mashed potatoes and gravy. Carli daintily picked up and bit into a crispy breast, the most heavenly taste she'd ever had. Mozelle returned with two glasses of sweet tea. "Y'all enjoy."

They didn't talk, just ate until Carli leaned back to take a breath. "That was delicious, but can I get a salad next time instead of all these carbs?"

"You eat what Mozelle serves. No substitutions. Want a rib?" He had a pile of used paper towels next to his plate.

"One bite, I guess." Carli had to admit the smells of Mozelle's kitchen would be something she'd dream about. He held out a rib and she took a bite right from the middle. The tender pork and tangy sauce blended together into a perfect combination.

"You have sauce on your nose." Lank picked up a clean napkin and leaned forward, gently wiping her face and then stopped. Their eyes met and locked. Carli's heart thundered out of her chest, and a panicked plea went through her mind. Don't lean in. Don't kiss me.

Lank paused, something flickered across his eyes, and he turned his attention back to his plate.

Carli was relieved. Kissing one of your employees was never appropriate. Her hands grew clammy and she suddenly felt parched. Without lifting her eyes, she drank the rest of her tea. But deep, deep down her heart still thudded and she was disappointed. She'd be thinking about that almost-kiss for the rest of her life.

Chapter Twenty-Five

The busy week of weaning was over and Saturday morning dawned a bit nippy, but the rest of the day promised to warm up to be clear, blue-skyed, and without too much of that Texas wind. Mentally checking off her To-Do List, Carli really wanted to ride Beau. But she needed to make an appointment with Patrick. Maybe if she drove to Amarillo and sat across his desk, she could get the listing agent confirmed. The sooner she could get back to Georgia, the better.

This ranch ownership was tedious at times, but she was learning a lot—ordering feed, paying the bills, the price of beef, and how the auction process worked.

Heading out her front door with several bags of trash, she noticed a group of women with Lola on the lawn near the cookhouse. They appeared to be stretching, each one in different poses. An array of colored pants and blouses brightened the scene. Once before she had participated with the yoga class and they were all nice, but today she had a lot to do.

"Morning, Carli!" Lola called to her. "Come join us."

She smiled at some of the women she recognized from last time. "I don't know. I've got work to do. And I need to check on Beau, maybe ride."

"It won't take long," said Lola. "It'll help loosen up your muscles. Get rid of some stress. It's a great way to start the day."

Many of the women nodded and smiled at Carli, some encouraged her to join them by waving her over.

Carli hated to say no. "Okay, let me toss this into the dumpster and then I'll be right there." She still wore stretchy pants before changing into her riding breeches and stepped into boots which sat by the door. She noticed some of the women were barefoot.

"Here's an extra mat," Lola spread it on the lawn for her. "Just take your boots off so you can stretch your toes."

Reluctantly Carli sat down to take off her boots. Her mind was buzzing with the things she needed to do today. Certainly not in the right mood to relax and focus on yoga.

"Thank you all for being here today. Let's get started," announced Lola.

"First, our sun salutation. Modified version. And we all know the Son we're saluting." They all smiled and chuckled.

Carli looked around at the group. Some were gray-haired, experienced in years but she noticed they were in great shape. Several women looked to be Carli's age or younger, one had bright purple hair. As Carli listened to the chit chat while they waited for the class to start, she found out the mothers with smaller kids brought them too; they were being watched by one young girl inside, a high school student whose mom was in the class. Every other Saturday they met at the Wild Cow for Lola's yoga class.

"Ladies, stand straight and tall, shoulders back,

feet slightly apart, and reach your arms straight to the sky, hands clasped. Take a deep breath, in through your nose, and let it out slowly through your mouth."

Carli wasn't sure what she had gotten herself into, but she had to admit it felt good to slow down and breathe.

"Now altogether, slowly bring your arms out and up. Breathe. Hold your arms up over your head. Tuck your chin to your chest and slowly, inch by inch, swan dive into a forward fold. Inhale. Exhale. Steady breaths. Let your arms hang down to your toes, but little by little. If you can't touch your toes, no worries. Just hang there, fingers pointed towards the ground. Feel the muscles in your back releasing, in your neck, your arms. A few more seconds. Let all the tension drain away. Now breathe and be thankful for God's blessings."

Carli liked Lola's soothing voice. It was mesmerizing. Pressing an app on her phone, Lola said, "Listen to this song, ladies, by Hillsong United. 'I've held everything together. And watched it shatter. Chased my heart adrift. And drifted home again. And every time I turn around. Lord You're still there.' That's us, ladies. He's always there. No matter what."

Carli took the words into her heart. I'm adrift. I don't know where my home is.

"Slowly return to an upright position," Lola said. "Inhale. Place your fingertips on your knees into a half standing forward bend. Extend the spine. Keep your tummy tight."

She walked into the group and put a hand on an older lady's back and said, "Slow and easy. You got it."

Lola stood facing the group. "That looked good, ladies. Now everyone, down on your mats. We'll have a Bible study discussion while we do core body stretches. Carli, since you're new, a little intro. I am a yoga junky but, in my class, I like to mix in a little Bible teaching as well. In our busy lives, remember breathing helps so much."

Carli didn't think she wanted to stay for any preaching, but she was trapped. How could she stand up and walk away in front of all these women without offending Lola? Carli seemed to be somewhat bombarded during these last few weeks. She had never thought about God this much before in her life. It seemed as though Buck and Lola had targeted her. All this religion mumbo-jumbo made her uneasy and feeling awkward.

"I want to talk about Proverbs 31. Hands and knees on the mat. Let's move into the cat pose. Exhale; pull in your belly and round your spine. Inhale, back to start. Repeat this five times."

Carli looked down at her mat and the grass, focusing on her yoga moves while Lola talked.

Lola opened her Bible. "The Book of Proverbs, which means parable, was believed to be written by King Solomon and others dealing with the art of living. Proverbs 31 tells us about a woman of noble character. This woman enjoys knitting and sewing. She's up before dawn, prepares breakfast for her family. She dresses for work, rolls up her sleeves, and is eager to get started. Diligent in homemaking, she also reaches out to help the poor. She mends her family's clothes and makes her own. She's never spiteful, always treats her husband generously. She is worth far more than rubies.

"Do you think she's too perfect?" Lola asked the group. "Is she too good to be true?"

Carli frowned. This is why the Bible wasn't her cup of tea. It was kind of putting women down, in a box, cooking and cleaning for a husband and children. What about women's lives, their own dreams and desires? It made her kind of angry. She didn't want to be a servant to some man.

Lola had them roll over on their backs and gave

them several poses for stretching and leg lifts. Carli focused on the muscles in her body.

One member spoke up. "Her kids like her, her husband thinks he's won the lottery with her. Sounds like they've got the perfect marriage, the perfect family. Is that really possible?"

The group laughed.

"We all strive to keep it together for our families, but no doubt some days are challenging," Lola said.

Carli let out a little "humpff" snort in agreement. "Yeah, really? Sounds like the perfect woman is a fairytale to me."

"Ladies, we know that God only wants the best for us, right? We also know that nothing in this broken world is perfect. But He gives us guidelines, commandments, and it's all for our own good. Verse 25 says, 'She is clothed with strength and dignity; she can laugh at the days to come'."

Carli smirked at that one. Clothed in strength and dignity doesn't get you by in this world. She was abandoned, never even knew her parents. She's been on her own from a young age. What did this so-called God ever do for her? If she wanted anything, she made her own way and worked for it.

Displaying a gentle smile, Lola continued. "This whole lesson isn't about being perfect. I think it's about doing our best. Loving and taking care of our family. Respecting our husbands. Doing all the things we can to keep our households in harmony. It's about loving our work, and loving to help and serve our family, not like 'servant' in a negative way, but in the kind, generous way Jesus taught us to love one another."

"I try to keep it all together, but sometimes feel guilty when I have to bring pizza home three nights in one week," said the girl with purple hair.

"Thank the Lord for boxed mac and cheese."

"I sent my kid to school on Monday in the same pants he'd worn the week before. Maybe I'll have time to do some laundry this afternoon."

"I've done that, too!" said another. The group laughed.

"It's not about a woman with a spotless house or having well-behaved children," Lola continued. "For all women, married or single, with children or not. Proverbs 31 tells us what we can strive for, but we also have help. Verse 25 tells us we are clothed in strength from the Good Lord, we are dressed in dignity and whatever life throws our way, with Him on our side we can laugh at the days to come. There are several verses throughout the Bible about 'spiritual clothing'. We're not afraid or anxious about the future. What a blessing our families are. What a joy it is to serve them."

The women nodded their heads in agreement.

"In verse 30 the word 'fear' refers to having a heart completely in awe of God; it doesn't mean being fearful of Him, it's respect. It describes a woman who honors God by seeking Him in everything she does and trusting Him completely with her life. She talks to God every day, about her big problems and the little ones. She asks His advice. She doesn't go through life alone."

Carli wasn't so sure. She found it interesting, but was any of this realistic? In her life she had to learn to take care of herself, no one else would. And people didn't serve her, they abandoned her, took advantage of her at times. Maybe for Lola and Buck this Proverbs 31 story worked, but for Carli it sounded like a bunch of hooey.

"Sure, we're not perfect and life's not all joyous times. Many terrible things can and do happen. But wouldn't you rather have Him holding your hand, walking with you through the fire, so to speak, rather than going it all alone?

"We can also learn from one another. Talk to another lady in the group. Some of you have amazing stories of how God has brought you through tough spots, even tragedies, to the other side. Share that testimony with others. Help them to see what you've learned. Families are such a blessing, although sometimes a challenge. We can encourage each other. We keep going, day after day. With God on our side, how can we fail?

"It's a lot to think about, I know, ladies. Right now, I'm going to say a prayer for all of us. Then we'll get back to some yoga."

After the prayer, Lola took them through more stretches and core work, and a cool down.

Carli stretched prone on her mat at the end of the class when Lola asked them all to relax and take deep breaths. She had worked up a sweat. Lola was a good instructor, but Carli's mind was jumbled with all the Bible words and stories. Were they real? She didn't know what to believe.

The women called out goodbyes, some told Carli they were glad to see her in the class. Young mothers collected their children from the cookhouse and drove away. Carli pulled on her boots and rolled up the mat, not sure where it should be stored.

Lola hugged some, waved at others, and then turned to Carli. "You can bring that inside the cookhouse. I have a closet where I keep extra yoga equipment."

Carli followed her across the lawn. Lola stopped to hold the door open for her. "I don't know a lot of details about your history, Carli, but from what I do know I think you are the perfect example of the verse today. You are clothed in strength. You have faced some hardships and accomplished many things in your young life. I admire you."

Tears pricked the back of Carli's eyes. Lola's comment took her by surprise.

"You may not believe it now, but someone is looking out for you. God loves you, and Buck and I are happy you're here. I just wish Ward and Jean had lived to see it." She gave Carli a quick hug and then showed her where the storage closet was.

Was God really looking out for her? She had so many decisions to make, so many choices about the direction of her life. She wished it were that easy, a big lightning bolt from above bringing a message that said, here's what you do. What was she going to decide about her future? Go or stay? Was she really as strong as Lola said?

Chapter Twenty-Six

On Saturday, Carli drove back to Dixon to satisfy her caffeine fix at the town's only coffee shop—B&R's Beanery and Buns. It was on the south side of the four-way stop at the junction of Main Street and Main Avenue. Carli took a second glance at the street signs. The town fathers couldn't think of any other names? That was just mixed up, but she laughed. The glass-fronted store with black trim sat on a tree-lined lot next to Roy's Grocery. Carli didn't need groceries, thank goodness.

She tried to be mad, but a smile tugged at her lips when she thought about Lank getting her stuck between the two brothers who owned the grocery stores. He was sneaky, yet she had to admit she had laughed more during these last few weeks than she'd ever remembered. Lank was laid back and fun. He was out for a good time; also easy on the eyes. Not intense like Mark who always zeroed in on work projects. In fact, she couldn't remember Mark having fun at much of anything. Always work, work, work. Even when they traveled to the horse shows, his desire to win or place took over everything else. It was almost as though he had something to prove or live up to. Talk about an over-achiever. She didn't know much about his upbringing but had learned over the years that oftentimes people's current issues and traits had something to do with how they were raised.

A bell tinkled when she stepped inside. Dark wood paneling lined the wall from floor to ceiling behind the counter, wide plank flooring in a warm honey oak, and worn wooden tables gave it a modern yet homey appeal. The tables were tall surrounded by black wooden chairs. In one corner, a stainless-steel roaster stood, modern and shiny. When she walked into the shop, the smell was nothing short of glorious and she inhaled deeply. Now if they just know how to make a Kona coffee latte, her joy would be complete.

"Hi, I'm Belinda," the barista said with a wide smile.

"Hello—" said Carli, but before she could introduce herself, of course the woman already knew her.

"You're Ward's granddaughter! It's nice to meet you."

"Thanks, you too. It's a little strange how everyone seems to know me around here."

Belinda smiled. "Well, everyone knows the Wild Cow Ranch."

Carli placed her order and then couldn't resist topping it off with a cinnamon bun. Quiet and relaxing without the peering eyes of the Wild Cow bunch, she finally relaxed. This was her time. Again, concern about her decisions filled her mind. Always nagging, always there. Was she going to make Texas her home? It was so different from Georgia. She'd be starting all over again.

"Is the latte to your liking?

The question interrupted her worries. "It's delicious. Thanks so much."

As Belinda went about her chores, Carli scrolled

through her contacts list and stopped at Mark's number. She hesitated. Anger swelled up inside for a minute, but then she thought about all they had been through together. The time and attention he had given to her and Beau. They had been friends for a lot of years.

Instead of calling, Carli thumbed through a magazine, Cowboys and Indians, she had picked up off the shelf. The bell on the door tinkled as customers came and went, their friendly chattering breaking the silence, but Carli rarely looked up. She remembered the ripped pages from previous issues that had decorated the walls of her tiny house in Georgia. There really wasn't all that much she missed there. It surprised her to realize she was getting acclimated to Texas. But could it become her home?

She could hardly remember the odd pieces of furniture from secondhand stores and flea markets she had picked up in Georgia, and then she thought about Jean and Ward's comfortable home with leather couches and heavy wooden tables. It was really beautiful. But she hadn't really explored the house at Wild Cow Ranch that much. Her days had been busy, and she slept soundly as soon as her head hit the pillow.

Absentmindedly she opened her contacts list again, and this time, with her heart racing, she punched Mark's number. It rang, and then went to voicemail. She froze. No words came to mind. Should she apologize? No, absolutely not. Ask how he's doing? If he made it back alright? She clicked off.

"It's Carli, right?" Belinda asked. "I'm sorry to disturb you but we're about to close. I need to take my son to soccer practice. We open every morning at six, but we close at noon on Saturdays."

"Oh, sure. I'm sorry. Time just got away from me." Carli gathered her purse, put the magazine back, and turned just before leaving. "This was a great latte. I'll be back."

"That's good to hear. We're glad you're part of the community. The Wild Cow holds a special place in so many people's hearts around here. Next time when we're open longer, maybe we can chat more."

"That'd be great. Thanks again."

Carli smiled and walked to her car. People seemed so nice around here. And, for once in her life, a sense of pride swelled in her chest. Being recognized as part of a hard-working family, as part of a higher purpose, wasn't so bad.

On Sunday she did laundry and tried to stay hidden in her house. Several times she thought about going through the huge hope chest that sat against one wall in her room, but it felt wrong. This wasn't her house. She was an intruder upon the lives of people she'd never had a chance to know. This wasn't her stuff, and this wasn't her home to claim. She made a mental note to call Patrick next week.

That night she could hardly settle down to sleep thinking about another week of riding alongside other cowboys, herding cattle, and being a part of the ranching community. She was learning so much and she loved every minute of it. She was determined to enjoy it until she could decide where she belonged—Georgia or Texas?

Chapter Twenty-Seven

On Monday Carli woke bright and early, anxious to spend another week riding behind cows. She met Lank at the saddle house in the predawn darkness. The silence was awkward after that almost-kiss, but she decided to push it out of her mind and focus on the work at hand.

Lank broke the silence. "Which horse you taking?"

"Let's start the week with Beau." He stood next to the pipe fence, his neck stretched as far as he could and his nose twitching, waiting for her to reach him.

"He always looks ready and willing to get started whenever you come around. He's a good horse." Lank unlocked the saddle house and they began carrying out their gear. Carli knocked her saddle blanket against a pole to shake loose the dust.

"Are you riding Blackie all week?"

"Yeah. There's no quit in him."

"Where'd you get him?" Carli walked over to the gelding as Lank slipped on his headstall. Solid black with not a spot of color anywhere, and, typical for a quarter horse, he had powerful hindquarters. Some people called it an "apple bum or butt" because of the well-shaped rear. Carli rubbed his muscled neck.

"Traded him after chores and horseshoeing work I did for an old man my dad knew. Got him as a three-year-old. He'd never been around people of any kind, so it took me forever to gain his trust. He's super smart. We had a battle of wills, but he's got good bloodlines and his natural instincts came through. He knows what to do around cows."

They loaded the horses in the trailer but before they left Lola appeared at the pickup truck window. "Here's some coffee and banana bread. You two have a safe ride."

"Thanks, Lola," they both said in unison, and waved as they drove away.

The Rafter O headquarters was east of the little town of Dixon, but Lank explained that they'd take the bumpy route through the Wild Cow and then across a cattle guard into the Olsen's place. The Wild Cow and the Olsen Rafter O Ranch shared a fence line.

They arrived at the Olsen's and before Carli could get her horse unloaded, Nathan was at her side.

"I'm glad you're here." He nodded his head in greeting to Lank and then held the trailer gate open for her.

"Thanks. I appreciate the invite. I'm looking forward to another week of riding."

***

The week was much the same as the week before on the Wild Cow. Moving cows and calves to a set of pens, sorting, and preg-checking mommas. Then pushing them back to their pastures. The calves were kept in a smaller trap, waiting for the sale date. They'd be shipped to the buyers in December.

Lank ignored her the entire week while they worked, but he was friendly enough every morning. Nathan barely left her side and she ignored him, focusing instead on the work to be done. Beau did well on Monday, and she rode him again on Tuesday but by then he needed a rest. She let him have several days off and took him back on Friday. He was turning into a ranch horse.

Nathan's sisters rode that week too and for the first time Carli felt a kinship with girls who held the same interests as she did. Within the horse show community, competition was always stiff, and the riders could be mean-spirited at times. But under the wide-open skies of Texas, there was no rivalry, only a pride for their ranch and a willingness to work hard for the brand.

The entire week was full of bawling cows, horse stories, laughter, and teasing, and she loved every minute.

Carli rode one of her ranch's cutting horses mid-week, and she was hooked. The skill to stay in the saddle while allowing the horse to follow its instincts to cut a cow off from running to the back forty and turning it back into the herd was difficult. Lots of stops and starts and whirl-arounds. But Carli held on.

On the ride back to the Wild Cow, Lank said, "You have a knack for this. There are quarter horse cutting competitions. Or if you want to rope, we can be a team."

"I don't know that I can give up my jumping time with Beau." She may never be able to sort any cows on Beau, but he seemed to understand what was required of him and was less anxious around the cows.

Before they made it back to the Wild Cow, Carli's phone buzzed. It was Patrick.

"Oh good, that's the attorney returning my call," she said before speaking into the phone. "Yes, I'll be back in about twenty minutes. Anytime this afternoon is fine."

She stuffed the phone in her pocket and turned to Lank. "Del is driving out to meet with me. Wonder what's going on?"

By the time Lank and Carli got back, unloaded the horses, and stowed the gear, Del was parked in front of the cookhouse.

Carli was parched and Lank followed. Lola always kept a jug of sweet tea in the walk-in fridge.

Del stepped out of her car as they approached, this time with bright purple hair.

"It's good to see you again," she said offering her hand. "I don't see anything left of the Georgia girl who came here several weeks ago. Appears you've settled in just fine," she laughed.

Carli shook hands, smiled, and looked down at dusty jeans and boots. Her face must be just as dirty. Spurs jangling as she stepped onto the porch. "We just got back from a neighbor's. I hope you have good news for me about a realtor."

Del frowned. "Not exactly good, I'm sorry to say." She pulled her briefcase from the back seat of the car.

They walked into the cookhouse. Lola shook Del's hand and they pulled up chairs around the largest table.

"Would you mind if we talk in private?" Del glanced at Lank and then Lola.

"My bad news affects them as well. Let's hear it," said Carli.

Del shuffled papers in her briefcase and pulled out several files. Before she could say anything more, Buck walked in. "How'd the morning go at the Olsen's?"

Lola looked at him and put her fingers up to her mouth.

"I'm sorry. Didn't know we had company. How're you doin' Ms. Fenwick?"

"Buck." Del nodded her head in his direction. "I brought bad news, but Carli says she wants you all to hear it, so you're welcome to join us."

With a puzzled expression on his face, Buck pulled up a chair. Lola wrinkled her brow. The jolly mood from the morning's work quickly turned to worry. Carli bit her lower lip.

Del cleared her throat and opened the file folder. "Billy's attorneys have petitioned the court to place all of the proceeds from livestock sales into an escrow account as he plans to appeal the ruling of your being the rightful heir. The judge granted his request."

Carli gasped and looked at the people's faces at the table. "How am I supposed to make payroll? What kind of supplies will we need for the winter?" Her stomach twisted in knots.

"Let's step back and stay calm," said Buck. "The hay barn is full, the freezer is stocked with food. One of the biggest expenses is meds and we won't need them until spring branding. As for a paycheck, Lola and I have survived on far less. We can make it a few months until you sort this out."

"What about utilities?" Carli asked.

"We have a little saved back," said Lola. "We run on a thin budget all year because the sale in December has to last us twelve months until the next weaning."

Carli rubbed the back of her neck. Anger and frustration suddenly swept over her and she couldn't help but think about her beloved Georgia. She should be riding through the hills and trees instead of facing the hassle of owning a stupid ranch. But she had more aggravation to face back there, too. Tears stung the back of her eyes at the thought of Mark and their friendship. Her life was going down the toilet fast.

"I want to put the Wild Cow up for sale as soon as possible and find a buyer. Can you make that happen?" Carli looked at Del directly, so there would be no question that she meant business.

Lola gasped.

Del cleared her throat and looked at her papers for a minute. "There's a problem. As long as Billy's appeal hangs over the place and the working cash flow is tied up, it's impossible to place the ranch on the market at this point in time. Buyers want a clear title."

Carli glanced at the faces of her employees. Lank leaned back in his chair, arms crossed over his chest, anger glinting from his eyes. He gave Carli a cold, hard stare. Lola's head hung down, but Buck met her gaze.

"We understand you're here under unusual circumstances and that you really don't want to be a part of the Wild Cow, but this is our home. We signed on and we'll do our job."

"We won't abandon you." Lola placed her hand on top of Carli's clasped fists.

Lank remained silent, his jaw clenched.

Why would these complete strangers show any kind of loyalty towards her? She was getting ready to sell the ranch out from under them, possibly at the cost of their jobs when the new owners take over. But her mind was made up.

"That's all I have." Del gathered her files, closed her briefcase, and pushed back. Chair legs scraped the cement, screeches echoing throughout the silent dining hall. The others rose. Lola went back into the kitchen with Buck close on her heels. Lank stomped across the floor, the door banging behind him. Carli followed Del to her car.

"I wish I had better news for you," Del said. "I'll keep you posted." She paused and then placed a hand on Carli's arm. "I know this seems overwhelming, but it will work out. The legal process moves slowly. Just be patient. In the short time I've known you, I've never seen you look happier than you did this morning as I watched you walk from the corral. Your face was beaming with a huge smile. You were glowing! You're happy here, I think. Texas suits you."

Carli gave her a half smile. "I'll be expecting an update."

The friendly smile disappeared from Del's face, she nodded her head, and got into her car.

Happy? Carli was the furthest thing from happy than she'd ever been in her life. She turned and walked towards the saddle house. Sure enough, that's where she found Lank sitting on a bale of alfalfa, rubbing oil on a halter.

"Out with it," she said. "I know you want to say something."

He turned to her, a coldness clouding his eyes, his lips flat. "You're the boss."

"For this moment I'm not the boss. You have the floor to say whatever it is on your mind." Carli was not leaving until she found out why he was so angry.

"There are tons of people who would give anything to own a place like this. The Wild Cow is important in this community. Jean and Ward, and even Billy, have devoted their entire lives to this ranch. It's yours now. Handed to you through no effort on your part. You don't even appreciate it."

"I don't want it," said Carli, anger warming her face.

"Well, too bad. You got it. So why not count your blessings and make the best of it? Why not carry on the legacy that your grandparents left you?"

"This isn't my legacy. These people had nothing to do with me. They didn't want me in their lives."

"That's not true and you know it. How many times has Buck mentioned that Jean and Ward spent their lives looking for you? Their only dream was to bring you home where you belonged. And now you're going to throw it all away?"

"This place will never be my home."

Lank jumped to his feet and walked to face her, nose to nose.

"You are a spoiled brat and the most irritating girl I've ever met in my life." He spun on his heels and left.

Carli clenched her lips tight to stop the trembling in her chin. Tears would not help the situation at all. She had faced worse things in her life and was alone for most of it. Now she knew the truth of what they all thought of her. This whole pretense of friendliness, working for the brand, was all for show, and they said God brought her to where she belonged. All a bunch of baloney.

If Buck and Lola's God had any influence in her life, why would He send her to the Wild Cow Ranch? She'd only made a worse mess of things for everybody. Why wasn't God looking out for Buck and Lola?

She wished she had never gotten on that plane with Del.

Who was she to trust now? And what in the world was she going to do?

Chapter Twenty-Eight

Carli and Lank rode in silence the next two days to the Olsen ranch, loading their horses in the predawn darkness. Despite her aggravation with the cowboy sitting next to her in the pickup, Carli wanted to finish out the week on the weaning crew. Riding was the only thing that kept her sane. His words still stung.

Even though she might not be able to put the ranch up for sale, according to Del, she could see no reason why she had to stay here. These people could care less about her, and they didn't need her. Not really. The operations would carry on and her presence here made no difference. Mark was right. She had an obligation to him and to their business. But could they still work together as friends and business partners? She would have to face that problem when she got back home.

Despite her homesickness for the wooded hills of Georgia, the morning work gave her an appreciation for the Texas Panhandle. When they climbed into the pickup, the sky was so dark she couldn't see her hand in front of her face and then the entire horizon suddenly glowed. This must be what poets wrote about. The colors she had seen, a different show every morning, took her breath away as she and Lank bumped across the pasture roads towards the eastern skyline. He drove slow because of the loaded livestock trailer they pulled.

In the silence it was just the two of them on the edge of the world. The unbroken sweep of grass that rose to touch the horizon. She could count on one hand the number of trees, except for an occasional clump of cottonwoods that clung to the narrow, dry creek beds. Crisp, cold air that stung her lungs if she breathed in too deep, but by midmorning she had to shed her jacket.

She wasn't overly friendly to Nathan or his family either, focusing on the task at hand and keeping to herself in silent frustration. The sooner she could get back to Georgia, the better.

One morning, the fog had hung like a gray curtain over the ocean of grass. They had sat patiently on their horses waiting for the sun to break through. It was too easy to get confused for those who were not familiar with the land; cowboys might ride for miles in the wrong direction. So, they had waited.

By late Friday afternoon on the last day, Lank and Carli loaded their horses and headed back to the Wild Cow. She watched the Rafter O headquarters through the rearview mirror until it disappeared behind a hill of grass. They were good neighbors, she had learned a lot in these past few weeks about working cattle ranches, and perhaps in another time she and Nathan might become closer than friends. At this point in her life, though, she did not need any more complications.

She and Lank unloaded the trailer, filled the troughs with oats for the horses, and then turned them out to their pasture for the night. She gave Beau a little extra. He had earned his keep this week. They worked in silence, and finally they walked to the cookhouse. Every bone in Carli's body ached, but she would remember these last two weeks the rest of her life.

"I can set the table," Carli said as she walked into the kitchen, delightful smells swirling around her head.

"Just sit, relax. You've had a busy week," Lola said.

"What's to eat, Lola?" Lank called out.

"Roast, green beans, mashed potatoes. Oh, and a big salad just for Carli."

Carli eyed the decadent looking chocolate cake displayed on the counter.

They were soon gathered around the table. Despite her wariness over what Lank had said, Carli couldn't help but smile. They all seemed so genuine, but she reminded herself this was all probably fake. Butter up the new boss, or the spoiled brat as Lank had called her, to save their jobs.

"Remember the first night Carli came to the ranch and Lank called the sheriff?" Buck laughed. It was contagious.

"It was an honest mistake. I didn't recognize her. Her hair was different, and I think she was wearing glasses," Lank said.

"I don't wear glasses, and you were wearing shorts and Crocs!" They all howled.

"What about the day with the coyote, Buck? I don't know what I would've done if you hadn't been there." Carli didn't want to think about the outcome if the coyote had attacked, or if Beau had panicked and run off leaving her on the ground and afoot.

Lola quietly spoke. "The Good Lord has protected us so many times. I have faith He'll continue to do so. We're glad you're here, Carli."

"Let's give thanks," said Buck. They linked hands, and he said the blessing over their food, thanking God for friends and family, for the ranch, for His provision and protection.

Despite her doubts, Carli felt comfortable with these people. Her guarded heart warmed at being part of the group. She did feel a connection since they knew her grandparents. Buck and Lola were almost like the family she never knew. Almost.

So much had happened since leaving Georgia. Carli had grown in so many ways—thought she might learn to trust, a daily challenge for her. Believing in others did not come easily because the people in her life always turned out to be something different than she had expected or hoped for. Then Lank had revealed his real feelings—called her a spoiled brat, but also nearly kissed her. Maybe this could be the family she never had, always wanted. Not to say that her guardians, the Fitzgeralds, weren't there for her. But it had only been the three of them. Carli had always longed to belong somewhere, to a real family, to have aunts, uncles, cousins. It felt good to be with the people here at the Wild Cow Ranch, but she still wasn't sure they would ever be a part of her future.

A faint scent of something burning invaded her nose and made her throat tickle. "Lola, is the oven still on? I smell something," Carli said.

Smiles disappeared and the laughter stopped abruptly. Buck looked at Lank and suddenly they jumped to their feet, chairs flying out behind them, crashing to the floor. They all ran for the door.

A blaze of bright red lit up the night sky. When Carli realized what was happening, she looked at Lola. "The barn! Beau!"

"It's the hay barn. Call the Fire Department!" shouted Lank over his shoulder as he ran in the direction of the glow.

Piles of round bales and alfalfa squares were stacked under a shed that was open on one side. As she ran, flames darted and climbed over the metal roof. Carli's heart raced at the sight. She remembered that the horses were in the pasture. At least they were far away from the fire.

As she got closer, she heard Buck yell. "How'd

the horses get in here?"

"No!" she screamed and ran.

Lank busted out of the saddle house with both hands full of headstalls and lead ropes, running towards the smoke. The opened gate he ran through was at the opposite end of where the fire burned. The bales now were glowing bright orange, with gray smoke billowing out from under the shed.

His face soot-covered, Buck emerged leading a bay mare and the gelding C.P.

"Stay back!" Buck yelled. He disappeared into the smoke.

"Is Beau in there?" As she shouted the words she sank to her knees. "God, if you're real, please hear me. Please protect Beau. Keep everyone safe."

Tears streamed down her cheeks. She'd never really prayed before, but this time her heart spoke the words. Her soul wanted to believe. She had to admit she couldn't handle everything on her own. It was too hard. And she was so tired of going it alone. She had watched Lola and Buck. Even though they had struggles like everyone does, they trusted God. They had a peace about them. She wanted that peace more than anything. She needed it desperately. A Father who loved her unconditionally, more than any earthly father ever had or ever could. She remembered the words of a song Lola had played during yoga: 'And every time I turn around, Lord You're still there.' Please be here for us, God, for me.

Lola appeared at her side and wrapped an arm around Carli's shoulders. "Father God, please watch over these men and our horses."

Carli let the tears pour out. "Lola, my Beau has to be all right! Where is he? And Lank? This is horrible. We must save them. What can we do?"

Lola held her and spoke softly. "God will help us no matter what happens. We have to trust Him. And pray, sweetheart."

Before the fire truck turned into ranch head-quarters, sirens rose in the distance above the crackle of the fire. A truck with "Dixon Volunteer Fire Department" painted on its side rolled into the gravel drive, lights flashing. Lola and Carli ran to open the gates wide so that the fire truck could drive up as close as possible. Following right behind, the sheriff's cruiser and several other pickup trucks. Men piled out and hurried to the blaze.

"At least we don't have a high wind tonight," shouted Sheriff Anderson. His face was bright in the glow from the burning hay, the perfect kindling. The entire headquarters was illuminated as if twenty floodlights had been turned on.

Just then Lank jogged out leading Beau and another horse. Beau was wide-eyed and high step-ping.

"Carli! He's okay," shouted Lank. "I've got to go back for Blackie!"

Carli hurried and took the lead ropes from him. "Be careful," she called out to his disappearing back. He dipped his wild rag into the water trough and tied it over his mouth. At a dead run towards the hay barn, the smoke encased him like a curtain.

"Hey! You can't go in there," a firefighter shouted as he passed.

Carli mouthed another quick prayer for Lank's safety and buried her face into Beau's neck. He smelled of smoke and horse sweat and panic. Her heart raced as fast as his.

As Carli got Beau into the corral with the other horses, she ran her hand quickly over his warm body to check for injuries. The other horses milled around in a circle, running from one end of the corral to the other. Their nostrils flared, heads up sniffing the air. Their eyes wide open in fright. The flashing lights and vehicles didn't help the animals' nervous state. Some snorted, some paced back and forth. Beau seemed to calm as she stood next to him and patted his neck.

Lola appeared at her side, yelled into her ear trying to be heard over the crackling fire and the backup beeping of the truck. "If we can get the animals out ourselves, that's most important. The barn can be rebuilt. Have you seen Buck? Did Lank come out yet?"

Just as she asked, Buck appeared. The two women hurried over to him as he led another horse out, this time he doubled over in a coughing fit.

Lola took the lead rope and soothed the frightened mare by whispering in her ear and stroking her neck.

"Where Lank?" Buck asked.

"He needs to get out of there now!" said Carli.

"Please don't try to go in there again!" said Lola as she patted his back. Sirens sounded in the distance. "More firemen are coming."

Buck ran to the firefighters. "We've got a man in there!" he sputtered in between coughs.

Canvas-clad men turned it up a notch as they hurried with the water hose. One group began wetting the grass around the sides of the barn.

Just then the roof gave way and a rafter crashed into the middle of the barn, flames leaping higher.

The two women shrieked. Tears streamed down Carli's face, the scene playing out before them made her stomach clinch.

"Dear Lord, please protect Lank," said Lola as she clasped her hands with Carli's. They stood frozen in time watching in horror.

"There he is!" Carli ran towards a shadow. In a cloud of gray smoke, Lank was crawling on his hands and knees, coughing uncontrollably to catch his breath. His face black with soot and his face shining with sweat.

"I couldn't get him! He balked. Wouldn't let me put a lead rope on him. I tried chasing him towards the door, but he ran back in. I couldn't get Blackie."

Lank collapsed, sprawled out on his belly in the dirt.

"There's an ambulance on the way." Sheriff Anderson kneeled beside him. "His pulse is strong."

The three of them surrounded Lank, Buck patted his back. "Lank. Can you hear me? It's okay. You did more than your best."

Lank's eyes fluttered open, they helped him to his feet.

Carli hugged him saying, "I'm so sorry about Blackie."

Lank held her tight and buried his face into her neck. She felt his warm tears. They stood there for several minutes, clinging to each other as raspy wheezing overtook Lank's body.

Just then sirens from two more volunteer fire departments screamed up the drive. The glow from the burning hay lit up the busy volunteers. Men jumped from the truck and lifted a heavy hose to a nearby concrete water tank. They moved a lever on the hose which proceeded to suck water from the tank to spray onto the barn. But everyone knew it was futile, there was no saving it.

One truck drove through the barbed wire gate out into the pasture, spraying water to wet the dry grass. An army of men surrounded the hay barn, being careful to stay out of the heat and smoke and dumping shovelfuls of dirt on sparks that glowed bright in the pasture.

Lola put her arm around Carli's shoulder and together they watched what was left of the metal sides of the barn curl in the heat, the wooden beams crumbling to the ground.

"I'm sorry, Carli. At least no human life was lost. We can rebuild. And look around, our neighbors are all here to help."

Carli viewed the many trucks, SUVs, and cars parked in the gravel and grass surrounding the headquarters. She was touched to her core.

More sirens, this time an ambulance as it raced over the hill towards them. Turning off the noise as they rolled to a stop, their flashers joined the blinking light show that surrounded the barn.

EMS personnel hauled out and hurried over to Lank who sat wheezing on a bench by the cookhouse. He refused the oxygen they offered. After they had examined him, they looked over Buck too. Because of Buck's age they wanted to take him to the hospital for a complete examination. Before they could finish with Buck, Lank doubled over in a fit of coughing, tumbling from the bench and landing on the porch. Passed smooth out.

Carli's heart stopped as she looked at Lank's pale face. The EMTs rushed to his side, fitting the oxygen mask over his mouth and nose. "Let's load him up," one said. Within minutes they had him on a stretcher and inside the ambulance.

Buck protested. "I really need to tend to things here. You girls go with Lank."

Lola and Carli stood firm.

"If I have to pull rank, I will," argued Carli. "Smoke inhalation is nothing to play around with. Now get in the ambulance."

Buck glanced at Lola with a sheepish look on his face, but she only glared back, a mean glint in her eyes and her arms tightly crossed. Buck climbed into the back. An attendant sat next to Lank, monitoring his oxygen mask.

"We'll be at the hospital as soon as we can," said Lola.

Watching the ambulance drive away, Carli's heart was half broken and half full.

"Let's go find out what they know," said Lola.

Carli followed her to one of the trucks where Sheriff Anderson stood.

"These men will stay here most of the night, keeping water on any hotspots, and making sure there are no flare-ups. That dried hay sure does burn hot," he said.

"Can they tell what started it?" asked Lola.

"I'll be back in the morning with the Fire Department Chief to look over what's left. We have to let it burn itself out before we can take a closer look. We'll try to get the horse carcass out as soon as we can."

Carli stifled a sob with her hand. Poor Blackie. Poor Lank.

"I understand. Thanks, Sheriff. We appreciate all you've done," Lola shook his hand. "We're heading to the hospital."

"I sure hope Buck and Lank are alright," he said.

Chapter Twenty-Nine

Lola and Carli grabbed their purses and piled into Buck's pickup truck. The drive to Amarillo seemed to take forever, the silence broken by their coughing. An overwhelming smell of smoke permeated the cab, making Carli's throat ache even worse. She sniffed her jacket, and even her hair smelled.

"Horrible thing about Blackie. Lank pushed thousands of cows on that horse," said Lola. They rode without saying another word until the lights of Amarillo came into view.

"I'm parched. We should've grabbed some waters." Carli flipped down the mirror. "Oh my! Have you seen me?"

Lola laughed. "Yes, and I was afraid to say anything, because I'm sure I look even worse."

A gray grit covered Carli's face and her hair stood out in every direction. Black smudges of mascara encircled each eye like an actress out of a horror film, smeared by recent tears caused by the smoke and emotion.

"There are wipes somewhere," said Lola.

Carli dug around in the console and breathed a sigh of relief when she found them. She wiped her face and hands and smoothed her hair, but it was dry and stiff with dust. "Does Buck have an extra cap in here?"

"Should be several in the back. Hand me one and a wipe, too, would you?"

Carli unbuckled her seatbelt and reached into the back. She shifted a box of livestock ear tags, a canvas jacket, and a vest. She handed Lola the first one she found. It read "Life is Better in Boots".

On the floor under a pair of rubber waders, Carli saw a gray denim ball cap, which would do fine. When she read the front, she wanted to ask Lola to switch but decided it would seem petty considering all they'd been through tonight. The cap had an outline of the state of Texas with only one word, "HOME".

They pulled into the medical center. Dead leaves swirled around her ankles as Carli followed Lola across the lighted parking lot to the front sliding glass doors, the only entrance kept unlocked at this hour. After they breezed through the hospital lobby, they stuffed dollar bills into the vending machines near the elevators. Their canned drinks made an echoing clunk in the quiet lobby as they dropped into the slot. A small waiting room stood vacant. The lingering smells of popped corn from the machine that now stood empty reminded Carli that their dinner had been interrupted. She downed a Coke in only a few large gulps and followed it with water from the fountain.

Due to the late hour, the information desk was deserted, so they followed the signs to Emergency in search of a nurses' station. By the time Carli and Lola found Lank's room, he was sitting up in bed sipping on ice water. His eyes were red and puffy, like he had a sunburn.

Lola patted him on the arm, stepping as close to the bed as she could get, and looking into his face. "Your color is good. How is the coughing? Any more fits?"

"No, ma'am. That oxygen helped. I don't feel lightheaded anymore, but I have a really bad headache." He took a long draw from the straw and glanced at Carli.

"I need to go find Buck," Lola said. "Carli, you can stay here if you want."

Carli sat on the edge of the chair next to the bed, not sure what to say or how to say it. Lank's hair stood on end, but his face didn't have that ashen appearance it had before they loaded him into the ambulance.

"That cap suits you," he said. The words tinged with a deep raspy sound, followed by wheezing and gasps for breath.

Carli pulled it down tighter over her head and tried not to grin. It was good to hear his voice. "I'm not so sure about that. I haven't decided if Texas is the place for me or not."

"How's Beau?"

Unshed tears closed her throat. She tried to get her wits together before she spoke. "He's good. I'm so sad about Blackie. I remember you said that you trained him from a colt. I wish he had let you guide him out."

Lank looked at her with glistening eyes.

She reached out and took his hand. She could tell he was trying to hold it all together. "And I want to thank you, Lank. You risked your life to save my Beau. I'll never be able to thank you enough."

Lank opened his mouth to speak, but in the next instant a wheezing fit overtook him. Carli handed him a tissue. He kept coughing, tears streaming down his cheeks, the white tissue stained black. After the fit subsided, he took deep gasps of air, making a raspy noise every time he tried to breathe in. He leaned back on the pillow.

"Take it easy, Lank. Let me know if you need anything."

"I'm as weak as a kitten," he closed his eyes. "And

losing Blackie...well, it just knocked the stuffing out of me."

Carli patted his hand. "Stop talking. Just rest." She stood. He needed quiet right now and she wanted to find Lola.

"Don't leave," Lank whispered, his raspy voice barely reaching her at the doorway. She turned.

"I'm not going anywhere." Carli pulled the chair closer to his bed with a screech of wood against tiles and sunk into the vinyl. She shifted several times trying to get comfortable, the crackling of the fake leather shattered the silence.

"Want one of my pillows?" He swung it out of the bed and let it fall into her lap.

"Thanks." Carli adjusted the pillow, coughed several times, and leaned back. The clock hanging high on the back wall read 4:30 A.M. What a night.

This community had surprised her. At times like this, everyone comes together. As she stared at Lank's sleeping face, Carli reflected on the number of men that had worked to save their barn, her barn. Without question and without complaints, they faced the danger. Most of the volunteer firefighters were neighbors, some she had met at one time or another since she had come to the ranch.

The horse community in Georgia would rally around others in a similar tragedy, but they were also super competitive about horse showing. People she had known for almost a decade. Instead of supporting her, they had been quick to believe that maybe she had drugged Beau to enhance his performance. Without even getting her side of the story. There's no way she would ever drug a horse. And even though she suspected that Savannah had something to do with it, how could she ever prove it? Carli remembered her parting words with complete clarity. "Looks like you were having some trouble with your horse. Maybe he had an extra nip of something in his water?" And then Savannah's face had slid into that nasty smirk of hers.

So many thoughts and memories swirled around in Carli's head. Lank had tried to get her arrested when she first arrived at the Wild Cow, had called her a spoiled brat and said other mean things, but then without any hesitation had run back into a fire to save her horse. Why would he do that? A few weeks ago, they had been strangers.

Carli realized that she had prayed more in the last hour than she had ever prayed in her entire life. It was hard to explain, but even though she had been scared, praying had given her comfort. As she whispered the words, she had felt peace, an experience new to her. A confidence had settled her spirit, helping her to understand that things would be okay. She had never felt that before. When bad things happened, she usually rode the wave of panic and dread, stressing over things and complaining for days. Just like she had lost sleep over who had drugged her horse. Maybe she should put her worries in God's hands?

She closed her eyes, her arm outstretched to rest on the bed, her fingers laced together with Lank's. And in the aftermath of the terror and fire, his strong hand brought her another sense of peace... maybe she could trust him. Trust this place. Home.

Lola's voice pierced her mental fog. "They've released Buck. Let's get some real food."

At the mention of food Carli's eyes snapped wide open. Lank had rolled over on one side to face her but he had not let go of her hand. She gently got her arm back and shook the feeling back into her shoulder.

"We're going home?" Lank's eyes opened as he slowly tried to sit up. But then grabbed his head and sank back into the pillows.

"Not you, cowboy," said Lola. "They want to keep you another night and monitor your oxygen levels. You breathed in a lot more smoke than Buck did."

Lank's face fell, his lips forming a pout like a spoiled schoolboy.

"We'll come back and check on you this evening." Lola tucked the covers up tighter under his chin. "Now, get some rest."

"Would you bring me a cheeseburger?"

They all laughed. "Maybe so," said Lola.

Carli, Lola, and Buck piled into the pickup. Buck drove to the IHOP, International House of Pancakes, where they ate their fill. Back on the highway and with a stuffed belly, Carli couldn't keep her eyes open. Buck and Lola talked in hushed tones, their voices muffled by Carli's foggy mind and her failed efforts to stay awake. She finally dozed in the back seat on the way back to the Wild Cow, her ranch.

Chapter Thirty

As news of the fire traveled from one neighbor to the next, the smoking pile of their destroyed hay supply drew onlookers to the ranch including Billy and Nicolette. Steam still rose from the hotspots every time the fire crew shifted their stream of water.

Carli stood in the corral next to the ranch's vet, Dr. Kearby. "Did you check him out last night?" she asked.

Dr. Kearby was barely over five feet, a bundle of energy with long brown hair pulled through the back vent of a baseball cap. Even with her small stature she had a commanding presence and a confidence in her own knowledge.

Maverick watched them from the smaller pen, his long tongue licking his nose while his eyes never left Carli. She reached a hand through the rails and touched the curly hair between his ears before turning her attention towards the vet.

"Yes. Just some scrapes on his legs, probably from him stepping all over himself, but nothing serious it appears." Carli knew there could be issues with

Beau's lungs, though.

"I'm more worried about smoke damage, but we'll listen and check him out. I am so sorry to hear about Blackie."

Carli swallowed her sadness over Lank's horse, a reply to the doc's comment caught in her throat, instead joining Buck and Lola who stood with Sheriff Anderson. Billy and Nicolette emerged from their vehicle to join the group as well. The sheriff tipped his hat in Carli's direction.

"Ms. Jameson, I'm very sorry for your loss." She could sense Billy's anger rising as the sheriff's attention turned to her, but he didn't say a word.

"I understand y'all lost one horse in the fire and that two of your men have gone to the hospital. Is that correct?"

"Yes," Buck spoke up. "I'm fine, and we're hoping Lank will be alright too, but he took in a lot of smoke when he went back in for Blackie. They wanted to keep him overnight."

"Blackie was a fine ranch horse," said Billy, genuine sadness reflecting in his eyes. Nicolette stood at his side, scrolling through her cell phone, her red hair piled in a messy bun and her makeup salon perfect.

"Smoke inhalation is nothing to take lightly, that's for sure." Looking towards what was left of the water-soaked barn, Sheriff Anderson continued. "We did identify the remains of one horse. If you need help, I'm sure there are enough people here to help you bury him. Just let us know where."

"Thank you, but we'll take care of it," said Buck.

"I think I'd like to ask Lank when he gets back from the hospital what he'd like to do with Blackie." Carli stuttered, emotion clogging her throat. "He might want to bury him in a special place."

"That's fine, Ms. Jameson. I just wanted to offer my help. I'm expecting the Fire Department Chief any minute, and we'll do a walkthrough of what remains. Try to determine a cause for you folks and then we'll need to do some paperwork."

"It's a total loss, that's for sure," said Buck.

"Looks like your winter feed is done for. Hopefully you can find a supplier before the first snow." The sheriff walked away, leaving a gloomy silence in the group that remained.

Walking over to Carli, Dr. Kearby said, "I just listened to Beau's lungs and they sound pretty good. I would like to keep a close watch on him. Or bring him to my place and give him some fluids. I might even put a nebulization mask on him just to help clear out any particulates. The same goes for the other horses. If you notice any coughing, let me know right away, and give him plenty of water, limit the dust around him. He should be fine."

"Thank you so much. I really appreciate your coming out so quickly. While you're here, could you check over Maverick. That's the little bull calf."

The vet nodded and walked back towards the corral.

Carli wandered over to the backside of the hay barn as the sheriff and several other men milled around. Buck and Lola visited with Billy and Nicolette.

Carli remembered the hot fire and the mountain of red flames. It had been one of the scariest nights of her life.

"Let's walk this way," said the sheriff.

The group followed him towards the back of a charred hill of straw. Carli side-stepped around black patches of burnt grass, ignited from the embers that had drifted out to the pasture. Billy left the group to chat with the vet. As rude as he had been since her arrival, Carli was surprised at the sincere concern he showed for the horses. She assumed several of them were his.

"It's a wonder it didn't ignite the place for miles, but, thanks to the quick response of the Dixon volunteers, they had it contained until the other fire departments could join them," Sheriff Anderson said.

"We really appreciate them," said Lola.

The sheriff kneeled on the ground just as the Fire Department Chief joined them. "Hey there, Mack."

Mack Griffitt was new to the job, according to Lola, but he knew fire after following his father around since an early age. His father had been the fire chief for close to fifty years. The tragedy that had taken his life was still talked about, a chemical plant explosion in a neighboring community and a sudden flash fire that killed several firefighters. The young Mack had high school and football practice after and hadn't been allowed to go with his father on that day.

Mack kneeled on the ground next to the sheriff. "That's the spot alright."

The sheriff nodded his head. "That's what I thought." He glanced up to Buck. "Looks like the fire started right here. A mixture of chemicals from the looks of it. See how the siding is melted and twisted. It burned hottest here in this spot."

Mack continued, "I agree." He took a pencil from his pocket and sifted through the ashes.

"But we still don't know how the horses got in here," said Buck.

"Is there only one gate in?" asked the sheriff.

"Yes," said Lola. "At the other end. The horses were in the pasture and we keep that gate latched and tied with rope."

"There's no way any of us would do that. If they got into the grain bins, they'd founder, and we know that. We can't take that chance. I don't believe for a minute anyone would be that careless." Buck crossed his arms, his face showing the frustration they all felt.

"Maybe it was intentional." All heads turned towards the sheriff.

Carli glanced over their shoulders as they studied the ground. She walked along what used to be the back side of the barn. Most of the metal was twisted or blackened from the flames. The heat that remained warmed her cheeks as she walked closer.

She stood at the back corner of the shed where a tin lid from an old bucket lay in the ash. Carli tipped it over with the toe of her boot and gasped at what she saw. Bending over, she carefully picked up a vape pen with two fingers. Blue and purple glass jewels, the same distinct pattern she had seen on Nicolette's device the afternoon of the tea.

Walking over to the sheriff, Carli held the pen out in front of her. "I found this," she said, keeping her eyes on Nicolette who continued to scroll on her phone, never looking up.

"Did Lank take up vaping?" asked Sheriff Anderson.

"Not that I know of," said Buck as he walked closer, peering intently at the item Carli held in front of her. "Sure is an unusual pattern."

"Probably an original design. Someone spent a lot of time bejeweling their vape pen," said Carli.

Nicolette's head snapped up and the color drained from her face when she looked at what Carli held. She then gaped at Carli with menacing eyes, daring her to make an accusation that she couldn't back up. Carli glared back. Waiting to see what she'd do next. The thing about the guilty, they aren't that smart, and they usually give up too much information. Just a little patience to see what story Nicolette would come up with. Carli didn't have to wait long.

"Yes, he did," said Nicolette. "Lank uses a vape pen. I've seen him and that's his."

Both Lola and Buck looked at her, surprise showing on their faces, but they didn't argue.

"I'll need to visit with Lank when he gets released from the hospital." The sheriff produced a plastic baggy from his pocket and held it open for Carli to drop in the evidence. He held the device up in the sun turning it over and over. "Sure is fancy for the likes of a cowpuncher like Lank."

"Some ole' gal gave it to him." This time Nicolette offered the information with conviction, her voice carrying a demanding tone. "I've SEEN him use it."

Carli stared at her, insides churning. Is everybody here that stupid they can't see through Nicolette's lies?

"Next thing we'll do is see if we can lift some fingerprints off this thing. I'd also like to get a set of prints from the gate that goes into the hay barn. Might be just Lank's prints, but then again it might be someone else's." Sheriff Anderson slipped the baggy into his coat pocket.

Mack nodded his head in agreement. "We also need to check with the local hardware stores and see if anyone has purchased a combination of odd chemicals that could have been used to ignite a fire."

"That's just silly," said Nicolette. "You can't start a fire with chemicals."

"Actually, you can, ma'am," said Mack. "You'd be surprised what combinations are available in your home. And you'd be surprised at how many criminals use their credit cards. It's not hard to find their trail."

Carli didn't know if she should shout or bust out laughing when she saw the look on Nicolette's face. If she were a betting girl, she'd put her money on the hardware store clerk remembering Nicolette.

Billy joined the group then. "Y'all figure anything out? I can tell you that I do not appreciate the outright criminal intent of some people." He stared at Carli. "Particularly with regards to my property."

"We can't say it was intentional," said the sheriff.

"There's no evidence of that. But we have a few leads, and we'll do our best to rule out arson."

Carli overlooked the claim Billy made, once again, about the ranch being his and kept her mouth shut.

"I'm ready to go home," said Nicolette as she placed a hand on Billy's arm. "Now."

"Hang on." Billy glanced over his shoulder at her before continuing. "It stands to reason there's only one person in this group who has any motive to destroy this ranch. She isn't the true heir. And I intend to prove that those lawyers are trying to keep me from my fair share of the Wild Cow. She knows it's just a matter of time before all of this is over, so she wants to destroy what she can before leaving." Billy never took his eyes off Carli, and she never took her eyes off his wife who stood just behind him. Her glaring red lipstick popped out on a pale face, that pea brain of hers obviously trying to sort out the lies.

"We did find this." Sheriff Anderson held up the baggy.

"What's he doing with your vape pen, babe?" Billy asked, as he glanced over his shoulder at Nicolette.

Her mouth opened but no words came out. Carli smiled. Here we go.

"She claims it's Lank's," said Lola.

Billy clamped his lips together and the look on his face was obvious as he realized how bad he had just messed up. "We need to get back to town."

"Just a minute," said Sheriff Anderson. "Where were you last evening, Mrs. Broderick?"

"That's not mine," said Nicolette. "I've seen Lank use it many, many times. Why would I be out here at midnight, of all places? That's just ridiculous."

"I didn't ask you about the time, ma'am. I just want to know where you were."

"At home." Nicolette crossed her arms, her

eyes wide before averting her gaze to the ground. "Watching television. Isn't that right, Billy?"

Carli's heart pounded out of her chest. The idea that she would blame the only person who wasn't here to speak for himself infuriated her. She stepped closer to Nicolette. "That's the vape pen I saw you using at the tea. It's not Lank's. He doesn't have one."

Nicolette's face went from pale to crimson. Rage turned her green eyes dark as she glared at Carli. She lunged. "You greedy witch! You've destroyed my life."

Carli tried to side-step, but she was too slow. Manicured fingers encircled her throat. Lime green nails dug into her tender flesh. Carli couldn't shake her off. She weaved down, then back up, but those hands clung to her like steel. She needed to cough or breathe in. She couldn't.

"Ten years of Pilates," screamed Nicolette. "You can't get away from me, can you?"

Within seconds the stunned faces turned into action, as they all came to Carli's aid. Sheriff Anderson took one hand and Buck took the other, as they pried Nicolette's fingers from Carli's throat. Carli bent over gasping for air, as Lola patted her back.

"Sweetheart?" Billy stood in frozen disbelief. "What did you do?"

"You spineless piece of—"

"Nicolette!" Billy cut her off as she jerked her arms free and turned on him. Billy took several steps back. The sheriff and Buck restrained her again.

"I promised my friends lakefront property. If Billy can't build his resort, I'll never be able to show my face in this community again. It's all her fault!" Nicolette screeched as she turned her attention to Carli, who backed away from the intense hatred.

"How'd you do it, Nicolette?" Sheriff Anderson

stepped in between them, blocking her view of Carli.

"It's like you said. A few chemicals mixed up in a bucket. It's a no-brainer. And no, I wasn't stupid enough to use my credit card. What kind of dolt would do that?" Nicolette snorted. Remorse suddenly crossed her perfect face. "I didn't mean to leave the gate open. I never intended to hurt any of the horses."

"Why would you do such a thing?" asked Billy. "I'm working with lawyers, Nicolette. You know that. The Wild Cow Ranch should be mine, and it will be, but we have to be patient and let the courts work it out."

"I wanted her gone. No hay for the winter. No money coming in from the sale of cattle to buy more, because that is owed to us. She'd have no money for payroll, they'd all quit her. She'd have to leave. We can't wait for the court system. We have to act now. Some of my friends have already put a down payment on their lots."

"You can't take money from our friends on a non-existent development, darlin'. What are you thinking?" Billy stared at her, his eyes bulged in surprise.

Sheriff Anderson pulled handcuffs from his belt and placed them around Nicolette's delicate wrists.

"Come on, you two. Let's get this sorted out at my office." He helped Nicolette into the back of his cruiser. Billy climbed into his truck, and they drove off.

For several minutes, Mack, Lola, Buck, and Carli stood in stunned silence. Buck turned to look at the charred barn, pushed his hat back, and scratched his forehead.

"What was all that?" asked Lola.

Carli turned her neck from side to side, feeling the ache getting worse by the minute. She coughed but couldn't think of an answer to Lola's question.

All she could think about was Lank and Blackie and red flames rising to sky, the heat burning her face. Never before had she been more scared for Beau or Maverick. Never before had she wished she had told a smart aleck cowboy what he meant to her. Never before had she wanted to trust in someone so much.

"I'm going to the hospital," said Carli.

Chapter Thirty-One

Carli tiptoed into Lank's hospital room. He slept on his back, sprawled over the mattress, one leg over the side. His eyes fluttered open and he stared at her for a few seconds before a grin crept over his face. "Hey."

Her heart melted as the smile on his face reached his eyes. "Hey yourself." Carli grabbed the arms of the guest chair and pulled it close to his bed. She squinted her eyes against the screech on the tile.

"They're letting me go in a few hours. Hopefully, before the dinner tray gets here. I really need a cheeseburger." Lank fumbled for the controls as he raised the head of his bed.

"That's good to hear. I'll drive you home then," offered Carli. She propped several extra pillows behind him.

"How are things, boss?"

"That's why I came here. To check on you, number one, and then to tell you that Sheriff Anderson and Mack, the Fire Chief, came by the ranch this morning."

"Is the fire out?"

"There are a few hotspots. A small crew of men have been working a hose through the night and all morning. I came by to tell you something."

"What's on your mind?"

"We haven't known each other that long. And with the fire and all that, there's something I have to say."

"If you're here to thank me again for running into the smoke to save your horse, you've already thanked me. Stop fretting over it." He smiled, and just as quickly his face turned to a frown. "I just wish Blackie would have come with me. He went kinda nuts and then I couldn't breathe."

"I am sorry about Blackie, but the horses are not what I want to talk about." Carli laid her hand on his arm.

"What's wrong with your throat?" Lank leaned up in bed and gently touched her neck. "It's bruised."

"I'll tell you about that later. What I want to say is you know I have trust issues."

"No. That's a shocker." Lank rolled his eyes. "You are a might standoffish."

She laughed. "Really. I don't trust people easily, particularly strangers, and I want you to know—"

Sheriff Anderson appeared in the doorway. "Excuse me. We've got Nicolette in a cell for now, but I still need to ask you a few questions, Lank."

"Billy's wife is in jail?" Lank looked from Carli to the sheriff and back to Carli. "Why didn't you tell me?"

"I didn't know where to start. It's been an interesting morning." Carli snapped her hand back. She moved to perch on one side of the bed and indicated the only chair in the room.

"To say the least." The fake leather crackled as Sheriff Anderson settled his bulk into the chair.

Not wasting any time, the sheriff got right to business. "Do you smoke, Lank?"

"What do you mean by smoke, exactly?" Lank

shifted and pulled himself up straighter in bed. "My uncle smoked anything and everything. He lived with us for a while before mom threw him out, and I just never had a yearn for it myself."

"More to the point, do you own a vape device?"

"A what? No." The confusion on Lank's face made Carli stifle a giggle.

"We found one at the fire and Nicolette says it's yours. We have probable evidence that it belongs to her." The sheriff cleared his throat. "Several people witnessed her using it." He winked at Carli.

"Wouldn't know how to use one," Lank said.

"That's what I figured."

A thought crossed Carli's mind as she watched the sheriff question Lank. "You knew it was Nicolette's all along, didn't you?"

"Off the record. Yes. Everybody in town has seen her use that blue and purple device. She takes it everywhere. I just needed her to confess, and you were the one that pushed her over the edge."

"Me?" Carli tried to remember the conversation again. What had she said that made the difference?

As if the sheriff read her mind, he explained. "When you told her it wasn't Lank's. We knew she lied. She knew that we knew it. That's when she lunged for you."

"The marks on your neck. Nicolette tried to choke you?" Lank's eyes widened in surprise. "What exactly happened at the ranch this morning, and somebody had better start from the beginning."

Carli laughed.

"You really should have a doc check that out, Carli. I've got nowhere to be." Sheriff Anderson shoved his chair back and stretched his long legs out, propping his boots on the end of the bed and crossing them at the ankle. Lank scooted over and Carli leaned against the pillows next to him.

What she needed to say to Lank was there in her mind, where it would stay. The moment had passed.

She'd be leaving soon to go back home to Georgia. Maybe words unsaid are best left that way.

He was a cowhand that worked for a ranch she had inherited, soon to be sold, and she would be out of the picture forever. She had no reason to even believe there was a future with Lank. If God were truly directing her life, their paths would never cross again. After she had prayed so fervently on the night of the fire, she had considered the idea that things worked out for the best. Thank goodness Beau was alright. It was obvious God had other plans for her, but it wouldn't be in Texas.

Carli settled in to listen to Sheriff Anderson's version of the morning investigation. Since he had a captive audience, he went over the events with much detail and liveliness. Despite the sadness of losing an exceptional ranch horse and the financial loss of hay, they couldn't help but laugh at the sheriff's continued adventures of other fires he had attended.

"What's going on in here? We could hear y'all at the far end of the hall as soon as we got off the elevator." Lola knocked gently on the door, walking in with Buck close on her heels. "You look good, Lank. I was so worried about you."

"Just regaling these youngsters with tales of a county sheriff." Sheriff Anderson polished his star with his shirt sleeve.

"More like long windy tales of the highly embellished kind," said Buck.

They all laughed.

Lola perched on the end of the bed and Buck kneeled, his back against the wall. He held his cowboy hat in his hands.

"Lola and I were just talking about finding a source for hay to get us through the winter. I'm not going to sugarcoat this, Carli. Since the judge placed the cash from this year's calf crop in escrow, we're in a tight crunch. The story goes just like Nicolette laid it out. As far as payroll, Lola and I have lived on the Wild Cow most of our married life. We have no other place to go. We'll stick with you until you get this thing sorted out." Buck beamed at her, kindness and loyalty shining in his eyes which made it even harder for her to say what she had to say.

"There's really nothing more to sort out. As soon as I can place the ranch on the market, I intend to do so. I wonder if the bank would make a short loan to get us through the winter?"

"That's a good idea. Ward and Jean have always had perfect credit. I'll get you the name of the banker tomorrow," Buck said. "Lola needs to show you the books, if you have any questions."

"I'll speak with the attorney as well first thing Monday," said Carli. "You have all been so kind, but I really don't fit in here. I feel like I'm leaving you all in the lurch, but my home is not here, and the Wild Cow is in good hands. I'm going back to Georgia as soon as possible. I've made up my mind."

Lola gasped, Buck snapped his head around to look at her in surprise, and Lank looked down at his lap. The room grew silent.

The nurse walked in at that moment. "Good news. You're out of here, Mr. Torres. I have discharge instructions for you."

"Thanks, ma'am." Lank looked at Carli. "I can catch a ride with Buck and Lola. Don't let me keep you from packing."

Tears stung the back of Carli's eyes. She stood. "I guess this is good night then. Glad you're doing better."

She did not remember how she found the elevator or the front entrance, but the cold night air stung her damp face as the sliding door opened. She hurried to her pickup truck and slammed the door shut before wiping the tears from her cheeks. That was that. What should she expect? She had made the decision to leave. These people owed her nothing, and she could never be a part of their world.

Chapter Thirty-Two

With jittery nerves and a heavy heart, Carli began gathering up her things. Nothing sounded good for breakfast, but the smell of the coffee calmed her nerves. She opened the cabinet to find a mug and noticed one from the Grand Canyon. Before she knew, she had taken every last one out of the cabinet to study them all. There were cups from various touristy spots, museums, funny country quotes, and several custom mugs with The Wild Cow Ranch logo stamped on the side.

Carli gasped when she discovered a mug from the Booth Western Art Museum in Georgia. The idea that her grandparents had been so close to where she lived made her eyes sting. When had they been there? Or did they order it online?

With the Booth mug full of steaming coffee in hand, she began wandering around Jean and Ward's home. She'd been here over three weeks and had never really noticed anything. The house was bulging with a lifetime of mementos, knick-knacks, Native American blankets, and oversized leather furniture. The Western art was much more impressive than the magazine pages she had tacked to her walls in Georgia.

She passed through the kitchen, refilled her mug, and wandered into a back room. She'd never noticed it before. Flipping on the switch, the room was a study or office. Bookcases lined one wall and on the other a glass display case was filled with buckles, plaques, and trophies from their rodeo days. She noticed a cord with a switch. One click and the entire trophy case lit up, the intricate silver buckles sparkling on the glass shelves. A solid wooden desk anchored the center of the room, and across from that, a red leather sofa. This was their sanctuary. She stood in the middle of the room feeling surrounded. She almost felt their presence and knew they had spent a lot of time in here. Every table, every inch of wall space was covered with something. She sank into the leather and took a sip from her mug.

A small plaque caught her attention. It wasn't anything fancy by any means. A plain square of sanded oak, varnished, and hanging next to a window by itself. She walked closer to read the words in handwritten lettering: "She never shook the stars from their appointed courses, but she loved good men and rode good horses." -Dr. Margot Liberty.

Carli sank to the nearest chair, her mouth open in shock. Was this a sign? Is this where she belonged? Still new and unsure about the praying thing, Carli opened her heart and mind to the possibilities that this house meant something to her. These people had been her family. She couldn't deny it any longer. With shaky legs she continued rummaging through Jean and Ward's ranch house.

Carli slowly opened another door located in the hall from the kitchen to the carport. She had assumed it was a storage closet but was surprised to see wooden stairs leading down into darkness. She felt around for a light switch. The stairs creaked as she slowly climbed down. She didn't want any mishaps that would put her out of commission and keep her from riding Beau.

When she surveyed the large room and saw all the boxes and other forgotten belongings, her mind reeled at what she might find.

Grandma Jean must've been an avid sewer, or was it seamstress? There was a fabric mannequin in the corner and a green sewing basket on four wooden legs next to an old black Singer machine. Carli remembered the closet upstairs of vests and split skirts and wondered if she had sewed her own clothes. Maybe she made her own rodeo shirts, Grandpa Ward's also.

Coughing at the mustiness, Carli lifted a moldy cloth cover to reveal an old show saddle replete with silver trim on the horn, cantle, and stirrups. She wondered how many years it had been kept here. It wasn't in such bad shape. She'd ask Buck about it later.

There must've been at least twenty cardboard boxes stacked against one wall, all of them neatly labeled with black marker block letters: DISHES, FABRIC, WOMEN'S BLOUSES, JEANS. Carli lifted two boxes marked "Thanksgiving decorations" towards the light. She thought this must just be the tip of the iceberg and remembered Lola had said once that her grandma loved decorating for the holidays. It would be Thanksgiving soon and the house would be empty this year. The familiar feeling of loneliness invaded Carli's mood for a moment. Time is not something you can turn back no matter how much you wish it.

Peeling loose the packing tape atop the Thanksgiving box, she discovered brown and rust colored centerpieces—accordion folded cardboard with crepe paper turkey feathers, spray-painted pinecones, and, protected by hand towels, pilgrim figurine salt and pepper shakers.

As much as she needed to finish packing, she couldn't stop herself from going through the boxes. Banners spelling out "Happy Thanksgiving" in foil letters, a plastic tablecloth that had seen better days after all these years, even a cookbook with recipes labeled "Jean's Favorites" of pumpkin pie, stuffing, and gravy. There was also a framed homemade picture with fall leaves and the handwritten words, "Welcome to the Ranch".

Carli began to enjoy herself, and longingly thought about what holidays might be like here. Her foster parents had not been much on celebration. Like a scavenger hunt or following a treasure map, but there were no directions; she was blindly navigating this path—a journey into her past, one she never knew had even existed. But she now wanted to know about these people. Who were they? Was she like them?

Before she could finish exploring the box labeled "Christmas", dust clogged her throat, still tender from the smoke, she needed a drink of water. She left the boxes in the middle of the floor and went back upstairs.

As she wandered out of the kitchen, her eyes went to the closed door of her grandparents' bedroom. She had peeked in there briefly when first at the ranch, but for some reason now, she felt an urge, a pull. She still felt like an intruder. Usually that's where people kept personal items—whether it be jewelry hidden in a sock drawer, or love letters from an earlier time. But Carli was curious.

Opening the door, she found the room dark, the shades drawn. It smelled stale, but with a lingering hint of Old Spice, she guessed from Grandpa Ward. The queen-sized bed was fitted into a wooden sleigh-styled frame, mahogany if she had to guess. A black and brown bedspread was emblazoned with a galloping horse.

She opened the drapes and watched dust particles float dreamily on the beams of light.

This room, like the others, left no surface uncovered, but it was a neat and orderly kind of clutter. A heavy, intricately carved cedar chest was at the foot of the bed, which Carli found to be locked. Now what? She was sure it must be filled with memories of some kind.

On the low dresser, sitting on top of a knitted doily, was a small replica of the larger chest. Inside was a necklace of small turquoise stones, rings, silver-etched bracelets, and a watch. As Carli used her forefinger to rummage around, she lifted the top tray to find more jewelry in the bottom of the box. A velvety pouch contained an old-fashioned key. Could it be that easy? What are the odds?

As luck would have it, it fit perfectly to open the bigger chest. Curiosity heightened, her fingers touched a lacy-edged pillowcase that had been neatly folded as if to protect what was beneath.

Numerous little yellow boxes containing photos and slides for a projector. Carli held some of the slides up to the light. She grinned at a young woman sitting atop a horse, probably Jean, with a smile as big as the sky and holding blue ribbons. Next, she opened envelopes of color prints. Thumbing through these, she saw familiar faces. She looked very much like her grandmother. One young face with Jean and Ward, she was sure belonged to her mother, Michelle, as a child of about ten. They were at a rodeo and Michelle looked especially grumpy. Carli tried to ponder the child's life—nearly every weekend at one horse show or another, driving all over with her parents as they competed in their events, while Michelle missed out on some of her school friends' sleepovers and other childhood activities back home.

With photo envelopes strewn all over the floor around her legs, Carli picked up a burgundy colored legal folder and unwound its little thread from the round clasp. Inside was a deed, Jean's Last Will, and a blue journal with gold-embossed design. The writing must be in Jean's script. She fanned through some of the pages, wanting to read it all right then, but determined to save it for later.

Finding a box marked "Michelle" caused Carli's heart to pound as tears welled up in her eyes. This was about her mother.

One yellow envelope held photographs. Michelle as a beautiful child, bright blondish long hair, cowgirl boots, a hint of a smile. Even at a young age, her face was stunning, and her personality showed through bright, shining eyes. She had been happy once. Later photos of her as a pre-teen, long-hair with neat braids, Western shirts, and sitting on a horse. The images slowly changed from cowgirl hat to frizzy hair, slouchy jeans, sandals, and wrinkled Tee-shirts. And so it had begun, Carli pondered, the teen angst and rebellion. She felt some sympathy for her mom and wished things could have turned out differently.

Then one envelope pierced her heart. Carli's hands trembled as she stared at it. "Birth Certificate—Carlotta Jean Jameson."

She wanted to read it but was terrified. This could change everything. It might have the name of her birth father. Was he still alive? She gazed intently at the written label. It took her several long minutes to gather her courage.

Seven-and-a-half pounds at birth. Baptist Saint Anthony's Hospital, Amarillo, Texas. Mother: Michelle Jean Jameson, 16 years old. Father: Taylor Miller, 18 years old.

There it was. The name she had wondered about all her life. Who was he? Where was he? Alive or dead? So many questions.

Carli quickly folded the document, returned it to its envelope, and cried.

Why didn't they want her? Why did they abandon her? Why didn't they love her?

The sobs caused her body to spasm, doubling her over into the fetal position. Physical pain consumed her, and she then moved to lay flat on her back clutching her heart, tan curls mixed with the dust on the floor.

Her arms encircled her body. She would hold herself tightly since her parents never did.

Chapter Thirty-Three

Shuffling to the kitchen after being woken by outside banging and the zinging sounds of an electric saw, Carli noticed Lola on her porch, a basket in her arms, about to knock on the front door.

"What are you doing here so early, Lola? It's barely six. And what in the world is all that racket?"

"Thought I'd bring you some cranberry muffins, fresh out of my oven. All that hammering is your neighbors rebuilding the hay barn. Have you put any coffee on yet?"

"Ugh. I'm barely awake. But yeah, I do need some caffeine. Thanks for the muffins. My favorites," she mumbled.

"Let me help." Lola was always so full of energy. Must be the yoga classes.

"Don't you have breakfast to fix for the men?" Carli rubbed her eyes. "Do you need help?"

"I made their coffee, put out some scrambled eggs, bacon, salsa, fruit, and muffins. They've got plenty. I just wanted to get you started and on the road. If you still have your mind set to leave."

Carli sipped the hot coffee, and her head began to clear. Her pickup truck was loaded, all she needed was to get Beau into his trailer.

"It sure is nice of the neighbors."

Lola put a muffin on a plate and pushed it towards Carli. "As the saying goes, 'that's what friends are for'. Good people helping one another. We have a lot of good folks around here."

Carli's heart still stung from the night before. She took another sip to summon courage, and then looked directly into Lola's eyes.

"I need answers and I want the truth," she said.

"I will try my best. What's on your mind?" Lola placed a muffin on a napkin and gently peeled the paper from around the outside.

"You and Buck have lived here most of your married life. Right? And you knew my mother. You said so. Why did Michelle abandon me?"

Lola choked on the bite she had just taken, surprise etching her face. She looked down, took a heavy sigh before answering. "You have a right to know, I suppose."

Carli clutched her hands together, willing patience until Lola could answer her question.

"It had nothing to do with you." Lola took a sip of coffee. "It had to do with Michelle rebelling against her parents. She just went through a wild period she never recovered from. When she got pregnant, the only thing we could figure out was that by hiding you, she thought that would hurt your grandparents the most. And she was right."

Carli swallowed the lump in her throat. What had been wrong with her mother to make her do something like that? Turn her back on her parents and her home?

"Please understand that Michelle was a lovely girl. So full of joy, she made the room sparkle every time she walked in. Your mother loved people, and she loved a good time, but at some point in her life, she decided cows were not for her. She hated living far from town and her friends."

Carli walked into the living room and motioned

for Lola to have a seat.

"Jean and Ward were busy with ropings and training their horses, and by the time they realized their daughter had gone her own way it was too late to change things. And then she disappeared just before you came along. She stayed involved with horses, but I guess the only way she could do that was to give you to another family. Jean used to call Michelle, 'My Wild Heart'."

Carli's phone buzzed, startling them both. "It's Mark. I'm sorry, but I need to take this."

"We are so thrilled to finally find you, Carli. Don't ever forget that. Don't be so hasty to turn your back on this place." Lola patted her shoulder. "Come say goodbye before you leave."

"Mark? Hello." Carli put him on speaker just as the noise of the front door clicked shut behind Lola.

"I'm glad you called." And Carli meant it too. She hoped they could still be friends despite his feelings for her.

"Don't say anything until you've heard what I have to say. I want to buy you out of our equine business and take on the clients myself. I've realized we can't work together anymore as friends, especially after you know how I really feel. Some new opportunities have just come up for me, and, without going into detail, I've decided to explore those options with new partners."

Carli was stunned into silence. The friendly tone was gone from Mark's voice. This was all serious business. He wanted her out of his life.

"I'll text you the number we're willing to pay. It's practically a done deal. I just need you to say yes."

"Alright." Carli managed to squeak out. "I'll call you back in a bit."

Almost immediately musical notes tinkled with a text message. He must have had it written already before he called, and then just hit send within seconds of the phone conversation.

She stared at the amount. Shocked at the generosity, sad to break up their partnership, but more than curious about the new opportunities. Also annoyed that she would not be included. She bowed her head and searched her heart. Is there really a God who knows me and has a purpose for my life? She desperately whispered a soft prayer, "God, what should I do? Where do I belong? Show me."

In the silence of Jean and Ward's kitchen, she placed her elbows on the table and rested her head in her hands. Suddenly she knew. She understood where and what she had to do. It was all so clear.

Carli jumped from the barstool and ran across the road to the cookhouse. She burst through the front entrance into the dining hall. "Where's Buck?" she called.

Lola wandered out from the kitchen. "He's helping the neighbors with the barn. Why?"

"Would this amount keep the ranch going until I can settle the inheritance issues with Billy?" Carli shoved her cellphone into Lola's face.

"That would certainly buy hay for the winter and then some. What's going on?"

"Mark wants to buy me out of our business, and this is the amount he wants to pay. I don't want to leave, Lola. I want to live here. At the Wild Cow Ranch."

Lola's eyes brimmed with tears. She grabbed Carli into a warm hug and held her for several minutes. "Thank God! Let's go tell Buck."

They giggled, clasped hands, and hurried out to what was left of the barn.

The air smelled sweet and musty at the same time with the lingering of smoke. She had never noticed the colors of the Texas land and sky so bright before. Her heart felt more joy than it ever had when she saw Beau standing at the pipe fence watching her. In the next pen, Maverick blinked and walked towards her.

This was home.

This was where her family had lived.

This was where she was meant to be. It just took her several decades to come back.

The next few minutes were a blur as they talked to Buck who laughed with delight and gave her a big hug as well. She also greeted and thanked some of the neighbor men, and several of their wives who had tagged along. One man was working on a back loader, hauling the burnt hay away. She thanked them all.

Lank appeared by her side carrying a saw, his face smudged with black ash.

"What's got Buck so fired up? What did you tell him?"

Carli explained and showed him the text message from Mark. Lank didn't have much to say, just looked at her with a big wide grin on his face.

Within the hour, she was back at the house and ready to leave. Instead of finishing the packing, she unloaded some stuff and carried it back inside. There was so much to do in Georgia, so many loose ends she had to take care of, but this time she was certain it was the right thing to do. The Wild Cow Ranch is where she belonged.

She backed her pickup to her livestock trailer. Lank walked over to help her.

"Will you really come back?" he asked. "You won't get to Georgia and change your mind, will ya?"

"I don't think so," said Carli. "I'll be back soon. Two weeks tops."

"How can you be sure? You never wanted to be here." He stopped cranking the handle to stare at her intently. "What's changed?"

"For one thing, I'm not taking everything with me," she said.

"What do you mean?"

"I'll be bringing back this trailer loaded with

my stuff. Which means I don't have any room for a horse."

Lank's eyes opened in surprise. "You're leaving Beau here?"

"Yes, and Maverick too. I expect you to take care of them until I'm back. That's an order."

"Yes, boss." He smiled and leaned closer to her face, and she didn't back away this time. His lips were warm and firm. She felt the kiss all the way to her toes.

"You're not that little, lost, lonely Maverick any longer, are you? You have somewhere to be and there are people waiting for you to come back. You've had a change of heart." Lank wrapped solid, muscled arms around her and she let him.

Neither said any more words.

As she drove away, he watched and waved, and Carli waved back. There were at least three people who had her back, and she had been wrong to doubt their sincerity. Riding for the brand was a code of the West that was taken seriously even today.

Adrenaline coursed through her veins at the new adventure she had waiting for her. There were so many things she wanted to do with the ranch, possibly even open her own equine center here in Texas. A wide grin spread over her face. Excitement filled her heart. Her mind buzzed as she drove over the caliche ranch roads towards the pavement.

Her mother suddenly invaded her thoughts. Whatever demons Michelle had faced were lost forever. There were some answers she was never meant to know or understand.

And then her father crossed her mind. "Are you out there somewhere Taylor Miller? Do you even know about me?" Carli whispered under her breath as she pulled onto Interstate I-40 heading east to Georgia.

Acknowledgments

Thanks to my co-author and friend, Denise McAllister. Your enthusiasm, skills, and willingness to work with me is greatly appreciated. Melding two writer brains together has been a challenge to say the least, but very rewarding, and now we have a fictional world with so many possibilities. I'm anxious to see where our muses take us on this journey.

Thanks to Lauren Bridges with CKN Christian Publishing. Your sincere interest was greatly appreciated when two crazy writers stalked you at the Western Writers of America (WWA) convention and gushed about a story they hoped to write one day. We thank you for your patience and guidance through this process, and we're thrilled to have you at our side.

Much love and thanks to my guys: Chris, Casey, and David. I really appreciate those conversations about the fictional characters that live in my head. Your support means everything to me.

Thanks to an awesome God who steered me on this path. Sometimes people and opportunities drop out of nowhere to turn dreams into reality. There's no time to contemplate the why or to question the reasons. Just whisper, "thank you" and get busy.

– Natalie Bright

My heart is full of gratitude to many who have helped and encouraged me in the writing of this fictional story. First and foremost, thanks be to God for giving me a creative mind and dreams. He gives us the desires of our heart. Since I was a young girl, I've wanted to be a writer, but life got in the way. To everyone out there with the desire to write, keep at it, make the time, no excuses, get up early, stay awake late, just write. Your dreams will come true.

What a blessing it has been to work with Natalie Bright. We met at the 2015 Western Writers of America convention in Lubbock, Texas. Already a successful author and blogger, she writes fiction and non-fiction. This book series was Natalie's idea. She described the story to me in February 2019, at the Booth Western Art Museum's Writers Guild in Cartersville, Georgia. I didn't realize then what a fun and educational journey we would take together. Thanks so much, Nat, for everything, especially your friendship!

Thank you to author Phil Mills, Jr. who spoke at the Booth Writers Guild in 2014 about the benefits and lifelong friendships to be made through the Western Writers of America. Without his passion for the WWA I would not have met Natalie, as well as so many other talented writers, and now, treasured friends. Thank you to everyone connected with the Western Writers of America—a fine organization since 1953!

Brad Gibby has been an American Quarter Horse (and Palomino) judge for "a gazillion" years. I have many fond memories of hanging out with Brad and other friends; he was my trainer for some time and hauled me and my various horses to shows (nervous nilly that I was back then.) During the writing of this book I reached out to Brad to research horse drugging scenarios. Before I could get our first idea out, Brad interrupted: "That would never happen." He was always straightforward with any advice, whether pertaining to horses or life in general. My co-author and I changed plot points in hopes of portraying real-world accuracy. But still, any error or unrealistic scene is solely our faux pas. I sincerely thank Brad for his counsel on this book, but mostly for his friendship of many years and for standing tall as a man of God.

Throughout my life, since age twelve, my dearest friend, Elisabeth (Lis) Ghyssels-Bragg-Klemis (I got all the names in!) has been my confidant, cheerleader, and prayer partner. Along with her husband, Tom Klemis, they are two of the best humans you will ever meet on this planet. Thank you, guys, for always being there for me. I hope "2-B" will always be available for me (their guest room.)

And thank you, Dear Reader, for taking the time to be immersed in Carli Jean Jameson's life journey. She has a lot more ups and downs to experience in upcoming books. Our prayer for you is that you will walk through life always holding onto the hand of your Heavenly Father. It's the best way to run the race and get to the finish line.

– Denise F. McAllister

Take a look at A Wild Cow Winter (Wild Cow Ranch 2)

New owner Carli Jameson is left in charge of the Wild Cow Ranch for a week. All she has to do is keep the livestock fed and tend to the ranch herd until everyone returns. How hard can it be?

Carli wants to prove to everyone that she can run the ranch she owns, but it seems that everything that can go wrong, does.

When a wicked Texas norther storm descends on Carli while she's out riding her horse, her life is suddenly in danger and she becomes stranded in a barn. Hungry, freezing, and full of doubt, she must rely on her growing faith to believe that she'll make it out alive.

The entire community comes together to find Carli – teaching her that sometimes you need a helping hand to find your way out of a desperate situation...sometimes you need God.

"An emotional story of courage and learning to rely on newfound faith."

COMING FEBRUARY 2021

About Natalie Bright

With roots firmly planted in the Texas Panhandle, Natalie Bright grew up obsessed with the Wild West and making up stories. The small farming community where she lived gave her a belief in hard-working, genuine people and a firm foundation of faith. She is the author of books for kids and adults, as well as numerous articles.

This author and blogger writes about small town heroes with complicated pasts and can-do attitudes, who navigate life's crazy misfortunes with humor and happy endings. A passionate supporter of history and libraries, Natalie loves exploring museums and collecting old books. Her ranch photography is featured in a chuck wagon cookbook. She lives on a dirt road with her husband, where they raise black and red Angus cattle and where the endless Texas sky continues to be her inspiration.

About Denise F. McAllister

Lovers of the West can be born in the most unlikely of places. For Denise F. McAllister, her start was in Miami, Florida, surrounded by beaches and the Everglades.

After being in the working world for some years, Denise F. McAllister decided to apply her life experience and study for her B.A. in communications and M.A. in professional writing. She loved going back to college "later in life" and hardly ever skipped a class as in her younger years. Growing up in the suburbs of Miami, Denise credits her love of horseback riding and showing in Atlanta, Georgia (15 years) for her heartfelt connection to all things Western.

Denise's faith is important to her and she loves to write about characters' journeys as they navigate real-world challenges. She prays that readers will enjoy her books, but most importantly experience a blessed connection with their Creator and Heavenly Father.